ESCHATON

INFINITY ENGINES BOOK III

ANDREW HASTIE

To everyone that believed I could.
Thank you

Other books in the Infinity Engines universe.

The Infinity Engines

Infinity Engines Origins

Infinity Engines Missions

FOREWORD

For all those that may need a quick reminder...

Josh and Caitlin were arrested while trying to change the course of history. They had planned to steal the skull of Daedalus and stop Dalton Eckhart from opening a breach into the maelstrom.

This event signified the third Eschaton Crisis. A theoretical set of events that would lead to the end of times. As a result, the Order was put under martial law by the Protectorate and Dalton was made head of the Eschaton Division by his mother, Ravana.

Before the founder was placed under house arrest, he told Josh to go in search of his father, and with Caitlin he follows the trail into the future, leaving her parents with an injured Daedalus and an Order in chaos.

1

COUP D'ÉTAT

Lord Dee stood silently in the centre of the Star Chamber while the other members of the council waved their ballot papers and called for calm. He was having trouble standing but refused the offer of a chair.

Dalton Eckhart smiled, as did his witch of a mother, Ravana, both taking great pleasure in this public humiliation as their Protectorate officers surrounded him and snapped the iron manacles around the old man's wrists.

'Order!' declared one of the clerks of the court, but no one took the slightest notice. Everyone was shouting, and the entire chamber was up on its feet, protesting at what Ravana had just done. Thousands of members were trying to make themselves heard.

This, thought the founder as he stood stoically observing the chaos around him, *was precisely what the Determinists had wanted* — the collapse of democracy within the Order. Ravana had spent years waiting to take control. At the point she indicted him, Grandmaster Derado and the rest of the Draconian guild had stormed out, refusing to take part in the mutiny, and left her so-called "Eschaton Martial Act" to be passed by the others.

It was evident that she'd been working on the divisions between the guilds behind his back, insinuating herself with the weaker members of the High Council, creating, for the first time in its long history, disunity within the Order. That fact, more than the irons that were clamped around his wrists, was the thing that disturbed Dee the most.

Ravana walked through the jeering crowd that was gathered around him. They moved aside, no one brave enough to challenge her directly until she was staring into his face.

'You're a fool,' she said with a smirk. 'Trapped in the past.'

He looked deep into her eyes. 'Better that than a world with no future.'

'Take him away,' she ordered.

The founder bowed his head and allowed her masked officers to escort him out through the crowd of protestors; he could only hope Joshua Jones had escaped.

2

EVERYTHING CHANGES

[Richmond, England. Date: 11.580]

Sim was still calculating the best escape route in his head when he grabbed his almanac and slide rule from his desk and hastily stuffed them inside his robes. He knew it was a mistake to go via the central hall, but he had to see it with his own eyes. His friend Astor had already warned him they were shutting down the difference engine, but he couldn't believe it.

Word of the founder's arrest had spread quickly through the Copernican news channels, and even though it was a shock, it paled next to the rumour that Professor Eddington had ordered the shutdown of the Copernican's computing system in protest.

Breathing deeply to steady his nerves he walked towards the centre of the vast, complex machine that formed their headquarters. The corridors that wove between the clock-work mechanisms were full of analysts and statisticians running around like frightened children with no sense of direction. Some were carrying everything they owned:

armfuls of journals, abacuses and strange collections of divination tools, while others wandered past with blank expressions following random people in the hope of finding someone who knew what to do, but no one did — the entire guild was in a state of panic.

When Sim reached the central computing hall, he heard a distinct change in the machine's pitch. The usual clack and clatter of the gears were winding down, and then, for the first time in its history, the hall of Copernicus fell silent.

Everyone stopped what they were doing and listened — it was as if time itself had frozen. Sim reached the gantry that overlooked the main atrium and saw for himself that the hands of the enormous clock that hung at the far end of the grand hall were still.

The silence was violently broken by the sound of the Protectorate storming into the building.

From high up in the gantries, Sim watched as the black-armoured guards flooded into the hall, arresting anyone who got in their way.

'We've got to go!' begged Astor, pulling Sim away from the balcony. 'Norman says Dalton is rounding up every Copernican he can find.'

Sim nodded to his friend and followed him back into their department.

'Where are you going to go?' Sim asked while Astor packed a rucksack with random things from his tiny cupboard of a desk.

Astor shrugged. 'Jefferson says the Protectorate want to control the continuum — that's why Eddington shut it down. I'm heading for the library — going to find the most obscure book I can and hide out in the dark ages somewhere. They won't go back there.'

Sim wondered how many Copernicans were thinking

precisely the same thing. The dark ages was a period most of them chose to avoid, being a statistical black-spot in their models and one that most actuaries excluded from their equations. It was the perfect hiding place unless of course, the entire guild had all decided to head for it.

He had his own escape plan, one that had already factored in the likelihood of others doing the same. His analytical brain had processed many different possibilities and reached the only feasible conclusion — he had to go forward, towards the frontier.

Although they always treated the past as if it were a vast and unexplored territory, it was still only accessible via known artefacts, whereas the frontier, the point where the future becomes the present, was chaos to most Copernicans and they abhorred it, even though they spent most of their careers trying to predict it.

Sim had decided he would hide amongst the linears: that unfortunate part of humanity who had to take each day as it came — not knowing what might happen next. It was something he'd always wanted to try, 'living on the edge', as Lyra called it, but it wasn't until he'd met Josh, that he knew it was something he had to do.

'Where are you going?' asked Astor, hefting his pack onto one shoulder.

'Not sure,' Sim lied, 'but before I go, I need to find Professor Eddington.'

Astor's face paled at the name. 'Haven't you heard?'

Sim shook his head. 'What?'

'They've taken him. He refused to hand over the keys to the map room. He's been hauled off by Dalton's Eschaton Division.'

That changes everything, thought Sim. Now he would have to follow Eddington's orders.

'Astor, I need you to do me a favour.'

Astor looked scared. 'What?'

Sim scribbled a series of numbers onto a scrap of paper. 'Find every book you can on the Eschaton and meet me at these coordinates.'

3

THE COLONEL

[Nautilus. Maelstrom]

Rufius' breathing was erratic and his pulse rapid; if she didn't know any better, she would have thought he'd taken a serious dose of amphetamines. Juliana Makepiece checked the clock and added another entry in her journal. Rereading her notes of the last few hours she could see he was deteriorating. His condition had declined dramatically since they'd pulled him out of the Cambridge mission.

'Thomas, we have to put him outside,' she said, turning to her husband. 'Get him out of linear time.'

'And do what exactly?' he replied, looking out into the swirling maelstrom through the large circular window.

'For starters, we could find someone who knows what they're doing. I'm not a medic.'

Thomas walked over to join her. He looked tired; neither of them had slept much in the last two days, and the stress was starting to show. 'But he was the last man to see Cat before she disappeared.'

'I know darling, but if he stays in here any longer he's going to die,' she warned.

She looked over at the photographs of the timesuit scattered across the table.

'Whatever technology that guy was using — I don't think it's a linear infection. Every drug I've tried so far simply reverts to an inert state. This pathogen isn't following any known pattern.'

'So who would know?'

She crossed her arms and frowned. 'Not Bedlam. This is way out of Crooke's field. We could go back and ask Dangerfield before he died, but I think our best bet is Alixia and the Xeno department.'

Thomas sucked air in through his teeth. 'Alixia De Freis? She's going to take some convincing.'

'But in the meantime, we need to keep him in stasis.'

'Where do you suggest?'

She looked up into the broiling clouds of chaos. 'How about that battleship cemetery we found near Cassiopeia? That looked like it'd been pretty stable for a century or so.'

'You mean the Cassandra nebula?'

She shrugged. 'That's why you're the navigator.'

'The one which just so happens to be where we stored the last of our chocolate supply?'

She held up her hands in surrender. 'Well, you've got to give a girl credit for trying.'

He put his arm around her. 'I do. I just hope our daughter has at least half your brains.'

'She certainly didn't get my taste in boys!'

Thomas smiled. 'I thought he was quite a decent chap.'

She punched him in the arm. 'Don't lie. I know what you were thinking.'

'His eyes were a bit shifty.'

4

MOTHER

[Protectorate HQ. Date: 11.890]

D alton looked up from the latest report and smiled as his mother walked into her office.

'Mother, how goes the war?' he asked, getting up out of her chair and coming forward to greet her

She winced at his snide remark, turning away as he kissed her cheek. Any maternal instinct had long since withered, and a thinly disguised animosity had taken its place.

'We have a lot to discuss,' snapped Ravana, taking off her long Protectorate cloak and hanging it carefully on the neat row of pegs. 'Who authorised the raid on the Copernicans?'

Dalton's smile vanished. 'I did.'

'Stupid boy!' She slapped him across the face. 'Are you trying to undermine everything I've worked for?'

He stood, unmoved by the attack, the red mark flaring up on his skin, staring defiantly at her. 'No, Mother, I was trying to ensure that we controlled the continuum,' he explained through tight lips.

Her cheeks flushed as she tried to control her rage. 'You

arrested Eddington! The one man who may actually be able to resolve the Eschaton Cascade!'

'He openly defied us by shutting down their difference engine! Surely it's better that he's in our custody.'

'Is he? Do you honestly believe for one second that he will cooperate with us now?'

Dalton smirked. 'There are ways to ensure his compliance, mother. But I don't see why you still concern yourself with that ridiculous theory — it was just a means to an end — you don't actually believe the sky is going to fall on our heads?'

She took her seat behind the desk and made a point of re-arranging the reports.

'I do, and for better reasons than you could possibly imagine. While the Order still believes it's a real threat we have their obedience; don't give them any reason to believe otherwise. I will try and persuade Eddington to continue his research for the good of the Order. You will do your best not to disrupt the status quo any further. Are we clear?'

'Yes, mother.'

He turned to leave.

'Wait,' she snapped.

Swearing silently under his breath Dalton span around on his heel.

'Since you've already read the report, tell me what the situation is with the Draconians?'

'They have retreated into the eighth. My agents tell me that they have set up blockades around all of the standard routes, and we're working on alternatives.'

'I was told they're entrenched around the Great Breach.'

'That's one of their strongholds. Apparently, they're concerned that the maelstrom is gathering its forces for another attack, but you know the Draconians — always looking for a fight.'

His mother's expression hardened. 'I know who I'd rather have at my side in a battle against the Djinn — at least Grandmaster Derado is taking the Eschaton seriously.'

Dalton glowered. 'Is that all?'

She waved a hand as if swatting a fly. 'You may go.'

Dalton ground his teeth as he took the elevator down to the main entrance.

His mother knew nothing of his plans. She was just like the other members of the council, too wrapped up in the old ways to see the real possibilities. For him, the Eschaton Cascade was nothing more than a myth, invented by a paranoid group of Copernicans to validate their existence.

But it had its uses, like any religion; if enough people believed, it gave it credibility and power — and with power came control — the entire Order was now under Protectorate supervision, and the founder was under house arrest. Dalton had access to all the resources he needed, resources that could help him realise his dream — to find the Book of Deadly Names and the future that Jones had foreseen.

5

MUGHAL EMPIRE

[Lucknow, India. Date: 11.764]

Eddington had told him to take the most obscure path from the Copernican Hall. Sim had taken a series of diversions from the Great Library before he found himself in Lucknow, during the Battle of Buxar, where he found himself walking alongside the army of the East India Company under the command of Major Hector Munro.

The road was lined with hundreds of wounded. Sim had adapted his travel robes to look like a priest and walked up the valley towards the fortified town.

The British forces had been outnumbered four to one by the combined army of the Mughals, Awadh and Mir Qasim — but the Indian allies had been uncoordinated; the boat bridge was still burning in the river below where Grand Vizier Shuja-ud-Daulah had destroyed it while retreating — abandoning the Mughal Emperor Shah Alam II and his men to their fate. Sim knew that Munro had lost less than forty of his European regiment and two hundred and fifty of the Indian Sepoys in the battle.

It was a devastating defeat for the Mughal empire as the British forces took control of the entire Ganges valley, but Eddington had told him it was also one of the only ways to access the history of Shuja-ud-Daulah, the Grand Vizier of Shah Alam II and holder of the golden key to the Fortress of Ajmer.

It took Sim nearly two days to get close to the grand vizier, who was busy negotiating the surrender of his emperor's army. Getting to the key was another challenge altogether.

He'd stolen a uniform from a dead British officer and joined the guards that waited idly outside the grand tent of Shah Alam, while the leaders of both sides held lengthy talks within. The soldiers were a mercenary group of men who talked of nothing but the alleged millions of rupees that the fleeing allies had left behind. Through the gaps in the silken tent walls, Sim watched the grand vizier counsel his emperor, who insisted on sitting on the imperial throne throughout the proceedings and who relied on his advisor for every decision. Major Munro and his lieutenants were making heavy demands, and the Shah was doing his best to save some small part of his dignity.

The key was on a chain around the vizier's neck; all Sim needed to do was touch it and make the jump, but the vizier remained close to the emperor, who still retained his own retinue of guards even though he was under British protection.

At four o'clock, tea was served, and the tension appeared to dissolve. Servants entered with ornate glasses of mint tea on silver trays, and while both parties helped themselves from the bowls of delicacies like Pinaca, a group of Urdubegis, his female bodyguards, entered the tent carrying a large wooden chest. Munro and his colleagues made space for the formidable warriors as they opened the case and took out a series of golden idols, gathering around as the emperor proudly exhibited his collection.

The distraction was all that he needed, and Sim stepped into the tent.

'These are the lightning stones of Indra, passed down from the Vedic kings,' Sim heard the Shah explain to the Major. 'Once said to have belonged to Vishvamitra himself.'

The grand vizier had stepped away while his emperor held court and was drinking tea when Sim approached him. There was a hint of suspicion in his eye as if he knew Sim wasn't really a British officer.

'Master,' Sim addressed him in Persian. 'I humbly beg a moment of your time.'

Sim could tell the grand vizier was genuinely impressed by his linguistic skills. Beneath the long moustache was the merest hint of a smile.

'Do you seek an audience with the Shah?' he replied.

Sim shook his head. 'No, my lord, I seek knowledge. About the Taragarh Fort.'

'You'll find little treasure left there my friend, the tunnels are many, and the maps are few.'

'I seek a book. One that once belonged to Dara Shukoh, eldest son of Shah Jahan.'

Shuja looked puzzled. 'Aurangzeb sent Shukoh's head to his father in a box, what could be so interesting about his books?'

'His translations of the ancient Sanskrit texts are said to be still held in the library at Rani Mahal.'

'As is the Majma-ul-Bahrain – the confluence of two seas, but it puzzles me as to why a young soldier would be so interested in the literary work of the heir-apparent of the fifth Mughal emperor.'

Sim was running out of time. The grand vizier was asking too many questions, and the emperor's demonstration was coming to an end.

'Because a year from now you're going to sign a treaty with the British that will cost you the districts of Kora and Allahabad. Your emperor will realise that he must remain allied with the East India Company if he's going to keep his throne. The major over there is a collector of rare books, I was hoping to present him one as a gift before the fort is ransacked.'

The grand vizier mulled over Sim's answer, his tea forgotten, cold in his hand.

'And how exactly do you think I can help you?'

'I was hoping you would allow me to examine the golden key of the fortress.' Sim pointed to the key dangling from the chain around his neck.

'This,' Shuja replied, holding the key up in front of Sim, 'is nothing more than a symbol of a better time.'

'May I?' asked Sim, holding out his hand.

'Be my guest.'

Sim touched the key and opened the timeline.

Eddington had told him that the fort at Ajmer was the historical seat of the Chauhan rulers and was one of the oldest hill forts in India, if not the world. Sim knew that there had once been a garrison of Draconians stationed here, but they were long gone by the time he arrived.

He'd instructed Sim to use the key to jump back to the seventeenth century, where an impressive cannon called 'Garbh Gunjam', or 'thunder from the womb', was still mounted on the battlements, a fearsome deterrent against the British forces. But Sim wasn't there for the gun.

Dara Shukoh was an enlightened mystic who'd devoted his life to finding a common language between Islam and Hinduism and was an avid collector of arcane artefacts which he kept in his library in Rani Mahal, the small palace that lay inside the walls of the fort.

When Eddington had first heard the news of the founder's arrest, he abandoned their lesson and sent everyone but Sim out of the lecture theatre.

'Simeon, do you know what a talisman is?'

Sim shook his head.

'As it should be,' he said with a sigh. 'There are more than a few secrets that may have to be revealed before this is over. A talisman is an ancient artefact — a type of vestige that can bestow certain powers on the user.'

'Powers, sir?'

The professor looked uncomfortable as he tried to explain. 'Access to preternatural abilities, from primaeval times. Anyway, what they do is irrelevant — they are something that cannot be allowed to fall into the hands of Master Eckhart and his friends. Fortunately, most have been lost, scattered throughout antiquity or buried in tombs of long forgotten kings. The founder knows the whereabouts of some, but I know of only one, and I may need you to find it.'

'Why me sir?'

Eddington's eyes glistened. 'Because there is a high probability that they will come for me, do you understand? He will be looking for information about that damned lost book, but once he reads my timeline he will know about the talisman, and I cannot let him have it. You are by far my best student, my most trusted amanuensis. If I am arrested, I leave it to you to remove it from his reach.'

He went on to describe the particular route he'd planned to reach Shukoh's collection and how to locate the talisman before Dalton and his newly acquired army got anywhere near it.

Running down towards the small, dilapidated palace, Sim hoped that Eddington hadn't sent him on a wild goose chase.

Stopping to catch his breath in the cool shade of the crumbling entrance hall, Sim found himself wondering what the fading murals and broken stained-glass windows would've looked like in their heyday. He was tempted to step back a few years and see for himself, but he knew his pale skin would cause too much of a stir; the East India Company had only just been established, and the sight of a European was still something of a novelty.

The palace seemed unusually quiet, beyond the occasional squawk of a peacock, there was no other sound as if the occupants had all stepped out for a moment.

Turning a corner, he found a servant standing in the inner courtyard holding a tray of food, staring at something on the other side of the quadrangle.

In the shade, below the canopied walkway, was a man, his face obscured by a dark mask — it was a Protectorate officer.

Sim moved quietly back into the shadows, his hand instinctively going to the rewind button on his tachyon. The Protectorate were here, which meant Eddington had already been interrogated.

6

EDDINGTON

[Protectorate HQ. Date: 11.890]

I t was the job of the seer to look into the lives of others, to read their potential futures and advise on ways in which they could improve their outcomes. Dalton had always been more interested in learning about their dirty little desires and deceits — it appealed to the darker parts of his psyche. He could hardly contain his excitement as he delved into Eddington's past; there were so many secrets, things that the professor had kept hidden for years in the dusty corners of his timeline.

It was like a museum of forbidden knowledge. Dalton tried hard to focus on the thing he desired the most, the location of the second book of the Djinn, and he found many conversations with the other members of the council on the subject of the book; heated debates on the validity of the Daedalus manuscripts. But try as he might he found nothing that indicated the professor knew any more about its whereabouts than he did.

Focussing on those meetings he discovered other, more

subtle moments, ones that Eddington had revisited multiple times — a particular word that cropped up in discussions with the founder and the head of the Antiquarians about a special kind of artefact; they kept referring to a 'talisman'.

'They must remain lost,' said the Antiquarian grandmaster.

'I agree,' said Eddington. 'They introduce an unpredictable element to our equations.'

Dalton watched through Eddington's eyes as the founder struggled to reach a decision.

'They are too valuable to leave in the hands of the linears.'

'At least they won't try and use them!' argued the Antiquarian. 'They can melt them down for base metal as far as I'm concerned.'

The founder shook his head. 'That's what worries me. They're a link to ancient times, ones that we may be in need of one day.'

'They're dangerous,' Eddington replied. 'Whatever connection they have to the lost civilisations of pre-history should remain exactly that — lost!'

'I disagree,' said the founder, shaking his head.

When Dalton extracted himself from Eddington's timeline the professor sighed, his head slumping forward onto his chest, and he would have fallen out of the chair had his arms and legs not been tied to it.

'So what exactly are talismans?' asked Dalton, pulling out the homunculus blade from the back of Eddington's neck and watching the agony revive him. He was using the same set of talons he'd interrogated Jones with, but this time they proved more effective. The Copernican professor was not as resilient as the Nemesis; pain wasn't something he seemed able to bear for more than a few minutes.

'Ancient objects. Antediluvian — from an older civilisation,' the professor said through sharp breaths.

'And they have power?'

Eddington nodded. 'The Antiquarians believe so.'

'Power over the Djinn?'

The professor grimaced and whimpered. 'So the founder says.'

'And where might I find one of these?' Dalton asked, picking up another talon and holding it above Eddington's knee.

'They are so rare, only the founder knows exactly.'

Dalton pushed the blade slowly into the old man's upper thigh, and he screamed.

'There's a ninety-four-percent probability of one within the Mughal dynasty.'

Dalton held up the Homunculus pin for Eddington to see. 'All you need to do is tell me where to find it and all the pain will vanish.'

'What an earth do you want with a talisman? It's nothing but cabalistic nonsense — witchcraft!'

He leaned in close and whispered in the professor's ear. 'I have a destiny. The Nemesis recounted it to me while sitting in this very chair, but to achieve it I must change the past, and for that I need the power of the Djinn. Now, tell me which part of the Mughal dynasty?'

'The collection of the fifth Mughal emperor, Shah Jahan.'

Dalton turned to leave.

'Wait!' Eddington groaned. 'You can't, the Eschaton Cascade predicts that —'

'That the barrier between the maelstrom and the continuum will be destroyed by awakening the Elder Gods? And you have the gall to accuse me of deluding myself with cabalistic nonsense!' Dalton laughed. 'You Copernicans are all so convinced that your calculations can't be wrong. What if the continuum is a lie? Have you ever stopped to consider that everything you've spent your life trying to predict is nothing more than a mathematical impossibility — that you've made no difference to the future whatsoever?'

He took the last blade and drove it deep into the professor's chest. 'Didn't see that coming, did we?'

7

ARRIVAL

[Kverkfjöll volcano, Iceland. Date: 12.418]

The hangar was a vast metal dome with circular tunnels arranged at various points around its circumference. The floor was nothing more than a network of metal gangways spanning across the deep shaft that fell away below them. There was a heavy metallic smell in the air, as if it were charged with electricity, and by the dull throbbing of machines Josh thought it safe to assume they were in some kind of power station. Thick cables snaked out from the central chasm and into each one of the individually numbered tunnels.

'When are we?' asked Caitlin, checking her tachyon and finding that the dials had frozen.

'No idea,' whispered Josh.

He was still holding Lenin's gun. It felt good to have a weapon, even if he had no idea how to use it.

There was no sign of Lenin, or anyone else for that matter. They'd simply appeared in the middle of this giant machine and he'd no idea what to do next — something he knew better than to admit to Caitlin.

'I thought the future would be different somehow,' Caitlin mused, looking around the structure. 'You know, all white and clean.'

'You've watched too many movies,' Josh replied, thinking back to the desolation he'd seen in the alternate reality of the Ascendancy; the future he'd witnessed there was far from idyllic.

'I guess you just assume everything is going to get better,' she said, taking off her fancy shoes and tying her hair back. This was always a sure sign she meant business. Her party dress and his tuxedo were completely impractical for a mission, and Josh wished he'd thought it through a little more before jumping.

'Yeah. It's called hope. No one wants to imagine things are going to get worse.'

He put down the gun and took off his jacket, hiding it with her shoes behind a metal duct. The temperature in the hangar was already beginning to make him sweat.

Josh picked up the gun and inspected it more closely, tapping a few buttons, but the thing was dead. He dropped it in with the clothes — it wasn't his style anyway.

The tunnel behind them had a sign with the code 'TE-3920' stamped into the tarnished metal. There was a thick layer of dust on it, and spots of rust. The shaft itself was dark and smelled like his grandad's shed; full of old electrical valves and parts of motors.

Caitlin walked part way into it, then stopped. 'It's a dead-end, it doesn't seem to go anywhere,' she observed.

The tunnel walls were made up of arches of coiled copper wiring, like giant magnets, with thick, heavy-duty electrical cables running between them.

'Don't touch anything,' she added, walking back out and looking around the space. 'There are hundreds of them.'

Suddenly, there was a power surge from deep in the shaft below and a circle of light appeared on the opposite side of the hangar. As they shrank into the shadows a figure stepped out of the glowing tunnel. Josh held Caitlin close to the wall and they watched as the new arrival paused for a moment before walking robotically into a well-lit corridor.

They both recognised the timesuit, the double-F logo etched on the side of its helmet, but neither said a word.

Josh could feel her heart beating fast against his chest.

'Did he just?'

'Appear out of thin air?' said Josh, picking up the gun again and looking back nervously at the portal they'd been using for a hiding place. 'I think we need to get out of here.'

8

TALISMAN

[Rani Mahal, Rajasthan, India. Date: 11.657]

The collection was housed within a tower at the southern end of the palace. A gilded, spiral staircase climbed up through the centre of the space, with spoke-like gantries coming off at various points to collections of dusty curiosities.

The intoxicating aroma of musty old leather mingled with the exotic oils burning in the lamps made Sim feel a little high as he climbed the golden stairs. The tower was an eclectic collection: hundreds of ancient books stacked beside complex astronomical instruments and idols of Hindu gods. Sim recognised a few of them: Brahma, Shiva and the elephant-headed Ganesha.

He'd retreated back in stages through the last few days, until he could be sure the Protectorate were nowhere to be seen. It was a dangerous gamble, and Sim knew they'd have procedures for locking down a site; ones that involved deploying a parenthesis around the time frame, guarding both before and after their temporal target.

There was little time and a lot of books. Fortunately, the Mughal prince was an intelligent man who took great care to organise his collection. It took Sim less than an hour to find the books on demons. There were three volumes, each with the pentacle carved into the binding — the seal of Solomon.

He sat on the steps and opened one of the tomes, finding the pages full of magical writing and invocations. Heavily annotated hexagrams listed the various components and ingredients required to summon a demon — it was an instruction manual for every kind of metaphysical experiment.

As Sim's fingers skimmed the pages he could feel the history unwind, the countless times the diagrams had been copied and re-copied by a hundred different scribes. He followed the knowledge back, feeling it change subtly with each transcription.

Finally, he located the reference to the ring — the talisman that Eddington had told him to find.

He heard the metallic clang of a steel-capped boot on the metal stair below, and he knew he had to go.

Grabbing the other two books, Sim ran up a few more rotations of the staircase, putting each one on a random shelf as he went.

Reluctantly, Sim tore the relevant page from the last book and hid the rest of it between a set of the Kama Sutra, hoping that the clean-living officers of the Protectorate would think twice before touching such a forbidden set of texts.

Then, using the timeline from the torn page, he found the location of the talisman and shifted into it.

9

LENIN

Walking cautiously around the metal walkway with their backs pressed against the outer wall, Josh and Caitlin came to the well-lit corridor the figure had disappeared into.

Caitlin looked back at Josh, raising an eyebrow at the gun as if wondering how the inert weapon was going to magically come to life.

There was another power surge, and across the hangar they saw another suited figure appear from a glowing tunnel.

They moved quickly into the corridor. It was a metal tube of corroding panels and exposed wires, with running lights down the edges of the walkway. There was nowhere to hide, only the exit at the other end of the passage. They ran hard towards it, as the sound of the stranger's steps echoed down the passage behind them.

The next room was like something from an abandoned spaceship, its walls stacked high with dirty, glass-fronted pods. Many were broken, but a few displayed flickering graphs of biometrics on their opaque doors. Caitlin approached the nearest working compartment and wiped away the grime and dust, stifling a scream as she jumped back.

There was a body inside.

Josh looked closely at the face of Lenin, whose eyes stared blankly out into the distance. A glowing light on his chest pulsed softly as though he was in some kind of stand-by mode and the power bar on the glass door indicated he was re-charging.

'What the hell is the place?' asked Caitlin, looking around at all the other occupied bays.

Josh went over to another cell and brushed away the dirt from the window. Again it was Lenin, but this time the body was much older.

The footsteps grew louder from the corridor behind them and Caitlin looked anxiously for a hiding place.

'In here,' she said, pointing to a darkened, empty unit.

Josh squeezed in beside her and closed the door as the figure arrived in the bay.

It was another timesuit, the smooth, silvered surface of the armour shimmering as the figure walked into the centre of the room and came to a stop. Josh heard the servos whine and watched the mirror field dissipate as the suit powered down.

A series of robotic arms dropped from the ceiling and removed the bolts that locked the headgear in place, pulling off the helmet to reveal the face of much older Lenin.

'Consciousness transfer initiated,' intoned a female voice, as a long cable was inserted into the back of his head.

Lenin's head jolted back and his eyes burned with a blue light as the procedure kicked in. A minute later the light faded and his head slumped down onto his chest-plate.

'Transfer complete. Unit X9010 expired. Recycle initiated.'

Just as it had done in the college grounds in Cambridge, the timesuit split open, but this time the emaciated body of the old gang leader fell out onto the floor. He looked as if he were in his nineties, strands of white hair clinging to his liver-spotted head and his arms were nothing but skin and bone.

Clamps descended and hoisted the suit away, leaving the feeble body of Lenin on the metal grill set into the middle of the floor.

'Commencing cellular reclamation,' instructed the voice.

The floor below Lenin split open and his body fell through the widening hole.

Josh went to leave the pod, but Caitlin held him back, shaking her head.

Only when the grill had closed and everything seemed to have returned to normal did she let go of his arm.

Josh went over to the spot where Lenin had been, careful not to step onto the aperture. Below the metal grid he could see a luminous vat of yellow fluid, and floating within it, the slowly dissolving body of the old gang leader.

'Clones?' asked Caitlin, coming to stand behind him.

'Maybe. But what's making them so old?' replied Josh.

Caitlin looked at the empty timesuits hanging above their heads, the space above them filled with an array of pods that stretched up into an unseen ceiling.

'Time.'

10

NAUTILUS

[Cassandra nebula, Maelstrom]

The *Nautilus* appeared silently inside a graveyard of old navy warships suspended in space like sharks out of water. Drifting past the silent hulks, Thomas read off their names, noting where the gaping holes in their grey steel hulls had been ripped open by torpedoes. Some were listing badly, as though they were still taking on water, but never quite sinking.

'I'm going to bring her in next to the *Enterprise*,' said his wife through the speaking tube. 'I think its medical bay is still intact.'

He watched the manoeuvres from the conning tower of the timeship, marvelling at the grand old destroyers. To him they were like monuments, each one a tomb and a memorial to a lost battle.

'Ten degrees down on your bow,' said Thomas, ducking to avoid the enormous propeller blade of a minesweeper which was still slowly gyrating. Once clear of the craft, the

Nautilus began to ascend towards the aircraft carrier floating high above them.

This was a sector of the maelstrom that they'd discovered early in their travels. At first, he'd assumed that all the ships had come from one battle, which would explain why they were collected in the same space, but after they'd spent a few months setting up a base, it was clear that this area had a dense magnetic field, and that large metal hulks like these ships were naturally drawn towards it.

Which also meant it was the easiest part of the chaotic realm to find — the needle of a compass would instantly turn towards it.

The *Nautilus* slowed alongside the *Enterprise,* one of the largest vessels in the forgotten fleet, and Thomas jumped onto the flight deck and secured the lines. Although there was no perceivable current or eddy to move their ship away, there was something within the magnetic flux that pulled at the vessels. More than once they had found their ship adrift in an otherwise stable space.

The deck of the carrier was a haunting museum of old WW2 aircraft: the painted smiles of Hellcats and Warhawks grinned menacingly at him as they sat chained to the deck, patiently waiting for pilots that would never come.

'Are you going to stare at those bloody planes all day?' asked his wife from a door she'd opened in the side of the ship.

Rufius was a heavy man, and even with Da Recco's help they only just managed to wrestle him onto a stretcher. His condition was unchanged since they re-entered the maelstrom, but his skin was sickly grey and his breathing was shallow.

Using one of the aviation elevators, they manoeuvred him down into a hangar and from there to the sick bay.

Juliana went off to search for supplies while Thomas and Da Recco made him comfortable.

'This is a metal ship?' marvelled Da Recco, touching the bulkhead.

'One of the finest aircraft carriers in the American Pacific Fleet.'

'And she floats?'

'Yes, and planes land on her.'

'What are planes?'

'Machines that fly — like a bird. Only with propellers instead of wings — but they have those too.' Thomas could see he was only making the poor man more confused.

'They fly how?'

'What happened to the prime directive?' asked his wife, coming back from the infirmary with an armful of medical supplies.

'I think we abandoned that when we rescued him in a timeship,' Thomas replied.

Juliana unpacked the saline drip and plugged it carefully into the Rufius' arm. 'This will need to be changed every few hours,' she said, laying out the extra packs of saline. 'One of us will have to stay.'

'I will,' volunteered Da Recco. 'I wish to explore this magnificent metal ship.'

'Fine,' agreed Juliana, glaring at her husband. 'But stay away from the gunnery sections — there may well be live ammo down there.'

As well as a bunch of dead seamen, thought Thomas with a shiver. The lower levels of the ship were haunted by the last few moments of the ship sinking, and even if you didn't believe in ghosts it was not a sight you forgot in a hurry.

11

SOLOMON'S TEMPLE

[Jerusalem. Date: 9.070]

The tomb seemed to have no entrance or exit; the walls were carved from heavy sandstone blocks, each finely cemented on top of the other so there was no discernible gap. Ancient Egyptian hieroglyphs were etched across the surface of the rock.

A golden throne sat at the far end of the chamber, with lions and eagles resting on the steps that led up to it. Sim used the light from his tachyon to move between the hundreds of grave goods until he reached the steps.

He had no idea how the ring had found its way to Solomon; Eddington hadn't really had the time to explain how he knew it was there.

The King was lying mummified inside the sarcophagus, his head covered with a golden death mask, and the staffs of office lay on his chest held down by his crossed arms. He was hours away from being sealed into his tomb and Sim knew that the priests would be returning soon to finish the ceremony.

The ring sat gleaming on his embalmed right hand, a pentagram engraved into its seal.

Putting on the gloves he'd brought especially for the task, Sim carefully prised the ring off the mummy's finger. He was probably now the most wanted man in the Order and also the most powerful. Sim had to restrain himself from opening its timeline and taking a look at the chronology. The thought that this was a talisman, an object from pre-history, was fascinating — that it alone could transport him millions of years into the past sent a shiver down his spine.

Eddington had instructed him to hide it in the most 'improbable place', and Sim had considered a number of options. The first was obvious: the Antiquarian archives, where it could be said to be lost in plain sight, but there was always the chance that some archivist might come across it while indexing. The other option was one of the out-of-the-way locations, secret paths that Sim's father had taken him through as a child — places that not even the Nautonniers knew of. But though they were tempting, they too did not feel safe. Most were archaic and the power contained in the ring could no doubt corrupt the timeline irreparably.

His statistical mind weighed the possibilities, assessing the risks until he found he'd rationalised them down to one.

He would take it home.

12

SWORD

'What do you mean it wasn't there?' screamed Dalton.

The three subordinates stared at their shoes, whilst Jarius tried to explain.

'There were latent traces, like someone had got there before us.'

'So go back earlier.'

'We did. There were no references to the talisman anywhere in the Shukoh's collection or the timeline.'

Dalton looked at them in disbelief. 'You mean it'd been redacted?'

Jarius nodded. 'Someone had taken great pains to remove any evidence of it ever existing.'

Dalton studied each of them in turn, unconsciously caressing the pommel of his sword with his thumb, as if considering which one to kill first.

'Bring me the Scriptorian Grandmaster,' he said calmly. 'I assume you won't have any trouble finding him.'

With relief they all turned to leave.

'Not you, Jarius.'

Once the others had gone, Dalton unbuckled his sword belt and placed it on his desk.

'Someone else got to the talisman before us,' he mused, taking the Katana out of its sheath. Jarius recognised it as the *Honjō Masamune*, made by the master swordsmith Masamune in 11.328 and supposedly lost at the end of the Second World War. Dalton had made no secret of wanting to own the sword ever since he'd seen it used during his internship with the Tokugawa shogunate. He'd issued a requisition order to the Antiquarians the moment he'd taken command.

The Protectorate were the only members given special privileges to carry a weapon at all times, although the Dreadnoughts were usually armed too, but that was because no one had the balls to tell them not to be.

'Eddington must have told someone,' agreed Jarius, eyeing the sword warily.

Dalton tilted the blade so it caught the light. 'Do you know what a Samurai would do if he failed his liege lord?'

Jarius shook his head.

'Seppuku. To restore honour in the face of defeat. The warrior would use a knife to open his stomach while another Samurai would take off his head.'

In one swift motion, Dalton swept the deadly blade to within a few millimetres of Jarius' neck.

'I have a small dilemma — Eddington is dead — making it rather difficult when it comes to finding out who he confided in — a situation that may allow you to redeem yourself.'

Jarius could feel the blood pumping through the artery in his neck as the cold steel hovered close to it. He realised exactly what Dalton was asking him to do and considered pushing himself onto the blade.

'But he's dead,' he whimpered.

Dalton lowered his weapon. 'Reaving is not a pleasant task, I have to admit, but sometimes these things have to be done — I suggest you get cracking.'

13

AVATAR

J osh stepped back from the steaming soup of body parts and looked around for another way out.

He spotted a metal door between two of the pods, which had a wheel in the centre, like a pressure door on a ship. Above it, stencilled into the tarnished grey metal, was the double-F logo.

Putting down the gun, he grabbed the wheel with both hands and tried to turn it, but the thing was rusted shut. By the look of the corrosion on the hinges it hadn't been opened in a hundred years.

'Lost your superpowers?' Caitlin asked with a chuckle.

'Do you have any better ideas?' he replied, giving up and kicking the door.

Caitlin was inspecting the other cabinets. 'We could start by moving back a few years. This all looks pretty degraded and badly maintained. I think this place has seen better days.'

Josh touched the wheel and felt the timeline unravel beneath his fingers.

Its chronology spanned at least four hundred years, but

Josh found it difficult to estimate exactly how far into the future they'd travelled. The facility had none of the temporal signposts a normal vestige would have, and its timeline was nothing like the ones the Copernicans created for the continuum.

From what he could understand they were inside some kind of massive industrial complex built into the base of a volcano. The energy shaft they had crossed earlier was a massive geo-thermal generator, constructed to power the entire base.

Josh chose a cluster of events at the end of the first century of operation and took Caitlin's hand.

'Let's see what this place looked like when it was at its prime.'

'This is more like it!' Caitlin said, as she looked around at the clean, brightly-lit room of glistening steel and glass. All the pods were empty — the dust and mildew that had coated them was gone.

Josh tried the door, and this time it opened easily.

'Whoever built this facility planned on it lasting a hell of a long time,' she observed.

Josh nodded. 'At least another three hundred years.'

'But what does it do?'

'That's what we're about to find out,' said Josh, stepping through the door.

Behind the door was a lift shaft. A metal platform floated in space where the floor should be, taking their weight without moving as they nervously stepped on to it.

As if triggered by their presence, a holographic model of

the facility appeared in the air between them, their location marked by a glowing red dot at the very bottom of the map. Caitlin quickly found that she could use her hands to rotate the model and zoom the layout. Many of the areas were marked with codes, numeric sequences or symbols that meant absolutely nothing to Josh.

Finally she pointed out an area labelled 'Central control'.

'I guess that's probably the best place to start?'

Josh nodded and she tapped the label and the lift started to ascend.

'Who were those guys in the timesuit? You seemed to know him — them.'

Josh shrugged. 'Just someone from way back.'

'A friend?'

Josh shook his head. 'Not exactly. We used to hang out together,' he lied, not wanting to have to explain his past, reminding himself that this version of Caitlin had never met Lenin, nor got shot by him in a gunfight.

'So, how on earth did he end up in this place?'

Josh had no idea what could have happened to Lenin in this timeline, nor why there seemed to be multiple versions of him.

'Some kind of cloning maybe?'

Caitlin's eyebrows furrowed, the way they always did when she was mulling over a problem.

'Sim once told me that the Copernicans had a prediction about genetics.' She paused as if struggling to remember the details. 'He said it was one of the potential wildcards from the O.D. — the Outliers Division.'

'What's an outlier?' asked Josh, as the lift changed direction and proceeded sideways.

She grabbed hold of his arm to steady herself. 'Outside

chances, small developments that can affect the whole time-line — left-field, wacky, conspiracy shit — Sim loved studying them.'

'And cloning was one of them?'

'One of many. It was going to revolutionise medical treatment and extend human life beyond one-hundred-and-fifty years.'

'Wow.'

'It also meant we were heading for over-population within two centuries. The O.D. had raised its threat level to a six.'

'Is that bad?'

'It's one below an extinction-level event.'

The elevator was beginning to slow, as an indicator on the holo-model showed them approaching the command centre.

The lift doors opened and they stepped out into something from Star Trek. It was like the bridge of a starship with giant curved screens displaying hundreds of images from different locations, each one labelled with the same numeric sequence they'd seen on the tunnels.

In the centre of the room a man was floating in a glass tube, his body held suspended in a clear liquid with cables and tubes plugged into vital points on his torso. He seemed totally unaware of their presence, his entire focus directed at the video feeds.

Caitlin walked towards the screens and Josh followed close behind. Neither spoke, both too intrigued by the scenes playing out on the monitors. Random parts of the past were projected across the displays, each filmed from a head-mounted camera. Josh caught glimpses of Nazi nuclear bunkers, Egyptian temples and what looked like the Thames on fire. It was like watching a hundred different versions of the history channel.

Small egg-shaped objects floated past their legs, emitting a faint blue halo. Caitlin moved aside as one came too close and its field turned to red. Josh decided against trying to touch it.

'How are they filming that?' Josh whispered, looking at footage of a Roman soldier marching out of view.

Caitlin looked puzzled. They both knew it shouldn't be possible to take that kind of tech back into the past.

'That's not video,' said a man's voice.

Josh span around to the body in the tank, but his gaze was still firmly fixed on the array of screens.

'Do not be alarmed,' the voice continued calmly, as a semi-translucent hologram flickered into life in front of them. 'I am a custodian sub-routine seven-sigma. May I ask how you arrived here?'

The man was in his mid-forties, with dark hair and black-rimmed spectacles. He wore a grey tunic with the double-F insignia on his breast pocket.

'We don't know,' lied Josh, winking at Caitlin.

'Interesting,' said seven-sigma thoughtfully. 'This may seem like a strange question, but when exactly are you from?'

Josh suddenly realised that the avatar looked remarkably like the professor from the university — the one who'd caught him after Lenin's stupid drugs heist, the one he'd left the tachyon with.

'Eighteenth century,' answered Caitlin.

'And you?' asked seven-sigma, turning to Josh.

Josh wasn't paying attention. Instead he was examining the face of the semi-transparent figure closely — a sense of dread growing in the pit of his stomach. 'What?'

'What year are you from?'

'Twenty-sixteen.'

The hologram faded for a moment, and Josh noticed that some of the screens flickered and went dark at the same time. As the image returned the old man in the tank shuddered and then went still.

'Is he okay?' asked Caitlin.

'A minor power issue, nothing to concern yourself with. We are quite safe up here. May I offer you something to drink? The professor has been expecting you, but he is currently in a restore cycle.'

The hologram waved them towards a space where a group of comfortable chairs appeared from the floor.

Caitlin raised her eyebrows at Josh, as if to ask if he had a clue what was going on.

14

CHAPTER HOUSE

[London. Date: Present day]

S im took his house key from his pocket and walked up to the front door of 71 Birkbeck Avenue. To any normal passer-by it was just another Victorian terraced house in a leafy part of Chiswick, and so it would remain until he turned the key anti-clockwise.

It was nothing more than a subtle change in the shape and colour of the door that signified the entrance to the Chapter House, but when he stepped over the threshold he knew he was home.

His father had built the house to be portable for just this kind of emergency. The random collection of rooms and floors could be detached and moved to another location in a matter of minutes. Sim had moved several times in the last few days, just as his father had told him to do when they had arrested his mother.

. . .

It felt strange not to be welcomed by Arcadin; their old butler had left with the rest of the staff just before the raid. It was over a week since the Protectorate had come and arrested the rest of his family and Sim had done his best to keep ahead of them ever since.

He'd considered hiding the ring in a number of places; at the bottom of the baths in the basement, beneath his bed with the festering underwear — but somehow it felt right to keep it in the roof garden, amongst his mother's collection of extinct carnivorous plants.

While he was burying it inside the pot labelled 'Archaeamphora', he felt the familiar nudge of a beak against his leg. It was Maximillian, his mother's dodo, whose constant chittering reminded Sim that he hadn't been fed for a few days.

The dodo followed Sim around the house and down into the larder where he found a tin of sardines.

'Where are they Max?' he asked the bird, dropping the last of the sardines into his open beak.

Max squawked his gratitude and waddled off.

'Big help you are.'

He was sure Dalton had arrested his mother for purely political reasons. The trumped up charge of fatecasting was just an excuse. She'd been far too outspoken about the Eschaton Division's heavy handed approach, and her loyalties lay with the Draconians, which made her a prime target.

Sim went back to his bedroom and took the note out of his almanac. It was the last message from his mother.

My dear boy, if you are reading this then the very worst has happened. I have been taken by the fascists. I have no time to explain, but it's imperative that you remain at large and move the house to somewhere safe. The Eschaton Cascade must be stopped. Find Caitlin and Josh — they will need all the help they can get.

Stay safe my brave boy. M x

Sitting on his bed he read it over again, looking for hidden codes or cyphers, but all he could glean from it were three instructions: move the house, stop the Eschaton Cascade and find Caitlin.

Then he remembered Astor.

'Where have you been?' asked his friend, shivering on platform 5 at Waterloo Station. 'I've been back here seven times.'

It was a chilly December in 11.866 and the morning commuters were just stepping off the 08:34 from Guildford.

'I'm sorry,' said Sim. 'I was doing something for Eddington. Were you followed?'

Astor looked furtively at the crowd of Victorian frock-coated men as they filed passed the steaming engine towards the exit. 'Not that I've noticed.'

He handed Sim a small stack of books neatly tied with string. 'This is everything I could find. The Eschaton Division had requisitioned nearly all of it, but the one by Peterson is quite good.'

'Thanks,' said Sim. 'Where will you go now?'

'I've got an aunt in Ethelred's court who's been studying the House of Wessex. I thought I could stay with her for a while.'

Sim smiled and patted Astor on the shoulder. 'Just keep an eye on those Danes.'

. . .

Astor was right about Peterson's treatise on the Eschaton Cascade. It was by far the most detailed thesis on the twelve crises. A slim volume of no more than a hundred or so pages, Sim spent the rest of the day familiarising himself with the theory.

It wasn't the easiest thing to follow; the formulae that Peterson used was not standard stochastic sequencing and his attempts to identify a unified thread that linked all of the crises together was tenuous to say the least.

Sim made notes of his own, separating out the facts from the conjecture until he had the basics. He divided the twelve crises into four parts and was just about to analyse the grouping when Maximilian jumped up on the bed. His mother would have gone berserk if she knew he was letting the bird have the run of the house, but Sim enjoyed his company.

'Not now Max!' Sim said, scowling at the ridiculous bird.

But Max wouldn't be told, and jumped up and down until Sim looked at him.

There was something shiny and silver in his beak — a key.

Sim had only ever seen this particular key once before; it was his father's most treasured possession.

The key to the Parabolic Chamber.

15

REAVING

Jarius stood over the pale corpse of Professor Eddington, trying to summon the courage to touch the body. The mortuary was a cold and soulless place, borrowed from the exhibition room of the Paris Morgue. Bodies were laid out on grey marble slabs, continuously sprayed from above with water from an antiquated sprinkler system.

He'd never come this close to a dead body, at least not a naked one. Seeing him laid out like an exhibit was very different to those casualties of war and plague they'd all witnessed during training. Those were more like props from a movie, or a photograph, and there was an unreal sense of detachment when you didn't know the victim personally.

This was different, more visceral, and the stench was making him gag.

Jarius was preparing himself to enter the timeline of a dead man, even though it went against everything he'd been taught. It was known as 'Reaving', and Bedlam was full of seers who'd gone insane from attempting it.

Eddington's skin was cold and waxy when he touched it,

the indentations made by his fingers remaining long after he lifted them away.

I can't do it, he thought, looking at the rose-like wound in the corpse's chest. *The man is too long dead.*

Yet, the alternative was to face Dalton and his damned sword. His leader wasn't going to show him any mercy for another failure. Jarius had watched him kill for less than this, and even though he knew many of his secrets, it was foolish to think he wouldn't make an example of him to the others.

The timeline was already quite degraded when he finally entered it. Skeins of memories and events moved in random eddies around the dark centre. The terminus was like a black hole, consuming everything around it and no matter how hard Jarius tried to avoid looking into the darkness, there was something drawing him in.

Frantically, like a kid snatching at butterflies, he grasped the last remnants of Eddington's life, hoping they would have some significance, but finding only snippets of random, unimportant memories: a picnic on a hill, the face of a lover, and the last words of a dying father: 'Nice to see you.'

There was nothing useful left except the black void, which seemed to speak to him of other terrible things, and Jarius felt himself give in to it.

16

PARABOLIC CHAMBER

The Parabolic Chamber was a circular room with a domed roof. The cylindrical walls were covered in mirror lenses configured to create an infinite number of reflections of any subject that stood at its centre — which was exactly where Sim appeared, still holding the key.

It was hard to focus on any one image, and Sim found it easier to close his eyes while he made his way to the side of the room.

His father was a temporal architect and had spent most of his adult life working on his 'experiment'. It was a complex arrangement of lensing prisms that was supposed to allow the operator to search the continuum for anything that had intersected with their own timeline.

His father described it as a kind of temporal telescope, letting you explore any part of history that you were even remotely connected to without having to go rummaging around in a museum or a library to find the relevant object — and it was very accurate.

And incredibly powerful.

Which was why his parents had never let their kids anywhere near it.

Sim took a deep breath and opened his eyes. The room seemed to shimmer as the lensing fields adjusted to his presence, so he closed them once more.

Lensing was not one of his favourite activities. The multi-layered vision of possibilities gave him motion sickness, and since it wasn't something any decent, upstanding Copernican should ever be seen doing, he'd managed to avoid throwing up over himself for quite some time.

But not now — now he had to find Caitlin.

Taking three steps away from the wall he opened his eyes. He was staring into an infinite number of copies of himself, and only by focussing on the memory of her could he make them fade away.

The chamber darkened as the first images of Caitlin appeared. Sitting at the dinner table next to Dalton, it was the last time Sim had seen her before she joined the Draconian Academy. He lingered in the moment, enjoying the banter between his friends and wondering where they all were now.

He focused in on her timeline and moved forward, following her through her training until he came to the moment she entered the maelstrom. The lines disappeared and he dare not follow them, but there was a tiny thread that reappeared later and he latched onto it and dived in.

The images were distorted and blurry, but Sim could just make out that she was at some kind of party. He could hear Josh's voice in the background, but everyone except her was an outline, a two-dimensional sketch. Caitlin seemed to be rocking out to some eighties classic, dancing like she did when she'd been drinking.

Sim shifted forward in time, following her through the gardens of some university towards an old college building. Rufius appeared in the periphery and they followed him into a wood, when something really odd happened.

Suddenly it was as though a thousand timelines converged on them at the same time — too many to count. The event became difficult to hold onto, the effort making Sim nauseous, and he fell to his knees.

He closed his eyes and reluctantly let go of her timeline.

When he opened them again he was staring at pale versions of himself kneeling on the floor.

Something bad had happened, and there was no more path to follow. Caitlin had simply disappeared from the continuum, which could only mean one of three things: either she'd died — which he didn't even want to contemplate, entered the maelstrom, or gone into the future. None of these options were anything he could do much about.

So Sim got to his feet and braced himself once more.

This time he focused on the letter from his mother.

Alixia was in her roof garden when the raid began. She was hiding the note in one of her more dangerous plants, which Sim could tell by the thick leather gauntlets she wore.

Suddenly, two Protectorate officers appeared in stillsuits and raised their weapons — she ignored them and finished the re-potting before gracefully removing the gloves and letting them lead her away.

Sim shifted to his father's office, where he too was standing passively between two heavy-set guards.

Lyra and Phileas were brought in, both struggling

against their captors. One word from Methuselah calmed them down and they were forced to stand beside them.

Then Dalton walked in.

Sim couldn't believe how much he'd changed since they'd last met. His head was shaved and the stark black uniform made him look like a member of the Gestapo.

It was too painful to watch in real-time, so Sim scanned forward along their timeline until he found their current location. They were locked in a cell, deep below the Protectorate headquarters. His father's face was bruised and cut, while the others looked scared and stressed but otherwise unhurt.

'Mum?' he cried, his heart breaking.

She looked up, as if she'd heard him.

The image of the timeline seemed to sharpen slightly, and it was as if he was in the cell with them.

'Sim!' she cried, tears forming in her eyes.

His father smiled and tried to stand but his legs were too weak.

Lyra and Phil's faces both lit up.

'You can see me?' asked Sim.

'A projection of you, yes,' his mother said, and nodded.

'What have they done to you?'

'There's no time for that now darling,' she said, wiping away the tears. 'You have to listen very carefully.'

Sim nodded, crying too, but he didn't care.

'Have you found Caitlin and Josh?'

His bottom lip began trembling. 'They're not in the continuum. I think they've gone into the maelstrom.'

His mother considered the idea and then smiled. 'Or maybe Joshua's taken her into the future.'

'Do you think he can?'

'Oh, I think that boy can do a lot more than that, but as long as he stays far away from Dalton we have a chance.'

'Dalton's taken Eddington,' Sim said quietly. 'The professor sent me to retrieve a talisman, because he wouldn't be able to hide it from him.'

'What kind of talisman?'

'A ring — it belonged to Solomon.'

Alixia smiled. 'Then it's good that you've kept it out of his reach.'

Sim sighed. 'The Protectorate were already searching for it, and they nearly caught me.'

'Then we don't have much time.'

'For what? The Eschaton Division are taking over everything.'

'Listen, you need to find a way to contact the Draconians and get us out of here. Can you do that for me? Find Derado and tell him about Caitlin, tell him to contact the Augurs.'

She reached out to touch his face, but he felt nothing.

'Yes mother, but how will I reach them? They've block-aded the past.'

'There is a secret way, through the moon garden,' his father replied.

Sim knew about the memorial to Caitlin's parents, but not that it had a connection to the Draconian Headquarters.

'How do you like the Parabolic?' asked Methuselah. 'Not making you feel too sick?'

'It's great, Dad,' replied Sim, his voice cracking as he tried to hold back the emotion.

'You'd better go,' said his mother.

'Alright. Love you.'

Their images faded away and Sim crumpled to the floor and wept.

17

___

BEDLAM

Through the small barred grille of the cell door Dalton watched Jarius, who was staring at the wall, rocking back and forth while murmuring to himself. The cell was covered with the crazed etchings of a hundred previous inmates, which Jarius seemed to be reading like a book.

'Is there anything you can do for him?' asked Dalton.

'No,' replied Doctor Crooke, 'the man is quite insane.'

'Did he mention anything regarding Eddington?'

The doctor looked puzzled.

Dalton's expression hardly changed as he continued. 'We suspect he murdered the professor. Apparently he was convinced that Eddington knew the location of the second book of the Djinn.'

Crooke closed the shutter on the cell door and turned to Dalton. 'His condition may improve over time, but this has all the hallmarks of a reaving. Not many come back from that, at least in my experience.'

Dalton shrugged and turned to leave.

'There was one thing,' added the doctor.

'Yes?' Dalton said impatiently.

'When he arrived he was quite manic, but there were some moments of lucidity. He asked for Simeon De Freis — Alixia's boy. I sent for him, but he's nowhere to be found. Did he know him?'

Dalton smiled. 'No, but Eddington did.'

18

FERMI

C aitlin was having trouble believing what Josh had just told her.

'What do you mean you left it behind?' she hissed under her breath.

While they'd been waiting, Josh had tried unsuccessfully to explain how he might have unintentionally left one of the Order's most valuable assets, his tachyon, in the hands of a quantum physicist.

'To be fair, I was unconscious.'

'And why exactly were you there in the first place?'

This was the question Josh was trying to avoid, the part of his past he thought he'd buried when the timeline had altered.

'It's complicated.'

'It always is with you. You're the epitome of random — Sim thinks it's part of the nature of the Nemesis. I think it's more like stupidity.'

She was right, of course. He always managed to screw things up, no matter how well planned. Bad things just seemed to happen to him — fate or destiny or whatever they wanted to call it never seemed to give him an easy time.

'Were you studying at the university?'

'No, not exactly,' he mumbled, trying not to look her in the eye.

'Did you work there?'

He shook his head. 'No, I was on a job — kind of free-lancing.'

Josh couldn't think of a better way to describe a getaway driver.

'So,' she began, her voice full of frustration, 'you think that maybe the old guy in the tank is the same professor, that you may have inadvertently given a temporal device to?'

Josh shrugged. 'Possibly. The hologram looks a lot like him.'

'Then I think we should leave, before we make this situation any worse.'

'What about my father?'

Caitlin looked over to the wizened old man in the tank. 'Well I hate to break it to you, but I think your old man might be a vegetable.'

Seven-sigma reappeared. 'The professor will see you now.'

Caitlin scowled at Josh as they followed their host over to the glass tank and stopped when it vanished inside.

The professor looked like a science experiment: hundreds of tubes and cables ran down from the top of the tank connecting to his white, skin-tight diving suit. His face was wrinkled, preserved like a dried old prune, and he was so thin and emaciated that Josh guessed he was probably looking at the oldest living man in history.

The professor raised his head and a spooky pair of milk-white eyes greeted them.

'Welcome,' said a disembodied voice, the thin white lips never moving. 'I have been expecting you.'

'So I've been told,' said Josh.

'Did you come alone?'

Josh realised then that the old man was blind. 'No,' he replied, as there seemed little reason to lie.

'Ah. My calculations predicted a thirty-three percent chance of another. Is she one of them?'

'One of who?' Caitlin interrupted.

'The engineers, I call them — the ones who created that magnificent device you gave me.'

Josh went to protest, but Caitlin's frown changed his mind.

'Yes, I'm from the Order,' she admitted.

'Excellent, I've always wanted to meet one of your kind. Even if you have been interfering in my experiments.'

'Experiments?' asked Caitlin, looking puzzled.

The professor's body began to thrash around inside the water, as if he were having a fit.

Seven-sigma reappeared. 'Please do not be alarmed, the episode will last momentarily,' he informed them in a calming tone and with a reassuring smile.

'What's wrong with him?' Josh asked. He'd seen enough of his mother's spasms to recognise an epileptic seizure.

The avatar's smile faded. 'The professor suffers from an advanced form of Alzheimer's disease. His treatment has managed to reduce the effects, but the therapy can result in mild seizures.'

Mild, thought Josh, *that was a grand mal.*

'Thanks to his advances in neural synchronisation most of his mental state was saved and integrated into the Fermian AI. Some of my neural network is based on his memory. I know for instance that you, Joshua, met the professor and have a perfect recall of the event.'

'Great,' said Josh under his breath. *I'd rather you didn't.*

'What's keeping him alive?' Caitlin asked as the tremors began to subside.

'The professor has developed technologies to extend the human lifespan far beyond its original design, although his physical body cannot leave the preservation chamber.' He pointed to the tank. 'But his mind is very active, and he can experience full physical and sensory input by migrating into a host.'

Josh looked at Caitlin. They were both thinking the same thing.

'You mean like another body?' asked Caitlin.

'Of a clone. Yes.'

Lenin, thought Josh, remembering the last time he'd seen the leader of the Ghost Squad was at the school. *How the hell did Lenin end up here?*

'The clone is the nearest I have come to immortality,' chimed the disembodied voice once more as the hologram faded away.

'I have spent the last hundred years trying to stimulate the technological development of the past in order to advance the present — and find a cure for this damned disease.'

An array of small red lights flashed on his collar and a dark liquid flowed down one of the transparent tubes and into his neck.

'The elixir of life,' the professor explained, 'one of my most significant discoveries and the only treatment that has managed to hold back the progression — although it comes with a heavy price.'

The veins lining his skull darkened as the medicine coursed through his body.

'When I realised you were somehow able to manipulate time, I became obsessed with trying to find a way into the future, but every one of my experiments failed. There were too many variables. So, I began to explore the past but it cost me dearly. Time is a harsh mistress and my condition worsened. The clones allow me to continue my work without suffering further physical deterioration, and I have learned so many things, yet the cure still eludes me.'

His eyes began to glow as the black liquid flowed into his pupils. There was something about it that reminded Josh of the Pharaoh — as though he were being possessed by a Djinn.

'I assume that since you're here, you have encountered one of my experiments. I wonder which timestream you're from. Do you remember the number of the tunnel you appeared in?'

Josh shook his head.

'Three-nine-two-zero,' said Caitlin.

'Interesting.' The corpse in the tank seemed to smile. 'Three hundred years from now. I assume that you have come back to find out who ruined your future?'

19

DERADO

[Ascension Island, Atlantic. Date: 11.927]

The headquarters of the Draconians was located in the tallest lighthouse Sim had ever seen. It was a vast tower, over half a mile high, that sat on Ascension Island in the middle of the Atlantic, two thousand miles from the nearest continent.

The water dragon sculpture in Caitlin's moon garden had taken him directly to the Firedrake that stood proudly in the central chamber of the Draconian command centre, where he found himself immediately surrounded by a group of fearsome-looking Dreadnoughts.

Sim looked into the barrels of their gunsabres and raised his hands. 'T-Tell the grandmaster I know where Caitlin M-Makepiece is,' he stuttered.

'Who are you?' demanded the grandmaster, two hours later, as the guards deposited him into a chair in his office. 'And how do you know my goddaughter?!'

The vast circular space at the very top of the lighthouse had been converted into a war room. Temporal maps and plans had been pinned around the walls, red notes scribbled at key points along the timelines.

'I'm Simeon De Freis,' Sim blurted, slightly upset the old man didn't remember him.

Derado's eyes narrowed, turning to one of the guards. 'Has Madame Besant confirmed his identity?'

The guard nodded. The Dreadnoughts had taken Sim to a seer after they'd searched him for weapons. The woman was nothing like Lyra; she had a hard face, one that had witnessed too many terrible things. Sim had complied with her instructions and let her read his timeline. He had nothing to hide, and in fact it saved a great deal of time not having to convince them of who he was.

'Good!' said the Draconian grandmaster, pouring two large glasses of brandy and handing one to Sim. 'You'll have to forgive our precautions — we're living in interesting times. So, tell me about my goddaughter. Is she safe?'

Sim sipped his drink, trying hard to ignore the burning sensation that was cauterising his throat.

'She's left the continuum.'

'Has she now?' Derado raised an eyebrow. 'Probably for the best. Do you know where, exactly?'

Sim shook his head. 'My mother believes she's gone into the future with the Nemesis.'

Derado sat down behind a large desk which was covered in reports, notes that were continuously rewriting themselves.

'And what do you think?' the grandmaster asked steepling his fingers in front of his face.

It was the first time anyone had ever asked Sim what he

thought. Usually adults told him what to do and when to do it. It took him a few moments to think of a response.

'I think there's an eighty-three-point-two percent probability that she's with him, and that they're working to stop the Eschaton crisis.'

Derado clapped his hands together. 'Spoken like a true Copernican! Tell me, how come the Eckharts haven't managed to lock you up in a cell with the rest of your guild?'

Sim's throat felt tight and hoarse, and he tried to clear it before speaking. 'Professor Eddington helped me escape.'

A dark cloud seemed to pass across Derado's face. 'Eddington was a good man.'

'Was?'

'I've had reports that he died while in Protectorate custody.'

Sim felt a cold knot tighten in his stomach. He took a large gulp of brandy and then nearly coughed most of it back up. 'He's dead?'

Derado drained his glass and went to refill it. 'Do you need another?'

Sim refused with a shake of his head. He was still trying to deal with the news. The professor was someone he'd always thought of as an immortal, the name they gave the old masters, ones who would always be there to guide them.

'You should know that his death will not go unpunished, once this crisis has been averted.'

'Dalton has arrested my family,' Sim said anxiously. 'My mother told me that you'd have a contingency plan — something to do with the Augurs?' he added, having no real idea what an Augur was.

Derado looked suspiciously at Sim. 'What do you know of the Citadel?'

'Nothing.'

The grandmaster grunted. 'Probably for the best — the Augurs aren't your concern, nor mine for that matter. They only report to the founder.'

'And my family?' asked Sim, trying not to sound too concerned.

Derado put down his glass. 'There's nothing I can do I'm afraid. We're only just able to keep the Protectorate away from the major breaches.'

Sim could feel his anger building, his analytical mind was being short-circuited by a sudden burst of emotion. 'But, Dalton will kill them, just like he did Eddington!'

The Draconian grandmaster patted him on the shoulder and sighed deeply. 'I warned the Founder that Ravana wasn't the dangerous one. He's always underestimated her son.'

Sim put his head in his hands. 'He's obsessed with the Djinn. Mum says his father was exactly the same.'

'Valtin? God help us all if we have to deal with another beast like that.'

Sim had never heard anything about Dalton's father, other than he'd died in some kind of hunting accident on their estate in the eleventh century. Dalton had never spoken about him, and they all knew better than to ask. He'd always been an arrogant bully — since as long as Sim could remember — but even so, he couldn't bring himself to imagine that Dalton would hurt Lyra or Phil, let alone his mother, who had welcomed Dalton into their home for years.

Sim stood up, a glimmer of defiance in his eyes. 'I have to try and get them out.'

Derado took a large register out of the desk and swept his hand down the page.

'I have very little in the way of spare resources, and my

regiments are stretched to the limit, blockading the paths into the second dynasty as well as containing four separate breach operations. Someone still has to defend us while all this goes on.'

'What about the recruits?'

Derado put on a pair of spectacles and squinted at the page. 'There were a few that passed through basic training who showed promise.'

'Thank you, sir,' said Sim.

'I wouldn't thank me just yet, as there is no guarantee this will work.'

20

DIFFERENCE ENGINE

[Richmond, England. Date: 11.580]

Dalton wasn't in the mood for another argument with his mother. She'd insisted that he join her at the Copernican hall to discuss the re-instatement of their difference engine with the chief engineer, an irascible fellow by the name of MacKenzie. The grease-stained chief was a plain-speaking northerner who had no problem showing his dislike for Dalton or the Protectorate in general.

'Chief MacKenzie,' his mother began.

'Ma'am,' MacKenzie replied gruffly, in a thick Yorkshire accent.

He was a short, round man with a fat jowly face and dark piercing eyes. His whiskers did their best to cover his many chins, but nothing could disguise the swell of his belly beneath his dirty robes.

'I've been informed that you cannot restart the calculus machine.'

'Difference Engine,' he corrected, 'requires a minimum of two hundred men to run. T'aint going to work with three-score and ten — can't bring her back to life with such a measly crew.'

He held up his hands; they were ingrained with black oil. 'I've but one pair of hands.'

Dalton folded his arms. 'You know the law regarding the gathering of groups of more than fifty.'

'Laws are meaningless. My engine knows nowt of your politicking. I'm telling thee that if thou wants the old girl back on her feet, I need more men.'

Ravana pursed her lips as she mulled it over. Dalton knew better than to interrupt her while she was thinking.

'Where is the Infinity Engine?'

MacKenzie's eyes narrowed a little, and there was a slight tremor to his voice when he answered. 'It's gone.'

'Gone?'

'Founder asked for it weeks ago.'

'Did he now,' Ravana said, glancing at Dalton.

'Aye,' said MacKenzie with a glint in his eye, obviously enjoying the fact that Lord Dee had outwitted them.

'You have two days,' ordered Ravana, turning to Dalton. 'Release another fifty men, and use fifty of your own.'

'But mother, I need them —'

She slapped him hard across the face. MacKenzie tried to hide his amusement as Dalton glowered at her.

'Everything you have is because of me,' his mother hissed. 'Never forget that.'

When they were gone, MacKenzie picked up the speaking tube and blew down the mouthpiece.

Far below in a sweltering furnace room, a whistle sounded.

A half-naked stoker, his skin glistening with sweat and

coal-dust, put down his shovel and picked up the speaking tube.

'Yes boss?'

'Tell your team to take the rest of the day off, master Dawson,' MacKenzie stated in a clear voice with no trace of an accent.

'But what about the boilers sir? If they're allowed to cool it will take weeks to get them back up to steam.'

'Duly noted,' said the chief, stoppering the pipe.

Dalton and his mother reached the founder's chambers an hour later.

'You're sure they've searched everything?' Ravana asked, picking up one of the brandy glasses and sniffing the contents — she clearly thought they hadn't.

Dalton looked abashed. 'Twenty men swept this place, five of them were seers. There's nothing here that he could've used to escape.'

She scowled. 'He's far too clever to have left it in plain sight. Anything you did find was because you were meant to. Damn the man! He's obviously been planning for something like this for months, if not years.'

'For the Eschaton?'

'No, for our coup. He knows that the most valuable asset in controlling the Order is the Infinity Engine. Without it, nothing the Copernicans do can be truly tested.'

'We don't need all of their bloody calculus,' Dalton said, picking up one of the founder's books and throwing it across the room. 'All of this theory and procrastination just holds us back. You're so bound up in tradition — trapped in the past — it's no wonder you can't see our future.'

Her hard expression mellowed, and taking his hand, she

said, 'Sometimes you remind me so much of your father — when he was younger he was all for dispensing with the continuum and following fate.'

Dalton grimaced. 'Was that before or after he used to beat you senseless?'

She flinched and took her hand away. 'He was a difficult man. Brilliant, but flawed.'

'He nearly killed us.'

'That doesn't excuse what you did.'

Nothing ever would, he thought. 'I killed the bastard before he went too far. It was only a matter of time.'

She went to slap his face, but Dalton caught her hand in mid-air.

'I think I've had enough punishment mother. It's about time you listened to me.'

21

LEVERAGE

There was something familiar about the hologram that expanded out to fill the control room. It reminded Josh of the model of the continuum, but without all the temporal notations.

There were millions of tiny lines, weaving around each other, all flowing within a sphere that looked a little like the Death Star.

'A multiverse,' the avatar explained, appearing like a ghost in the centre of the globe. 'The result of a hundred years of systematic exploration. The professor has mapped thousands of alternate realities. Each has been categorised and recorded, and not one of them has produced the outcome we require.'

The avatar waved his hand and many of the lines faded away, leaving one group of branching ribbons of orange energy. 'This is three-nine-two-zero. The projections show that this alternate will most likely suffer corruption from non-linear space.'

'The maelstrom,' Caitlin translated for Josh.

The avatar considered the phrase. 'Yes, that is a fitting term. You're chronology will become infected.'

Josh looked puzzled. 'Like a virus?'

Caitlin leaned in closer to study the branching lines.

'No,' she said, narrowing her eyes. 'The maelstrom introduces too many variables, which will make it too difficult to predict.'

The avatar smiled. 'Exactly.'

'So these are all different versions of the same reality?' asked Josh, trying to get his head around the concept.

'It is the most complex model ever created. Built on machine learning, the system on which it runs is a singularity, a self-aware machine. I am one small part of it.'

'You're sentient?' asked Caitlin.

'Indeed. A by-product of the experiment. The entire complex you stand within is now dedicated to my consciousness.'

'So why were we expected?'

The model zoomed in and another set of blue lines were overlaid on the orange.

'I have processed billions of separate scenarios, looking for a way to accelerate the past, and each time something has failed.'

He waved his hand and the lines followed his fingers back until they were a single thread.

'No matter what I've tried, there is not enough time. Ironic I know, but the last Ice Age presents too great a barrier, and even with all my power I cannot change the climate.'

The lines died out beneath his fingers and scenes of ruined cities, full of slums and starving children, appeared in front of him.

'The past hundred years have been challenging. The

world beyond these walls is in decline. Energy supplies and food shortages have led to civil unrest and the breakdown of society. I calculate that in less than two hundred years from now, life on this planet will have devolved into total anarchy.'

'Couldn't you stop it?' asked Caitlin.

'The burden of progress. The changes I have introduced to the timeline are only for the enhancement of certain technologies: quantum physics, power generation and temporal mechanics. They don't factor the impact on the population or the environment. It would vastly increase the data set and go way beyond my processing capability.'

'If energy is in such short supply, how are you powering this?'

'This facility is run on geothermal energy, but the power required to distort time requires something of a significantly higher magnitude.'

'Nuclear?' wondered Josh.

'Nuclear fission was outlawed after the second Fukushima disaster of 2022. No, the professor found a far more plentiful energy source — dark matter.'

Caitlin frowned. 'It's never been actually proven to exist — except by implication.'

Seven-sigma waved his hand and the model changed to display a map of the maelstrom, or at least parts that Josh recognised from the colonel's observatory.

'Non-linear space gave us more than the ability to travel through time.'

'You've mapped the maelstrom?' asked Caitlin, looking astonished.

The avatar nodded. 'As well as anyone can record a chaotic realm. However, we have harnessed the limitless dark energies of the universe.'

'Yet you won't use them to save the human race?'

'Of course we will! Once we have found the cure.'

Josh thought about what he'd seen in the timeline of the laboratory and how it was still searching three hundred years from now. 'What if you never find it?'

'That is not part of my mission objective. This facility can run indefinitely unless ended by an external factor — such as yourselves.'

'You think we came to stop you?' asked Josh.

'It would be the logical thing to assume.'

The floating egg-shaped spheres had silently surrounded Caitlin and Josh, their fields all glowing red.

'It is my duty to ensure optimal conditions for the experiment are maintained. You are an external factor that must be neutralised. Please do not resist.'

Josh felt something sting the back of his leg and the world faded away.

22

BENTLEY

Bentley sat staring at the invertor. It was a brand new design he was working on, and the copper wiring that he'd wound so carefully around the ferrous cores gleamed in the lamp-light.

Fiftieth winding, he wrote in his journal, *added 20mm of carbon.*

He picked up the soldering iron and fused a small carbon tube onto the copper. He was concentrating so hard on his latest invention that he hardly noticed the arrival of the grandmaster or the boy that came with him.

'Samuel Bentley?' stated Derado, so abruptly that Bentley jumped and dropped the hot iron, which immediately began to burn into the table.

'Sir!' Bentley said, standing to attention.

'This is Simeon De Freis,' he said, nodding to Sim. 'I believe you may be able to assist him.'

Bentley had only ever met Derado once before, after the first trial at the academy. He'd been so nervous then. It was like meeting a god, or a superhero — basically the most important person you could think of. The man just seemed to exude authority.

'Simeon, I'll leave you to explain the situation, as there are certain rather pressing matters that I must attend to.' He patted Sim on the shoulder. 'I hope your family will be safe.'

And with that he disappeared.

Bentley stared at Sim with wide cow-like eyes, both boys unsure of what to do next.

'Do you know Caitlin?' Sim asked awkwardly.

Bentley smiled. 'Yes, and Josh.'

Sim relaxed a little. 'They call me Sim,' he said, holding out his hand.

'Bentley,' he replied, shaking it firmly. 'Artificer, second class.'

'Only second?' Sim looked puzzled.

'Temporarily. I had a slight accident with a Hubble invertor.' He pointed to the disassembled device on the table. 'Have to re-sit my assemblage course to get my grade points up.'

'You haven't graduated?' asked Sim, a hint of surprise in his voice.

'No, but they passed me on account of having seen some action.'

'Really? You've seen a breach?' Sim couldn't contain his curiosity.

Bentley nodded proudly. 'And I've helped to catch a Wyrrm too.'

Sim's eyes went wide. 'A Wyrrm?'

'Yeah, during the DDS trials,' Bentley said with a chuckle. 'It won us the second round, you should have seen the look on Dalton's face when his team lost.'

Sim's enthusiasm waned. 'He's got my family.'

'Ahh.'

'And I need your help to get them back.'

Without another word, Bentley grabbed a leather bag and began to rummage through his drawers, stuffing strange-looking devices into it.

23

WITCH TRIALS

[Chelmsford. Date: 11.645]

The sun was setting over the castle walls, casting the last of its rays across the courtyard and onto the four figures standing on the gallows. The De Freis family stood in the warm glow of the evening with nooses draped around their necks. It was a sight that Dalton had fantasised about since he'd first met the self-righteous Alixia and her brood six years ago. He hated the way she regarded him as if seeing the darkness inside — silently judging him.

But it was different now.

Now, she looked like a frightened rabbit, like the ones he used to find in his snares as a boy. The ones he used to kill very slowly.

He knew that Sim wouldn't be able to stay away. The boy's love for his family would override any instructions that Eddington would have given him.

It took less than an hour for the boy to arrive.

Dalton weighed the ring in his hand; the gold felt unusually warm, even through his glove. 'You did the right thing.'

Sim stood before him, flanked by two of Dalton's guards, his eyes cast down at his feet.

'What choice did I have? You were going to kill them,' snapped Sim, showing more backbone than Dalton would've given him credit for.

Dalton smirked at the scar on the back of Sim's hand — the date was still faintly legible. 'I knew you would evaluate the options. All I had to do was make the stakes high enough so your little Copernican brain would have no choice but to choose the most logical path.'

Sim tested the bindings around his wrists, but the hemp rope tightened as he flexed his muscles, biting into his skin. He looked up to his family standing on the gallows behind Dalton. His mother was staring at him with tired, sad eyes. She knew the choices he'd had to make, the sacrifice he wasn't willing to go through.

'What happens now?' Sim asked weakly.

Dalton smirked, taking off his glove and placing the ring on his index finger.

'Now I have a talisman that can control the Djinn? I think we both know what happens next.'

Dalton turned to the hooded executioners and nodded. The two men grabbed Sim and dragged him up to the scaffold.

'But you said you would let them go!' screamed Sim.

Dalton wasn't listening. He was too busy admiring his new toy.

. . .

'Hi,' Lyra said, a sad smile on her face as they placed a noose around Sim's neck.

'Hi,' replied Sim, trying to be brave.

'What day is it?' she asked tamely.

'Friday, I think. Does it matter?'

She shrugged. 'Always thought I would die on a Sunday. Not sure why.'

His mother and father nodded stoically at him over Lyra's head.

The thirteenth century crowd that gathered around the gallows was becoming impatient. They'd come to see some witches hang, and the delay created by Sim's arrival had clearly postponed their enjoyment and many were beginning to mutter and curse under their breaths.

'Ladies and Gentlemen,' Dalton began in old English, 'there stands before thee today the most seditious coven of witches and warlocks that I have ever had the misfortune to meet.'

He was playing the part of the notorious Witchfinder General, Matthew Hopkins, the son of a puritanical clergyman and the self-appointed investigator of witchcraft in East Anglia. Sim remembered Dalton boasting about how he loved to go back and impersonate the man and all his cruel practices on women.

'They all bear the Devil's mark,' he said, nodding to one of his guards, who was dressed in a long cloak with a black cowl masking his face. The man reached up and tore open Phileas' shirt to show his birthmark. It was a port wine stain in the shape of a crescent moon, one which they'd always joked about being a sign of a werewolf in another life. The crowd drew back a little at the sight of it — Sim could sense the hysteria as Dalton stirred them up.

The witch finder held up an almanac. Sim recognised it

immediately as his mother's — full of sketches of dinosaurs and other extinct creatures.

'They have made their pact with Lucifer, learned the names of demons and consorted with all manner of beasts. Do they deserve to live?'

'No!' came the crowd's unanimous reply.

Dalton nodded sternly. 'Then let us pray for their souls,' he said, bowing his head. 'I have come into the world as a light, so that no one who believes in me should stay in darkness. If anyone hears my words but does not keep them, I do not judge that person. For I did not come to judge the world, but to save the world. Amen'

He turned and walked off into the crowd.

Sim saw the fervour in the faces of those who let him pass. They treated him as if he were some kind of messiah, even trying to touch his coat as he strode away.

As he felt the floor beneath his feet fall away and the noose tighten he prayed that Bentley knew what he was doing.

Dalton admired the ring. There was something about the way the gold glimmered, even out of the sunlight — as if it were internally powered, but only when it was against his skin.

He'd taken to wearing leather gloves after the "accident" when his father had lost his temper and plunged his hand into a boiling pot. The fingers of his left hand had been badly scalded, withering the skin like an old man. Those that saw it never quite managed to hide their pity and he couldn't stand that — he wanted to be strong and respected, even feared. The gloves had given him that, and more besides — as a seer he hated physical contact with others, as the slightest touch meant catching moments of their pathetic lives, and no matter how hard he tried to block them out, they were always an anathema to him.

He'd taken off his left glove and pushed the ring onto his gnarled finger. It slipped over the scars with ease, as if expanding to glide over the swollen joints. Once in place he felt it contract, fixing itself tight against the skin.

Then the healing began.

Dalton watched in surprise as the layers of scar tissue smoothed out, returning his hand to the youthful version it should have been. Vitality returned to his fingers, and when he compared it with his right hand, they were both the same.

He was whole once more, or at least as whole as he could ever be — thanks to his father.

When his father had lay dying, shot by his own gun, Dalton had taken great delight in entering his degrading timeline. He made himself witness the moments of his past brutality as they vanished into the dark void, hoping that he would find some kind of closure as they died. The scars of his childhood refused to heal, and nothing changed except for the singular feeling of dread and despair that he experienced at the end of his father's timeline, one that had intrigued him ever since. The impression that there was something beyond the veil.

His father was an angry man, who seemed to blame his only son for all the things that were wrong with his life. Dalton had borne the brunt of his inadequacies for sixteen years, suffering in silence, pretending this was somehow normal family life — and his mother stood by and let it happen.

Until the hunting accident.

On that day in 11.817 they had been stalking wild boar through the forests of the lower Rhine. It was something Dalton got to do once a year, on his birthday, and every year his father had promised that one day he would have his own gun.

And on his sixteenth birthday, in keeping with the long family tradition, he got one.

It was a Purdey, a fine, sporting shotgun, chased in silver with the family crest inscribed into the stock. There was nothing to compare with the feeling of carrying his own weapon through the thick, resinous pines of the valley. It was as if he'd finally been accepted by his father, that the feeling of being a failure could now be laid to rest.

The shot was a simple one, and it should have been a clean kill.

But Dalton clipped the boar, and the second shot was off by a mile. He tried to blame the gun, but the look on his father's face as he shouldered his own weapon left little doubt as to how he felt.

The grand old boar turned towards them and charged.

It was a fearsome beast, at least 90 kilos and with tusks as long as Dalton's forearm. As it crashed through the undergrowth towards them, his father calmly took aim, waiting for the shot.

Dalton reloaded his rifle quickly and raised it, sighting on the beast as it thundered down the trail towards them. He didn't want his father to think he was weak — he still had time to take the shot.

His father was shouting something at him, telling him to move to higher ground or climb a tree. Dalton always remembered that moment as the first and last time he had ever heard his father try to protect him.

He emptied the first barrel into his father's back and, as he fell, the second shot went into the boar.

Both lay dying at his feet as he broke his gun and let the cartridges fly out into the bush.

The wild pig panted hoarsely. Dalton could hear the blood filling its lungs with every breath, and gave it a merciful death with a carefully placed knife between the ribs.

His father was shown no such favour.

Kneeling down beside him, Dalton carefully removed the rifle from his grip, and as bright red blood bubbled up out of his father's mouth, he grasped his hand.

'Papa,' he whispered into his ear, 'I will never forgive you.'

Then Dalton let his mind descend into the last moments of his father's timeline.

24

RESCUE

[London. Date: Present day]

Sim came up last. He wasn't the strongest of swimmers and the drop had taken him deeper than he'd estimated, leaving him gasping for air when he surfaced.

Turning around he saw the others already swimming towards the side, where Bentley was standing holding a large bundle of towels.

'You took your time,' said the beaming red-headed boy, putting down the towel and grabbing hold of Sim's hand.

Sim could still feel the graze of the rope against his neck and shivered at the thought of what might have happened if Bentley had got it wrong.

They had landed in the baths in the basement of the Chapter House. Bentley had hooked up a series of apertures in the trapdoors the night before the execution.

Sim wished he could have seen the faces of the god-fearing crowds as the bodies disappeared from the nooses. He could imagine all kinds of legends being born from that day, and made a mental note to look up the Chelmsford witch trials when he got the chance.

It was a terrible thing to have to put his family through, but warning them meant there was always a chance Dalton would've found out. Sim had based his predictions on Dalton's obsession for the talisman overriding his usual paranoia. He calculated that the sight of the ring would distract him enough, and of course Sim had counted on the probability that he would never hold up his side of the deal.

Dalton was too much of a coward to stay and witness their deaths. Though his speech had been slightly shorter than Sim had estimated, he'd built in a contingency. Dalton had to believe they were being executed, which meant leaving just enough time between his exit and the hanging.

Dalton's threat had appeared on the back of Sim's hand a few hours after Derado had left him with Bentley, which was timely, since neither of them could agree on the best way to rescue his family.

Bentley explained how he could create almost any kind of temporal device, including a breacher, and punch a hole into another part of time. The problem they faced was that Sim's family were being held in the Protectorate's high-security unit, a prison buried deep below their headquarters that was shielded by an array of temporal defences. Other than the Parabolic Chamber, there was no way in or out of their cell without alerting the guards.

'Their timelines are off-limits,' said Bentley, lying on the roof of the building opposite and studying the Protectorate building with a pair of modified binoculars. Looking through them, Sim felt immediately ill, like he did with most lensing equipment, but what he did catch was the lack of temporal variance in the building itself. While everything around it changed and fluctuated, their headquarters stood unchanging.

They'd gone back fifty years before the Protectorate had acquired the building. Bentley called it a 'safe distance', but Sim wasn't convinced and kept looking over his shoulder.

'I just need to get an idea of the structure,' Bentley explained as they walked down the fire escape and down onto Lexington Avenue.

The Chrysler building was a grand, art-deco skyscraper that dominated the east side of midtown Manhattan.

'Steel,' Bentley moaned as they walked past the entrance, 'not my favourite material. It acts like a Faraday cage, bloody impossible to breach. They knew what they were doing when they chose this building.'

Sim suddenly felt a pain lance through his hand and looked down to see the date '11.645' appear in white scar tissue across the back of it.

'What the —' swore Bentley as he caught sight of the wound. 'Someone wants to get your attention.'

'Dalton,' said Sim, rubbing the scar with his thumb. It was at least seven or eight years old. Dalton had gone back into his timeline and carved it onto his younger self. It was called a 'cicatrix', and was a serious violation of one of their basic laws — interfering in another's timeline.

'What's so important about that date?'

Sim knew the moment he saw it. 'Witch trials.'

His mother and father were engaged in a serious conversation, so Sim dumped his wet clothes and went to sit with Lyra and Phileas. They both looked as if they were still in shock and Bentley had given them hot drinks which were slowly cooling, untouched in their hands.

'What did you give him?' asked Phileas.

'A talisman. A kind of ancient vestige.'

'One that can command the Djinn,' warned Lyra, still shivering.

'Perhaps,' said Sim, taking a steaming mug of hot chocolate from Bentley, 'but first he has to create a breach and all the known ones are being guarded by Dreadnoughts. The only way he can reach the Djinn is to create one, and he can't do that without the help of the Draconians.'

Lyra didn't look convinced. 'How long before he works out how to do that?'

Sim shrugged. 'No idea.'

His parents walked over to join them.

His mother gathered Sim up in her arms and hugged him tightly. 'Well done, my brave boy. I knew you would find a way,' she whispered into his ear.

It took Sim half-an-hour to explain how he and Bentley had planned their rescue. There were many questions, especially from his father, who was fascinated by what Bentley had done with the trapdoors.

When he'd finished, his mother stood up and smoothed down her dress, which seemed to have dried out remarkably quickly.

'Darlings, your father and I have decided that we should seek sanctuary with the Draconians until this nonsense resolves itself. Bentley has generously offered to escort us back to the lighthouse.'

It felt like they were running away to Sim, and his mother could see he was confused.

'This is not the end my brave one,' she added, stroking his cheek. 'The resistance will take many forms, but we must regroup and have time to formulate a strategy.'

Sim smiled weakly. His mother was right, as always. They'd been taken by surprise and to react too quickly could end in disaster.

Bentley strode over to them. 'We have to go, Madam.'

Alixia nodded and pulled all of her children to her. 'Be safe my little ones.'

Sim realised then that she wasn't coming with them.

25

FUTURES

Josh woke to find that they were in some kind of operating theatre, surrounded by clinical steel devices and medical equipment.

He tried to move his arms, but they felt like lead weights. His head was the only thing that wasn't strapped down, and when he turned it he saw Caitlin strapped onto a white table beside him.

Her eyes were wild and the veins stood out in her neck as she tried desperately to move away from the needle-like probes that were hovering next to her temples.

'It will be less painful if you don't struggle.' The voice of the professor sounded odd coming from the expressionless face of Lenin. 'I have added a mild sedative to compensate for the anxiety.'

A band of light scanned along her body, creating a holographic model of her internal physiology in increasing levels of detail above her.

'Interesting,' observed Lenin, studying the hologram. 'She's quite normal — no sign of temporal degradation. Whatever genetic abnormality allows you to move through time will be a vast improvement on the Lenin model.' He tapped an icon and the needles began to move inwards.

The white-coated Lenin turned towards Josh. 'So, I wonder what we'll discover within your biology?'

A vicious array of sharp instruments descended from the ceiling and Josh struggled against his own bindings, but the clamps held fast.

'What do you want?' Josh shouted.

'You're the first visitors to have returned from one of my experiments. There's a great deal I can learn from the effects of the time dilation — and I'm always interested in upgrading my hosts.'

Josh realised then that Fermi had no idea about his mother; for whatever reason it hadn't happened yet.

Lenin initiated the same scan on Josh. 'I'm especially interested in what it does to the structure of the brain.'

Josh felt a warm band of energy move along his body as Fermi studied the results. He seemed unimpressed with what he saw, which Josh took as a positive until the needles in the unit deployed.

26

FOUNDER

[Date: -654,000,000]

It had been a while since the founder had walked the timelines and the aching in his joints reminded him exactly how long it had been. He knew all the old paths well enough — the ancient ways that others had forgotten — but there was still something to be said for actually traversing them.

He was tired and cold, as there'd been no time to prepare for this journey and his robes were thin, letting the icy winds cut through them like a knife.

It had taken two days to travel here, taking diversions to ensure that no one would be able to follow his path, especially Ravana and her pack of wolves. He'd selected the most obscure routes through history, sometimes doubling back on himself just to conceal his destination.

Bumping against his hip in a small leather bag was the Infinity Engine. He gripped the strap with both hands as he began the descent down the snow-covered ridge and into the white valley beyond.

The Marinoan Ice-Age was one of the only places he knew where the device would be safe. A blank space in the map of the continuum. No one could navigate accurately through the millions of years of glaciation without a suitable vestige and an object that could be used to reach this far back was extremely rare. There were still a few talismans of his own that he kept earmarked for just such an occasion and he tried to find some comfort in the fact that he'd never had to use one until now.

His boots made deep impressions in the snow as he reached the bottom of the valley. It was a long, deep cut between the mountains, covered in a glistening blanket of purest white. The place he sought was at the northern end of the defile and half way up the mountain, somewhere that could only be reached by foot, and without snowshoes it would be hard going. The drifts were already coming over his knees and he hadn't reached the worst of it yet.

The founder put down the bag and blew on his hands, the air from his breath creating clouds of ice crystals as it froze. The earth at this time was a truly barren, inhospitable place, and he marvelled at the fact life had managed to survive this period at all.

Taking the old locket out of his cloak he sat down upon a rock and read the inscription.

'The future belongs to the dreamers.'

His wife had given it to him on the day they were married; it was the only thing left from that life and it always made him smile. It was also his personal key, with a limited range of no more than a few years either side of a very special location. Opening up its history he felt time slide under his fingers, flowing back to the moment he first arrived in this world — the day he stepped into this timeline.

27

E.R.D

Walking through the underground vaults of his Eschaton Research Department, Dalton could feel the power of the ring pulsing against his palm. It was calling to him, inviting him to open its chronology, but he resisted, knowing that once he succumbed there would be no going back.

His mother was too busy with the council to take any notice of what he was really doing with his research. Everyone involved had been instructed that their work was classified top secret, kept apart from the other Protectorate departments to reduce the chances of escalating the crisis, or at least that was the lie they chose to believe.

The research department was established after the Augurs revealed that the first three crises of the cascade had taken place. Using the power of the Eschaton Martial Act, Dalton immediately sequestered every expert on the Djinn and the maelstrom that he could find within the Order.

He had no time for the Augurs. They were a superstitious group who treated the Eschaton Cascade like it was some kind of religious doctrine. A secretive sect that dressed in long robes like monks and refused to answer any of his questions regarding the crises — something that Dalton hoped would give him a better idea of how to enter the maelstrom.

They were all so mysterious and enigmatic, with an annoying air of those who knew all the secrets but refused to tell.

Now Dalton had over a hundred officers at his disposal and most of them were handpicked for their specialist skills and abilities, many for their knowledge of the chaos realm.

Ever since the interrogation of Jones and his revelations about the future, Dalton had become determined to find a way into the maelstrom. The prophecy had been correct about one thing; the Nemesis was a bringer of change, and he finally knew what his destiny was to be. The version of the timeline Jones had seen was out there somewhere, waiting for him. All he needed to do was find a way to reach it, and for that he needed the power of the Djinn.

His intelligence reports were clear that there was no chance of leaving through any of the existing breaches. Every one of them was under Draconian control, and since they had annexed themselves from the Order, they were not responding to any of the Protectorate directives. Dalton had considered attacking one of their positions, but he couldn't come up with a plausible reason that would satisfy his mother.

His only option was to create a breach of his own. He'd considered using Daedalus' skull, but since the Augurs caught Caitlin and the Nemesis trying to steal it, his mother had placed it in a secure vault under twenty-four hour guard. Dalton needed another way to cross over, one that didn't raise too many questions or involve drawing too much attention upon himself or his team.

The Draconians had a specialist unit for dealing with breaches, the Dreadnoughts, who were dedicated to defending the weak points in the chronosphere rather than causing them, but he knew they must have a good understanding of how to create one.

Especially their artificers, and one in particular had crossed his path during training.

Bentley.

28

DRACONIAN HQ

I t was midnight, and Sim was sitting in the observation deck at the top of the lighthouse, staring out through the glass walls at a vast ocean of stars.

'Where do you think Caitlin is right now?' wondered Lyra, who was curled up beside him on the sofa.

Sim let out a long, mournful sigh; it was the question he'd been pondering all day. 'I don't know.'

'Do you think she's really gone into the future?'

Sim looked down and took her hand. 'I guess so. Mum isn't usually wrong about this kind of stuff.'

Lyra turned his hand over to study the scar. The date was still clearly visible, carved in sharp white marks.

'I can't believe Dalton went back and did that to you. He's turning into a monster.'

'I think he's always been one. We were just too nice to point it out.'

'What do you think he's going to do with the talisman now?'

'Try and get into the maelstrom somehow.'

Lyra shivered. 'I can't think of anywhere I'd like to go less.'

'From what Bentley told me, there are Dreadnoughts stationed at every breach for the last ten thousand years. Dalton's only a fifth millennial, so he's got a limited range. He can't go back past 7.000.'

'Maybe that's why he's so obsessed with the Djinn — he wants to use them to go back further.'

'You think he's got some kind of inferiority complex?' asked Sim, holding up his little finger and wiggling it.

Lyra laughed. 'Oh yeah. He wouldn't ever admit it, but his reach has always held him back. Seers usually have an unlimited range — it kind of comes with the package.'

They watched the falling stars arc across the night sky for a while, thinking about the furthest back they'd been in time.

'Do you know what a talisman is?' asked Lyra after a few minutes.

'Not really. Eddington just told me that it was too dangerous to let Dalton anywhere near one.'

'I can't believe he's dead,' Lyra said with a shake of her head.

'And Dalton has the ring now.'

'That wasn't your fault. You did the right thing.'

Bentley walked into the room, carrying a tray of food. 'Sorry, the kitchen's closed, so I had to raid the larder.'

There was honeyed bread, cheese and slices of various meats as well as large glasses of cider. Sim and Lyra clapped their hands and grunted their gratitude as they began to tuck in.

Bentley nodded and went to leave.

'Is there any news from my mother?' asked Lyra, spreading butter over the warm bread.

'Nothing. But to be honest, I'm the last person they would tell.'

'Why?'

Bentley flushed a little at the question, his gaze dropping to his feet. 'Everyone's busy, and I'm the most junior rating here, so important stuff tends to take a while to drift down to me, unless it involves catering.'

'I know the feeling,' agreed Sim through a mouthful of cheese.

Bentley's eyes lit up and he leaned in. 'I did hear that the founder has disappeared with the Infinity Engine.'

'Good,' Sim said, 'at least that means Dalton's as blind as we are when it comes to the next crisis.'

'I don't think he cares about the Eschaton Cascade,' said Lyra, who was constructing the largest sandwich Bentley had ever seen.

'Really?' Bentley looked surprised. 'Why not?'

'He's never believed in it,' Sim explained. 'He thinks that Copernicans create problems out of some need to find them. He's a determinist, so the idea of predicting the future of a chaotic universe is abhorrent to him.'

'Whereas you're a natural-born worrier,' said Lyra.

Sim smiled. 'I can't help being risk averse.'

'He gets that from his mother,' she added, 'who I'm guessing is probably planning some kind of counter-attack as we speak.'

29

XENO

[Royal Zoological Gardens, London. Date: 11.828]

The Xenobiology department was off-limits to most members of the Order, mainly because it held some of the most deadly and dangerous creatures from the maelstrom, or storm-kin, within its cells.

Alixia had taken extra precautions on her route to their laboratory. She'd correctly assumed that the main entry points would be being watched. Dalton wasn't stupid enough to try and raid it, but she knew that he had a talisman now and would be considering trying to use it on one of their specimens in the hope of creating a breach.

She had to warn Doctor Shika, the head of the Xeno department.

The lab was hidden deep below London Zoo, in Regent's Park, and housed over four hundred species from the maelstrom. It had been created by Daniel Dangerfield years ago to better understand the chaotic, non-linear realm by studying the hideous creatures that lived within it.

Daniel had died the previous year, killed by a chimæra, a hybrid of man and maelstrom — which was thought to be another precursor to the Eschaton Cascade.

Kaori Shika had been promoted to his position on Alixia's recommendation. Her role had always been a supporting one within the Xenos; although not actively involved in their management, Alixia had helped Dangerfield to develop the techniques for storm-kin capture and containment.

Alixia was an extinction curator, which focussed on the study of long-dead species, and had dedicated her life to understanding the reasons behind their eradication, which in most cases also meant bringing them back to life.

'Alixia, how lovely to see you,' Kaori said, greeting her with a formal bow.

Alixia put her arms around the small Japanese doctor and hugged her.

'How are you?' she asked when Alixia stepped back. 'I heard a ridiculous story about your family being hanged?'

Alixia subconsciously rubbed her neck. 'I am dead, at least in the eyes of the Eschaton Division, but other than that I'm quite well. There will be time for details later. Right now we must discuss your security.'

She took Kaori's arm and they walked into the central hall. It was an enormous round chamber with iron staircases rising up along the high curved walls. Thick glass panelled cells that lined the ground floor were filled with strange and terrifying beasts, each one guarded by a Xeno technician in a heavily shielded suit.

'As you can see, I have imposed a lockdown as you instructed.'

'Good, and are all the access portals sealed? Even the secret ones?'

Kaori nodded.

Alixia's keen eyes scanned the laboratory, catching glimpses of hideous creatures moving silently behind reinforced glass. 'Have the storm-kin showed any abnormal activity?'

Kaori looked puzzled. 'No more than usual. Are you expecting some kind of trouble?'

'I believe they may be the first indicator of a breach, and they'll be more sensitive to any maelstrom activity. We must remain vigilant — these are our canaries.'

Kaori nodded. 'You suspect there's going to be an attack from the maelstrom?'

'No,' Alixia said and shook her head. 'I believe someone on this side is going to initiate one.'

Suddenly, an alarm went off, sending the guards into a frenzy of activity, men and women in armoured suits running in from all corners of the building, carrying an array of large calibre weapons. They formed a cordon around Alixia and Kaori, whose tiny body had metamorphosed, and was completely enclosed within the spectral shell of a terrifying horned monster.

A shimmering portal expanded in the air in front of them and two rather flustered people stepped through it.

'Madam De Freis?' probed the man nervously, his features reminding Alixia of Caitlin.

She studied the woman, whose eyes confirmed her suspicions. 'Mr and Mrs Makepiece I believe?'

'We need your help,' Caitlin's mother said with a hint of desperation. 'Caitlin has disappeared and the only man who can help us has been badly injured.'

Alixia nodded, turning back to Kaori. 'Let me know the moment you detect any abnormal behaviour.'

Kaori, who was still shrouded in the ghostly aura of her creature, simply bowed.

30

FERMI

Josh heard someone cry out. His vision was blurry from the drugs, but he could just make out another clone of Lenin standing over him. This one was naked except for a tattoo on his neck that read 'Xooor', and he was holding a knife in one hand which was covered in blood.

The clone was staring at him and saying something, but Josh couldn't hear what it was, then he felt a sharp pain in his leg and lost consciousness again.

'Wake up!' insisted someone from deep within his dream.

'Josh — wake up! I think this place is going to blow!'

It was Caitlin. She was shaking him and slapping his face.

'Okay!' he said, opening his eyes.

'Get up!' she demanded, something in her voice telling him she was scared.

The world swam a little as he swung his legs off the operating table, and he put his hand on her shoulder to stop the room spinning. There was something silver sticking out of his thigh.

'What happened?' she asked, pointing at the knife in his leg.

'I think he was operating on me,' he said, nodding to the body on the floor.

It was Lenin, the one the professor had been using, his white coat was stained with red.

'There was another one. Another Lenin. I think he killed him.'

A loud explosion shook the room and the lights went out, plunging the operating theatre into darkness. A few seconds passed before the emergency lighting kicked in.

Lenin lay dead in the middle of the room, his face completely blank, as if someone had just taken out his batteries. A dark stain spreading across his chest where he'd been stabbed.

'We need to get out of here. Do you think you can walk?' Caitlin put his arm around her shoulder.

Josh nodded, then winced as he tried to put his weight on the injured leg. 'You're going to have to pull it out.'

Caitlin searched the drawers for anything useful, but most were full of devices she'd no idea how to use. Then she found something that looked like a bandage.

Gripping the handle of the knife, she told him to take a deep breath and pulled. The blade was sharp and came out easily, as did the blood. She applied the largest dressing and pressed hard, watching the white gauze turn red.

'Hold that,' she ordered, opening a packet of plasters as he took over.

Josh was looking very pale. Caitlin knew she had to work fast before his blood pressure became a problem. She placed the first plaster over the dressing and was amazed to see it expand around the wound as if it knew what to do, and they both watched in silence as the band-aid secured itself and sealed the bleed.

'Wow,' she said. 'That's one benefit of being in the future then.'

The colour was returning to Josh's cheeks. 'I can't feel anything,' he shrugged.

'Probably some kind of built-in anaesthetic. Does that mean you can walk? We need to leave here before he sends another clone,' she said, looking around for an escape route.

Josh limped to the door. The lack of power on the control panel told him it was out of action too. 'We can go back the way we came?' he suggested, tapping the metal door with his knuckle.

'No, that future won't exist at this rate,' she said, examining the knife. 'This has a basic chronology we can use to get back to those time tunnels.'

'It's like the one he used on my mum,' said Josh, taking it from her.

'Some kind of DNA extraction tool I guess.'

31

TIBET

[Spiti Valley, Tibet. Date: 11.587]

The founder paused to watch a golden eagle soar effortlessly on air currents that swept down from Everest and into the steep, rocky sides of the Spiti valley. He spied the Ki Monastery standing on top of a hill, dwarfed by the broken-toothed mountains of the Himalayas.

He stretched his back, kneading the knotted muscles at the base of his spine. Parts of Ki were over a thousand years old, cracked and crumbling; he knew exactly how they must feel. Its ancient stone walls were built more in the style of a fortress than a religious sanctuary for good reason, as the monastery and surrounding village had survived numerous attacks from Mongol armies, not to mention earthquakes and fires.

He'd moved forward millions of years in the blink of an eye. Like a time-lapse film, he had watched the ice-sheets and glaciers that had once covered the landscape melt away, leaving nothing but the meandering river that wound through the accumulated shale and boulders that were scattered across the valley floor.

As he climbed the stairs to the stone battlements, an old Buddhist monk, dressed in traditional gold and maroon robes, stepped out of the temple doorway and bowed to him.

'Lord,' he said, greeting him in Zhe-sa, the polite, respectful style of Tibetan.

The founder bowed low. 'Master.'

'You carry the worries of the world on your shoulders,' the old monk said, his eyes studying the founder's empty bag. 'Has the time come?'

The founder sighed. 'As you predicted it would. I'm afraid I must seek the sanctuary of the Citadel.'

The monk closed his eyes and spoke quietly. 'Do not dwell in the past, do not dream of the future, concentrate the mind on the present moment.'

He stepped aside and allowed Dee into his temple.

There was always a sense of serenity that came over him when he walked through the corridors of the temple. Hundreds of columns lined the passageways that led to the inner sanctum, each one elaborately decorated in relief of Buddhist stories: of cause and effect or flying goddesses and powerful deities.

With each step he found himself reflecting on the plans he'd made. If this truly were the beginning of the Eschaton Cascade, then everything he'd prepared for would be tested. This wasn't the first time he'd witnessed the end of a timeline, and the founder shuddered at the memory of what could be facing them if they didn't manage to correct the course they were on.

The Djinn were not the worst of things that lived outside of time.

32

THE LETTER

Bentley hadn't seen or spoken to his family since he'd joined the Draconian Defence trials, and for all they knew he was still at the Academy trying to complete his training.

His father was a retired Draconian engineer, and his mother was a Scriptorian who worked at the Bibliothèque Mazarine in Paris. He had a brother and two sisters who were all much older than him and had followed their mother into the Scriptoria — he was the only one who'd joined his father's guild.

Or at least he'd tried to.

Bentley had a sneaking suspicion that if it hadn't been for his actions with the Wyrrm, he'd never have made the grade. He was proud of how they had trapped the creature, even if it had cost Darkling his life, but he couldn't shake the feeling that he wasn't really cut out to be a Dreadnought.

The thought of having to deal with those kinds of terrors every day made him break out in a cold sweat. He was much happier making stuff, like his father before him — they were inventors, not fighters, and even though he'd proved himself in battle, Bentley felt it was probably better for all if he stepped down from the front line.

The problem was that he hadn't found a way to tell his commanding officer.

Since rescuing Sim's family, the threat level had been raised to severe, which meant that the entire guild had gone into a permanent state of combat readiness, and every guild member was mobilised — ready at all times for battle. It was over a week now and Bentley had grown tired of carrying the cumbersome gunsabre around with him; the rifle weighed a ton and his body armour was bulky and uncomfortable.

He was stationed with the garrison on Ascension Island, which was more like a prison than a dormitory, and Bentley, who was by far the youngest of the squad, felt like a complete fraud surrounded by so many veterans.

At lunch, a letter arrived from his father, and Bentley felt his spirits rise. He'd written to him only the day before to ask his advice on what he should do, and was so eager to read his reply that he gave away the rest of his rations.

Taking the note, he slipped out of the canteen and took the elevator up to the observation deck, which was deserted, so he settled down to read in peace.

'*My dear boy,*' his father began, '*please do not be alarmed, but we have been taken by the Protectorate and are currently being held against our will.*'

His dad was rather old-fashioned, having been born in the late-seventeenth century, and his turn of phrase tended to be a little understated. What he really meant to say was: 'Help! We've been taken prisoner!'

'*Our captors have been quite fair-handed thus far, and we are for the most part unharmed.*'

Bentley's hand shook with anger as he read on.

'*I have been instructed to implore you to attend us at your earliest convenience, and for the sake of your mother's nerves, it would be most agreeable if you would come directly.*

Tell no one. D.'

Bentley's knuckles were white as he opened the timeline attached to the letter.

It was a simple task to unwind its chronology and find his family sitting shivering in a dark cell somewhere beneath the Protectorate headquarters.

Bentley knew better than to jump straight into it, even though every nerve in his body was telling him to do so. Tears filled his eyes as he stood hovering on the edge of the event watching his father write the note while Dalton's henchmen stood menacingly over him.

Why would Dalton want me? he wondered, thinking back to the time he'd met the arrogant bully and his gang of Daedalans in the lower dungeons of the academy.

As he disconnected from the timeline, another message appeared in a different hand below his father's writing.

'*Don't take too long.*'

It was signed in blood.

33

JUSTICE

Fermi observed Lenin's entrance through a hundred different video feeds.

The man was naked, and his gleaming, well-muscled body was everything that the old professor was not.

Fermi remembered the first time he'd occupied that body, wearing it as if it were a set of clothes, feeling the skin and muscle of his arms, touching and flexing his fingers as his mind integrated with the neural pathways.

The sensation of standing on two feet again as he stepped out of the gestation pod had been a revelation — like being reborn. To breath air without the assistance of a machine, to feel the weight of gravity on his body, all sensations he'd never thought to experience again.

Not until he'd discovered dark energy.

Then everything changed.

His work on the time portals had given him the ability to change the past. Fermi had used it to accelerate many different areas of research, teaching young scientists knowledge they should never have had, using multiple pasts to improve their theories. It was the ultimate scientific method, and every iteration brought him closer to his goal, closer to the cure.

One particular area of study was in quantum fluctuation. The waves of space-time were creating energy, a limitless supply of energy. When he learned how to harness this dark power source his range became extraordinary, he could suddenly reach parts of the past that were well beyond the scope of his original machine.

Fermi soon realised he could move beyond time altogether and it was then that he first felt the alien presence. There was no real physical element to their connection, merely the existence of another entity. It had no shape, no real consciousness, but somehow from within the dark energy that flowed through his suit, an awareness surfaced, an insidious collection of thoughts and memories permeating his own like a virus.

The memories of a thousand lifetimes poured into his augmented mind. He had absorbed them all, and like a petulant child at Christmas, he would open each one and devour it. There were so many stories, so many lifetimes to share. The entity taught him of the other universes, ancient timelines that had died before his own was even begun. The alien showed him ways to use his technology, to move his mind into Lenin and to harness the dark energy to power the portals.

Now Lenin stood on the other side of the glass tank, his hand on the controls, smearing its pristine surface with blood. Fermi watched as Lenin began to disable the safety protocols on his life support. He felt the supply of dark energy slowing, felt the creature within him begin to hunger.

Lenin turned to the main control desk as Seven-sigma materialised.

'You will refrain from any further action,' it said politely to the clone.

Lenin ignored it, staring at the screens that were still displaying live feeds of his brothers out in the field. He picked up one of the small egg-shaped robots and shook it until the field turned to a deep shade of red, and then threw it hard into the main desk.

The explosion ripped through the unit as if it were made of paper, and flames seared his skin, but he felt no pain. Fermi had engineered them that way so that they could endure the most extreme conditions.

As the life support drained away, it somehow seemed fitting that Lenin should be the one to end it. The facilities' alarms were activating, a core breach was imminent, but as Fermi felt the cold seeping into his body, he realised he didn't care, for the other mind had shown him what was to come and it wasn't a future he wanted to be part of.

34

EXECUTION

Bentley tried and failed to hide the shock of finding his father on his knees before Dalton. The rest of his family were nowhere to be seen, but the sword that lay across his father's neck was enough of a threat to focus his attention.

'Your father tells me you are one of the brightest artificers of your generation,' said Dalton, sneering. 'A glowing commendation from such a respected engineer. I wonder if you're as good as he says — you know what dads are like.'

Bentley had no idea that his father thought of him like that, and he could still remember the day that he'd told him he wanted to join the Dreadnoughts. The look of disbelief on his father's face was nearly enough to make him change his mind, but he hadn't, and now it seemed he might be their only hope.

Dalton had taken over an old church, somewhere in the fourteenth century. It was a solemn, gothic building with gargoyles and saints staring blindly down at them from the vaulted ceiling. For some reason, it reminded Bentley of the plague church they'd used to capture the Wyrrm.

Dalton laughed. 'I wondered how long it would take you to realise where we are. I hear that it was one of your finest moments, although I'm sure Darkling would disagree.'

This is the place, thought Bentley, *before we arrived — but how long?*

Dalton lifted the sword away from his father's neck.

'I have a little problem that I'm hoping you can resolve,' he began. 'You see, I wish to enter the maelstrom and those annoying Draconians have blocked every path bar one.'

'The W-Wyrrm?' Bentley stuttered.

'Exactly,' Dalton agreed, pointing the sword directly at Bentley's head, 'and you're the man that caught it. So I thought it fitting that you should be the one to release it.'

'I can't — ' Bentley began to say but stopped as the sword flashed, Dalton bringing the blade to within a millimetre of his father's skull.

'That's the wrong answer,' Dalton snapped, his face like thunder. 'I have no quarrel with you or your family. All I ask is that you open a breach, and my experts tell me that a Wyrrm can be used for such things.'

Bentley shook his head. 'You don't understand, the stasis field and the spike are closed loops, so I cannot unmake them.'

Dalton lifted the blade, and taking the fighting stance of a samurai, he held it high above his head. 'Not even if your father's life depended on it?'

Bentley's brain didn't work well under stress, especially fear, and as he tried to think of a solution all he came up with was: 'Time. I need more time!'

'Part of the reason we came back forty-eight hours earlier.'

Bentley shook his head, trying to think clearly. His father stared at him, the way he used to do when he was telling him off — willing him not to do it.

'Forward! We need to go forward to after it's been captured. If I invert the spike it may open a path through the Wyrrm's chronology. You could follow that into the maelstrom.'

'See!' Dalton whispered to Bentley's father. 'He's a genius after all! Bravo, Bentley junior.'

Then with one swift movement he brought the sword down on his father's neck and sliced off his head.

Bentley screamed.

Dalton's men grabbed his arms before Bentley could attack him.

'You can of course change the outcome. Just get me in there and my men have been instructed to alter this event. He can still live — but it's up to you now!'

35

COLONEL

[Cassandra nebula, Maelstrom]

Alixia took her hand away from Rufius' pale forehead and replaced the poultice. 'Do you know who he is?'

'His name is Rufius Westinghouse, but Caitlin calls him Daedalus.'

Alixia's eyes widened in surprise. 'And where exactly did you find him?'

'In the maelstrom, fighting the elder gods — Djinn, I think you call them.'

'And they did this to him?'

'No, this happened in the linear. When Josh was trying to discover who his father was.'

'Did he succeed?'

Juliana shrugged. 'We haven't seen him or Caitlin since.'

Alixia picked up his notes and flicked through them. 'And you don't know what attacked him?'

'There'd been some kind of temporal disruption,' said Juliana, handing her a Polaroid of the timesuit. 'This was standing next to his body when we found him.'

Alixia took the image and studied it carefully. 'This came through from the maelstrom?'

The Makepieces nodded.

'I believe it's a time suit,' said Thomas, a little too enthusiastically. 'Much like our ship.'

Alixia hadn't had time to come to terms with the fact that she was in the sickbay of a WW2 battleship in the middle of the maelstrom, much less how they'd got her there. The events of the last few days had been manic, and she'd hardly had time to change her clothes, let alone form a plan — that would have to come later, once she'd saved the Makepieces' friend and found Caitlin.

She crossed her arms and allowed her medical training to take over. 'He's tachycardic, pulse weak, and I don't like the sound of his breathing. Which all point towards systemic infection.' She pulled back the sheet to examine the blackened wound. 'This is no linear contagion. I've seen similar patterns in Xenos who've been attacked by storm-kin. He's been infected by something from the maelstrom.'

Juliana gave her husband the 'told-you-so' look.

'I would need their laboratory to diagnose this, and the best we can do now is try to isolate whatever it is that's got into his system and try and remove it. My daughter, Lyra, is far more adept at this kind of healing. I take it we can reach her? She's at Draconian headquarters.'

'The *Nautilus* can go virtually anywhere,' Thomas said proudly.

'Good. Let's get him back on board, as there's no point keeping him here,' she said, looking around at the grey bulkheads. 'It's full of ghosts.'

36

ESCAPE

J osh hobbled after Caitlin as fast as he could. He could feel the anaesthetic wearing off as the muscles in his leg were beginning to ache, and every time he put any weight on it the pain lanced up his spine.

Caitlin had climbed into one of the timesuits and used its powered exoskeleton to race ahead, reaching the entrance to the tunnel chamber long before him.

'Come on slowcoach!' she shouted, her voice enhanced by the speakers in the helmet. 'We're out of time.'

The floor shook as another explosion detonated below them and the lights went out for good. Electricity sparked along the fractured conduits above his head, split open by the force of the power surge.

Josh forced himself forward, ignoring the pain and focussing on the mirrored suit that was waving at him through the smoke-filled corridor.

The edges of his vision were going dark, and he knew he wasn't going to make it.

'Just go!' he shouted at her, as his leg gave way and he fell to his knees.

There was another blast, and he felt the metal gantry they were standing on beginning to give way. Somewhere far off Josh could hear the countdown of the self-destruct that the real Lenin must have triggered.

'THIRTEEN, TWELVE, ELEVEN.'

It was too late. They were never going to make it.

37

WYRRM

The contorted body of Darkling hung limply in mid-air, his eyes staring blankly out of a face frozen in the middle of a scream. Bentley could still see the phantom mandibles of the Wrrym's mouth where they pierced his limbs. They were both enclosed within a shimmering sphere of energy — known as a 'spike'; it was simply a containment field that froze a tiny fragment of time.

The bodies of the unfortunate Xeno research team lay scattered around the edges of the field where Dalton's soldiers had cut them down. There was no mercy for the scientists; they would've been the only witnesses to his plan and Bentley's betrayal.

The Xenos had brought their own containment units, and twelve of them were positioned around the sphere like a clock face. Bentley recognised the modified Hubble invertors immediately. It was a design his father had helped to develop, one that created an infinite loop of a nanosecond of time — effectively freezing anything trapped inside it.

Bentley was aware that collapsing a Hubble sphere wasn't a simple thing to do; it was generally thought to be suicidal by most temporal engineers. Once these devices were deployed, they were not supposed to be reversed. They were designed to keep things locked down — permanently.

All Bentley could think about was the look on his father's face as his head had rolled across the floor. He had no choice but to do this, and even if he couldn't save his dad, Dalton's men still had the rest of his family.

The Wyrrm's head took up most of the knave of the church. Dalton was busy admiring the creature, walking around the perimeter with the sword over one shoulder, the blood still gleaming on the blade.

'Such a magnificent creature,' Dalton observed. 'You really can't begin to appreciate what the maelstrom is capable of until you see it in the flesh.'

The rest of his squad, a mixture of hard-faced soldiers and scientists, were busy unpacking their equipment from black bags and strapping on unusual pieces of body armour.

Bentley knelt down beside one of the containment generators and took out his set of screwdrivers. They were made in the late tenth century and given to him as a present for his sixteenth birthday. A sob caught in his throat as he read the inscription on the side of the handle.

Modos et cunctarum rerum mensuras audebo — 'I dare to give the methods and measures of all things.'

It was the motto of the artificers and one that his father had quoted to him on more than one late night in his workshop.

He wiped his eyes when Dalton wasn't looking and got to work.

.   .   .

Two hours later Bentley had everything aligned correctly. The adjustments he'd made to the field had weakened it enough for the Wyrrm to move a little, making the body of Darkling dance awkwardly in mid-air.

Dalton seemed fascinated by the way the creature had merged with the Augur's body, studying it from different angles and more than once trying to poke it with his sword.

The first time Darkling had twitched the entire Protectorate team had jumped. Bentley had to hide his amusement at the sight of the battle-hardened soldiers flinching like scared children. Dalton turned it into a joke, making fun of the 'meat marionette' as he called it.

'It's ready,' said Bentley, when the creature had settled.

'Are you sure? It looks awfully like it's going to devour us the second we step in.'

'I'm sure. My father's life depends on it.'

'So it does,' Dalton said, tapping the handle of the sword, which was now cleaned and safely back in its scabbard.

'How will I know you will let them go?' asked Bentley, holding up the master switch.

Dalton's smile twisted. 'You're wiser than you look. Here, take this.' He tossed Bentley a coin with the words 'THE FUTURE IS NOT YET WRITTEN' around the edge. 'It will be more than enough.'

Bentley pocketed the coin and went back to his post.

Dalton took off his gloves. There was a golden ring on his left hand that seemed to glow when he brought it near the Wyrrm. Bentley didn't have a clue what it was, but the others seemed to treat it with a great deal of respect.

'Gentleman, we stand at the edge of the abyss. Beyond lies all manner of dangers, most of which you'll never have encountered before and will undoubtedly attempt to kill you.'

He held the ring up for them all to see. 'But we have an advantage; this talisman will protect us. With it I shall command them, with it we shall claim dominion over the Djinn.'

His men cheered, beating their fists against their body armour. Bentley threw the final switch, and the field dropped.

Several things happened at once.

As Bentley expected, reversing the containment field instantly freed the Wyrrm, who immediately attempted to break out of its prison; only to find it could move neither forward nor backward in time. Dalton's ring was glowing brightly as he held it up towards the creature.

The walls of the church shook as the creature thrashed around, trying to break free of his control.

Dalton's grin widened as he realised the power he had over it, and Bentley thought he caught the faintest glimmer of madness in his eyes.

'Be gone!' Dalton declared, his voice full of other words in half-whispered tongues.

The Wyrrm took the only route open to it and retreated through the chronosphere, creating a large circular aperture in the skin of time.

As it disappeared into the maelstrom, Dalton and his team leapt forward, charging down the tunnel of swirling chaos that it left in its wake.

Bentley saw his chance and grabbed the body of Darkling, dragging him to one side and placing his broken body on one of the pews.

'I'll come back for you,' he said to the ravaged corpse, turning to see Dalton and his entire team disappear.

Then he took out the coin and opened its timeline.

38

TITANIC

[Atlantic Ocean. Date: 14th April 11.912]

'You need to drink this,' implored Caitlin, holding the cup up to Josh's dry, papery lips.

His eyes flickered open, and for a moment he had a vague, faraway stare, then Josh did as he was told, gulping the water down — it tasted good after all the smoke he'd inhaled.

He tried to move his legs, but the pain brought tears to his eyes.

'Don't try and get up yet. I dissolved some painkillers into the water, but they'll take a few minutes to kick in.'

Relaxing back into the bunk, Josh closed his eyes and listened to the little sounds she made as she moved around the room, soothing sounds made more soporific by the faint thrum of engines.

He woke an hour later, and there was still a dull throbbing in his leg, but his head was clearer now.

'Where are we?' he asked.

'On a ship,' she said nonchalantly, helping him sit up and adjusting the pillows behind his back.

That explained the noise of the engines, he thought. 'And how did we get on a ship?'

'After you passed out I took you through the nearest portal. The whole place was falling apart, and we were lucky it still had enough power to function.'

'Do you know when?'

'By the looks of the décor, I would say early twentieth century. I've been waiting for you to wake up before going out for a recce.'

She gave him some more tablets and another glass of water. He didn't ask where she'd got them from, or how. Their cabin looked like a hotel suite from an old 1920s movie, so he guessed it came with room service.

Ten minutes later the pain in his leg eased. 'Nice place,' he said, shifting his weight so he could sit up on the bed.

Caitlin was reading in a chair on the other side of the state room.

'Don't get up or you'll burst your stitches.'

Josh looked down at his leg. His trousers were gone, and the band-aid from Fermi's lab was missing, leaving a long black wound running down the side of his thigh.

'Should it be that colour?'

'I was thinking the same thing,' she said, coming over to inspect it. 'It might be infected. I cleaned it up as well as I could.' She pointed to an empty bottle of vodka on the side table. 'I think you should see a doctor. There'll be one on board, as this is an Olympic-class ocean liner on its maiden voyage — according to the welcome pack.'

Caitlin showed him the booklet.

Josh read the words on the cover. 'RMS Titanic?'

'She's the largest ship in the White Star Line. She's on her way to New York. By the time we get there, you should be healed enough to walk. I thought it would be nice to get some RnR.'

'We can't stay on this boat, Cat,' he said through gritted teeth, trying to stand.

'Sit down!'

'We have to get off this ship!'

'We're in the middle of the Atlantic...' She opened the brochure at a map of the voyage.

'Have you never heard of the Titanic?'

She shrugged. 'No, what's so important?'

Josh looked worried. 'In my timeline it hit an iceberg and sank — over half of the passengers died!'

'Well, it didn't happen in mine.'

Josh sank back onto the bed. 'So how do we know which one we're in?'

'Probably better not to leave it to chance.' She stood up and went to look through one of the large portholes at a sky full of stars.

'I would say we're just south of Newfoundland. Do you know when it happened?'

'No. Can you see any large white floaty things?'

'I know what an iceberg is, and no, there aren't any.'

He laughed. 'That's what the Captain said just before it hit the ship.'

'Can you see if you can find us a way out of here? I tried, but that bloody timesuit has messed up my ability to weave.' She waved at the suit standing in the corner, looking like someone had attacked it with a chainsaw.

Josh reached out to the nearest man-made object, a small lamp next to his bed. The jewelled beading rattled on the shade as the ship suddenly shuddered. Josh tried to find a timeline from it, his face a mask of concentration. 'No. The drugs might be throwing me off.'

'Shit.'

There was another, deeper tremor this time accompanied by the keening sound of distorting metal.

'Bad timeline,' coughed Josh, who was looking very pale. 'You need to get up to the deck.'

'I'm not leaving you.'

'Women and children first,' Josh explained, 'they left most of the men behind.'

Caitlin looked horrified. 'You're not playing the martyr card — you're too bloody important.'

39

TIMESHIP

Da Recco held Rufius' hand as Lyra inserted the needles carefully into position along imaginary lines in his arm.

The Italian navigator whispered prayers under his breath as she worked.

'When are you from?' Lyra asked without looking up.

'A time of religious fools. Thirteen hundred and fifty-four.'

'And Josh rescued you?'

'Si, from the hands of the holy tormentors.'

Lyra wasn't quite sure what that meant, but she smiled all the same. 'Was Caitlin with him?'

Da Recco nodded. 'They go off to some party, with the colonel,' he said in his heavy Italian accent, annunciating in all the wrong places. 'And this is all that came back.'

The old man's body was still in remarkably good shape, though the virus was taking its toll, Rufius was a big bear of a man and a natural fighter.

Her mother stood behind Lyra, watching every move like a hawk.

'How many are you planning on using?' she asked in the annoying way parents did when you were trying to concentrate.

'As many as it takes,' Lyra muttered without looking up. 'I will need to anchor myself while I'm looking for it.'

'And what are you planning to do with "it" when you do?'

'Well, first I'm going to put it in that,' she said, pointing at the large glass specimen jar on the side table. It was covered in runes and esoteric symbols that Lyra had spent the last hour etching into the glass. 'Then I'm going to take it back to the Xenos and see if we can borrow their non-corporeal lab. Does that sound like a plan?'

Alixia seemed satisfied with Lyra's response and let her continue.

Lyra closed her eyes and let her hand linger on the last pin. She slowly and carefully eased her mind into the old man's timeline.

Usually, when Lyra entered another's chronology, she would immediately get an empathic sense of the essence of the person. Some seers referred to it as their soul, but she preferred to think of it as the distillation of their experiences; their life condensed down into a purified series of sensations and emotions. It always had a colour and luminosity. Some were like stars in a nebulae, while more troubled individuals, would be like stormy thunderclouds.

Rufius' essence was like a night on some cold, barren planet a million years from the sun.

She shivered inadvertently and felt her mother's hand on her arm.

'I'm okay,' she whispered.

The usual lines associated with a man of his age and experience were gone, his chronology devoid of any events. It was as though they'd petrified and crumbled into a cloud of dust that had been blown across the surface of that dead planet.

It was something Lyra had never encountered, not even in the victims of a Monad attack — which could suck the life-force out of its victim's past in seconds.

Like black snow, the dark swirling fragments swarmed around her. She tried to dig deeper into his timeline, but it was impossible to catch anything more than a tiny moment of his life, and Lyra was about to give up when she spotted a glimmer of light.

Far off, fading in and out of sight, a beacon glowed in the darkness. She pushed her mind towards it, feeling the malevolence around her increasing the deeper she went.

Her defences were too strong for the evil presence. The pins she'd set into place were like anchors into her past: strong memories and emotions that she could call on to protect her — to remind her who she was. They surrounded her psyche like shields, holding back the leeching effect of the contagion, but she could feel their energy being drawn off — it would not be too long before they would be used up.

She would have to reach him soon.

As she approached the glowing nexus of energy she felt an essence reach out, a warm aura that enveloped her — it was his, and she moved inside the event, the only piece of his life that was still intact.

'There's a problem,' Lyra explained to the old man as they sat in the waiting area. From what she could gather, his wife was inside the consulting room with Doctor Crooke, having an examination, while Rufius, who looked much younger and less world-weary, was made to sit outside and wait for the results.

This was one of his most precious memories, full of emotional energy and he'd obviously retreated into it when all else was collapsing around him.

'What kind of problem?' he asked, looking for all the world like nothing else could ruin his day.

'You're being attacked, some kind of virus from the maelstrom. Everything we have tried has failed to stop it.'

His smiled faded and his eyes grew distant as he tried to access his own timeline.

'From the maelstrom, you say,' he said thoughtfully.

'I don't have all the details, but Caitlin's mother told me you were involved in a breach.'

He shrugged. 'I've no memory of that.'

She coughed. 'I'm not surprised. Your chronology has lost all its cohesion. I'm not sure what we can do.'

'The founder will know. You must take me to him,' Rufius instructed.

Lyra felt the last of her defensive anchors giving out.

'I have to go,' she said sadly, holding his hand.

He smiled. 'Don't worry my dear, I've had worse.'

Lyra seriously doubted that.

40

BROTHER VALIENT

The floor began to tilt, a couple of degrees every few minutes. Tremors shook the ship as the seawater caused the boilers to explode, and with each shock, they could hear the hysteria of the passengers echo down the corridors. The sounds of the frightened people drowned out the instructions of the officers who were trying to calm them over the tannoy system.

'You have to go,' said Josh into her hair as she hugged him.

'No I don't,' she whispered. 'Maybe in a couple of minutes we'll get our abilities back and we can both just jump out.' The stress in her voice was making it higher than usual.

He could feel her heart beating hard in her chest. 'Yeah, or maybe not. Better that you find out before we sink under the water though?'

'I'm not leaving you and that's final. If we're going down, we go together. That's what being in love means.'

'What did you just say?'

'Are we really going to do this now?'

'You started it.'

She pulled away from him, wiping tears from her eyes. 'Well, I don't think there's going to be many more chances to say I love you.'

He smiled weakly, the pain in his leg obviously worse than he was letting on, Caitlin thought.

'I know.'

She punched him hard in the arm. 'No, you don't. You say it!'

'Okay! I love you too.'

She kissed him hard, holding his face in her hands. Her cheeks were wet with tears.

'Now, do you think you can walk?'

He grimaced at the thought of it. 'Not far.'

'I have a theory. I think we need to get away from the suit,' she said, putting his arm around her shoulders. 'There may be some kind of latent field coming off it that's blocking our ability to weave.'

Josh shifted himself off the bed, trying not to put any weight on his leg.

'Shit!' he hissed through his teeth.

She tried to support him as they moved to the cabin door. The sound of the mayhem outside had calmed a little as the passengers moved to the other side of the boat. Caitlin realised from the upward angle they were on the wrong side of the ship.

As she opened the door, she tested the handle for any sign of a timeline, but still there was nothing.

The oak-panelled corridor was strewn with a jumbled collection of discarded belongings, lifejackets and broken crockery, all of which was slowly inching itself up the side of one wall. The camber made it harder for Josh to keep off his bad leg and Caitlin could feel him leaning on her more heavily with every step.

'Let's just get to the stairs and then we can rest,' she said, trying to sound encouraging.

'Okay,' he replied, panting through the pain and putting his other hand against the wall.

There was a loud groan from somewhere deep below, and Josh imagined the large jagged hole the iceberg was making in the hull. Screams echoed up from the lower decks as the ship pitched further over.

'Anything yet?' Josh asked as Caitlin touched the door of another cabin.

She shook her head and they continued.

They came to a junction with another corridor, one that led to the other side of the ship, and halfway along the passage a priest was administering the last rights to someone lying on the floor.

Or at least that's what Caitlin thought he was doing.

The priest looked up from the corpse, and she saw the book he was reading from. Even from a distance she recognised the temporal patterns updating themselves across the page, and the shapes were unmistakable; he was holding an almanac.

'Hey!' she shouted. 'Tempus fugit!'

The man crossed himself, put away the book and got up off his knees. Holding on to the side rails, he carefully made his way down the sloping passage towards them.

'You shouldn't be here,' he said in a strong Scottish accent. He was a thin, gaunt-faced man with haunting eyes that reminded Caitlin of Edward Kelly, the Grand Seer.

'We can't weave,' she explained, 'and Josh is too weak to make it to the lifeboats.'

The priest nodded. 'Temporal exclusion. This event is not to be meddled with.'

'Can you help us?'

He looked around furtively, checking to see if anyone was watching.

'I can, but there may be consequences.'

'Worse than staying on a sinking ship?' Josh groaned.

The priest stared at Josh, his eyes narrowing like a snake deciding where to strike.

'When have you come from?'

'Twentieth,' Caitlin lied before Josh had a chance to respond.

The ship pitched further over, and they moved aside as a pile of rubbish slid down the passage along with the body he'd been ministering to.

'You're not from this timeline,' he said, looking at Caitlin.

'And you are?' she replied defiantly.

'I'm your only chance of surviving this event,' he said, taking out his tachyon and checking the dials. 'Now, in the time we have left I would appreciate the truth.'

Caitlin was confused. The man was no Draconian, nor from any other guild she could think of. He could be a watchman, but most of them had visited the Chapter house, and none of them were religious types — nor did they like to get too close to dead bodies.

'You're a reaver aren't you?' she declared. 'You're here for the dead?'

'Don't try and judge what you don't understand, girl,' he said and sneered. 'The future of the continuum hangs in the balance, and my research may save us. Now I'll have the truth, or I'll leave you here to drown.'

'My name is Caitlin Makepiece,' she said in a tone of self-importance, but the priest's face remained impassive, so she decided to play the only other ace she had. 'And this is Joshua Jones. The Paradox or Nemesis, depending on which timeline you come from.'

His eyes widened as she spoke.

'The Paradox?' he repeated.

Josh smiled weakly. 'In the flesh. So, can we leave now?'

The man grasped Josh's arm, and his eyes rolled back into his skull.

Caitlin went to push him away, but Josh shook his head. The man was a seer, there was no doubt, but Josh couldn't feel his presence in his timeline at all, it was as if he was a ghost.

The priest was gone for over a minute before his eyes returned and he came out of his trance.

'So it is true, the Eschaton has begun,' he whispered to himself.

Josh felt the ship shift once more. 'Time to go, my friend.'

'Brother Valient,' the man said as a way of introduction, pulling back the sleeve of his cassock to reveal the number eleven surrounded by the most beautifully complex set of temporal tattoos.

'Augur of the eleventh crisis,' he added, running his fingers along his forearm, and as he did, the symbols seemed to come to life.

Seawater began to pour into the corridor, and Valient gripped them both by the hand. 'This may be my favourite moment.'

41

MAELSTROM

Sometimes, in the quiet, dark hours before dawn, Dalton wondered what it would be like to enter the maelstrom. He'd always thought of it as a place of pure chaos, but with his limited understanding of the realm, he imagined it would still have a set of rules like physics and gravity.

Now, as he was tossed around in the swirling storms of disjointed time, he realised how naïve he'd been, how nothing could have prepared him for this place.

Without the limitations of time, everything could happen at once, or not at all — worse still, it could happen entirely out of sequence.

One moment he would be standing in the middle of a city surrounded by buildings from different ages, each sitting side-by-side like the work of some absent-minded architect, and then a heartbeat later, his entire company were floating in a forgotten ocean miles from land.

Moments of time collected around them like shoals of fish, gathering and then dispersing at the slightest change.

His men's faces were all covered by the Protectorate

battle masks, so it was impossible to tell if they were as scared as he was. Dalton tried not to show it; as their leader he knew he must stay strong. But there was a voice inside his head screaming for it all to stop. He tried desperately to make sense of what was happening, his mind searching for a pattern, but it was too much for his brain to process, and they were all going to be driven insane.

The ring seemed powerless, glowing weakly now and then as if sensing the Djinn were nearby, but nothing ever appeared.

42

SHIMMERING SEA

[Ascension Island, Atlantic. Date: 11.927]

W hen the *Nautilus* returned to the Draconian
headquarters, they learned that the founder was
missing.

Edward Kelly had sought sanctuary within the walls of
the lighthouse and brought news of events from the Order,
as well as a large contingent of seers.

Grandmaster Derado had clearly had enough of the
man's cryptic conversations by the time Alixia joined them
in his war room.

'Ravana has taken control of the Copernican difference
engine. The Grand Seer tells me she's determined to get the
system running again, but the founder has disappeared, as,
it seems, has the Infinity Engine.'

Kelly was sitting opposite Derado, wearing a black hat
with a veil that made him look like a Victorian widow.

'Time is out of joint,' he observed.

'Now is not the time for your foolish riddles!' barked the
grandmaster.

Alixia could feel the tension between them. They were like oil and water, a soldier and a poet, neither capable of understanding the other's point of view.

'Do you know where he is?' she asked Kelly.

'Beyond the shimmering silver sea,' he replied, wiggling the fingers of his hand like waves.

Alixia ground her teeth as she held back the urge to shout herself.

'Master Kelly, we have little time to decipher your riddles. A man's life hangs in the balance. One who may have answers to the whereabouts of the Nemesis. Can you speak plainly for once?'

The seer lifted his veil, revealing raven-black eyes.

'In the room of no return, sits a citadel in a silver sea. The tulku will know the way.'

'What's a tulku?'

'A Tibetan Buddhist term,' came another voice. It was Sim. 'The Dalai Lama is one.'

Alixia smiled at her son, who seemed uncomfortable in the Draconian armour. It made him look more like a man, but yet still he was her little boy. She had to stop herself from running over and hugging him.

'Thank you, master De Freis. At last a straight answer,' said Derado, sighing. 'Your son has been a most helpful assistant since he arrived.'

Sim was not great at taking compliments, and she saw the colour rise in his cheeks.

'So where is the founder?'

'With the Augurs,' said Kelly, shocking everyone with a reasonable reply.

43

BERGSON

Finally, after they'd travelled through a hundred battlefields, deserted cities and a thousand other forgotten moments, things began to slow. Dalton felt the vertigo receding, their free fall through the mayhem decelerated, spending longer in each world, until they came to rest in a necropolis of gothic churches and tombs.

'Form a perimeter,' Dalton barked to the others as he got to his feet. Some had taken off their headgear and were throwing up, while others were staring like awestruck tourists at their surroundings which continued to shift and change. 'Deploy the stabilisers.'

Dalton's research team had done their homework. They'd combed through the hundreds of theories on the maelstrom, mostly inspired by the works of Daedalus, and although many of them were nothing but crackpot fantasists, like Belsarus, imagining a strange and unusual neverland, there were some that seemed to have a scientific basis. Dalton focused on those concerned with the control of time in non-linear environments, and particularly the work of a young Copernican by the name of Eric Bergson.

Bergson was only in his early twenties when he published his first work, 'On the fluidity of Time'. It was ignored by many, and those that did bother to read it claimed the work was too theoretical. Since it made no reference to the Djinn or Daedalus, many Daedalans ignored it entirely, but Dalton saw the man's genius and knew that if he were going to survive in the chaos realm, he would need Bergson's help.

Bergson was nearer thirty now, and Dalton watched him organise the men as they assembled his prototype stabilising arrays, driving the long metal stakes into the shifting earth to help anchor the basecamp.

It was a simple concept; all the best ones were. To create a static field within a non-linear universe one had to induce a coalescing field, a strange attractor, and the dynamics of chaos would do the rest.

The mausoleums around them shifted slightly as they worked. Smaller structures were randomly replaced by larger ones, as though an unseen architect were refining a model of his work, while others aged rapidly and crumbled before their eyes.

'We have achieved a stable time field,' reported Bergson in his curt Norwegian accent. The man was nearly ten years older than him but seemed more naïve somehow.

Dalton nodded his approval. 'Now all we can do is wait.'

His men moved within the boundaries of the temporal field and started to unpack supplies. A guard duty rota was agreed, and the first watch took their places as the world around them continued to evolve.

Dalton sat staring at his ring, watching for any signs of Djinn. There was a terrible power within its history, and he sensed the long lines stretching back into a distant past, but he wasn't ready to find out what powers were waiting there.

The rations were passed around, and everyone began to relax as they acclimatised to their environment. It was an uneasy peace though; these were highly trained men who kept one eye on the shadows, always wary of the threat of an attack.

'I have spent the last ten years dreaming of this moment,' said Bergson, looking around at the chaos. 'Nothing in my wildest dreams could have come close to this.'

Dalton wondered if he'd made a mistake bringing the scientist. 'The maelstrom is nothing more than a temporal scrap heap, a junkyard of abandoned moments, so what on earth can you find so endearing about such a place?'

'It's the ultimate foil. Everything we believe to be normal within the continuum is missing in this place. We are opposites, and you cannot have one without the other.'

'You sound exactly like my mother!' Dalton scoffed. 'Why does everything have to be in some kind of cosmic balance? What all of you fail to admit is that you have no idea why this exists and spend all your time trying to validate your position by hiding behind some equation.'

44

CITADEL

[Spiti Valley, Tibet. Date: 11.587]

A calm serenity filled the temple as the third Dalai Lama, Sonam Gyatso, knelt praying in the chaitya. The ancient walls were carved a thousand years before he was born, yet the sacred texts etched into their columns were as relevant now as they had been the day they'd been struck.

His daily ritual always ended with a walk between the columns of the great prayer hall, a practice known as pradakhshina, where he reflected on their enlightened wisdom.

The arrival of the founder had troubled him. His presence, though always welcome, was like that of a harbinger, a bringer of change, and the old monk had spent many hours contemplating what it could mean.

'Do not dwell in the past, do not dream of the future, concentrate the mind on the present moment,' he repeated the words of Buddha to himself.

There were times when the monk had wondered what kind of future his old friend was trying to protect.

It had been an unusual request to make on the day they'd first met. Sonam was only nineteen-years-old when the founder walked into their monastery with his book of forbidden knowledge and told him that one day he would be the spiritual leader of the Tibetan people. Fifteen years later Altan Khan invited him to Mongolia to teach his people the ways of Buddhism.

Now, as Sonam felt the ache in his old bones, the founder had returned to enter the room he'd hidden for all those years, never allowing anyone to disturb it.

His reverie was broken by a tremor that shook the stones beneath his knees. At first, he thought it might be an earthquake. They were quite rare and his temple had survived long enough to know it could stand all but the most violent shocks.

But the vibrations grew stronger as if a herd of yaks were stampeding across the plains of the valley below.

The old monk got slowly to his feet as the dust began to drift down through the shafts of sunlight. *Perhaps*, he thought, *I would be safer outside.*

As he turned to leave, the conning tower of a small submarine broke through the floor of the temple.

There had been a moment when they had stepped out of the timeship when the old monk had considered it wiser to retreat. The strangers who had destroyed his beloved temple floor were dressed in unusual clothes and looked desperate.

There were two women, a girl and two men carrying a wounded man on a stretcher. The men were nervous, their eyes searching the room as if they were being hunted.

A lady approached him and bowed respectfully. She had a kind face, her eyes full of questions, but her smile spoke of peace and friendship.

'Holy one. We require sanctuary,' she said in fluent Mandarin.

The Dalai Lama bowed in return. 'Of course, my house is yours. What is left of it.'

She nodded her thanks and turned to her companions.

Her instructions were in some other language, but her intentions were clear. The other woman, dressed in men's clothes, took out a metal device and their ship retreated below the stones once more, leaving them as if they had never been disturbed.

He bent down to touch the slabs, marvelling at their restoration.

'What is this magic?' he asked.

'Time flows in two directions,' the lady replied.

They were the watchwords, the passphrase that the founder had told him was a signal of his allies.

'My master?' she asked. 'Is he still here?'

The monk shook his head. 'No he has entered the room of no return.'

Her expression became thoughtful. 'We need his help. Can you show us this room?'

.   .   .

'The founder left it with me many years ago,' the Dalai Lama explained as he stood before the ancient-looking door. 'He instructed me to allow no one to touch it.'

Alixia smiled sympathetically at the old monk. 'I'm assuming he revoked that order when he returned.'

The monk nodded. 'He told me that others would follow and that I would know the ones by their words.'

Standing before the door, he studied the other members of her group: the two men carrying the injured one were eager to be gone; the man was obviously gravely ill. Sonam had tried to examine him, but they wouldn't let him touch their patient. The lady explained that he had some kind of plague and that only the founder would know how to cure it.

The young girl they called 'Lyra' seemed fascinated by the temple and by him. Her eyes had been wide and full of wonder when she arrived, and they had hardly changed since.

He blessed them all and opened the door to the room, knowing full well that he would never see any of them again.

The room was a simple stone cell with a metal plinth at the centre. On it rested a shallow copper basin filled with a silver liquid.

'Mercury?' asked Lyra, going up to inspect the bowl.

'The silver sea,' Alixia muttered.

'Mercury was thought to prolong life — they found a massive cache of it in a Teotihuacan pyramid. The ancient civilisations were obsessed with its healing properties,' explained Thomas, lowering Rufius down onto the floor.

'Don't touch it,' warned Alixia. 'Quicksilver is highly toxic.'

'The founder wouldn't use mercury as a vestige,' Juliana said, going over to join Lyra.

Alixia looked around the cell. 'There's hardly anything else in the room to use. Kelly told me he was here.'

'Whatever it is, we need to find it quickly,' Thomas interrupted. 'All this linear time is not helping Rufius' condition.'

Alixia went over to examine him. His skin was ashen, and his hands were drawn up and claw-like where they had gone into spasm.

'His pulse is feeble. Thomas is right. We need to locate the founder as soon as we can.'

'It's not quicksilver,' Da Recco said, holding his hand just above the rippling liquid. 'This is hot, while mercury is cold to the touch.'

'And how would you know that?' Lyra asked with a sly smile.

'A night in the arms of Venus leads to a lifetime of mercury?' Da Recco raised one eyebrow. 'It is true that many of my crew had used it for the treatment of the pox — but myself, I am a navigator, and the barometer is an essential tool of my calculations.'

'He's right,' Juliana confirmed. 'This is molten metal being kept in a liquid state.'

'Too hot to touch. A perfect way to keep anyone from using it as a vestige,' agreed Thomas.

Alixia stared at the bowl. 'What would keep it in this way?'

Juliana was inspecting the base of the pedestal, which seemed to be cast out of iron. She tentatively touched the stand feeling, the temperature as she moved up towards the basin. 'It's cold.'

'You're thinking about this too linearly,' said Lyra.

Alixia snapped her fingers. 'Of course.'

She approached the basin and put her hands on both sides, searching for a timeline

'Well?' asked Juliana impatiently.

'You were right,' Alixia said, smiling proudly at her daughter. 'There's a switch hidden in its past.' They watched as the silver solidified, returning to its original form. It was a tower made up of concentric levels, each one smaller than the last.

'A citadel?' wondered Lyra.

'Molten silver, using an induction loop — no need for heat at all,' noted Juliana, tapping the copper bowl and making it chime.

'Exactly,' Alixia said, turning to Da Recco and Thomas. 'Now you're going to have to carry him I'm afraid.'

Between them they managed to raise the unconscious man, each taking one arm over their shoulder.

'Let's see where this takes us,' said Alixia, opening the timeline of the silver statue.

45

REVERSE EXORCISM

The passage of time was impossible to measure within the maelstrom. Bergson had brought a variety of chronometers with him, but they'd all failed, even his tachyon had stopped at the moment they had left the chronosphere.

By Dalton's estimation two days had elapsed, and still there was no sign of the legendary Djinn. The initial excitement they'd experienced when they arrived was quickly turning to disappointment, and the sustained apprehension was beginning to tell on the men.

The guard still patrolled the edge of the stabilising field, watching the ever-changing, hypnotic landscape around them. More than once his officers had reported seeing 'strange things' on the periphery, but nothing came close. Whatever was out there was being cautious, staying out of range of the talisman at least.

By the end of the third day, Dalton was growing bored. The provisions they had brought would last another week or so, but the lack of action was bad for morale, and he could see the tension taking its toll on their mood. Men were beginning to have disagreements over nothing, and fights broke out over stupid remarks that would have been shrugged off in any other situation.

'We need to drop the barrier,' Dalton suggested to Bergson.

'But we will lose temporal cohesion.'

'I didn't come here for a bloody sight-seeing tour. The Djinn are here, I can feel them. But your damn field is keeping them at bay.'

Bergson shook his head. 'I don't think it's wise —'

In one fluid motion, Dalton took out his sword and held it against Bergson's neck.

'Shut down the grid,' he ordered through gritted teeth. 'Or I'll feed you to the first Djinn we see.'

Bergson nodded and ran off to his equipment.

'Mallary!' Dalton barked at his lieutenant who was sleeping, slumped against one of the kit bags. 'Get the men ready. We're going to drop the shield.'

There followed a rush of activity, as his well-drilled team donned their battle armour and prepared their weapons.

As the others formed themselves into a circle around Dalton, Bergson flipped the switch, and they felt time begin to drain away. Like air slowly leaking from a balloon. Each man sighted along his gunsabre, scanning their surroundings for any sign of attack.

But nothing came.

Bergson seemed to relax, walking around the perimeter as he checked his equipment.

'Are they all down?' asked Dalton.

The scientist nodded.

'Interesting. I believe what we need now could be referred to as a reverse exorcism. Lieutenant Mallary, please be so good as to shoot Mr Bergson.'

'But —'

The next words never left his lips as a bullet ripped through his chest.

Bergson was thrown back over the perimeter and out of what was left of linear time, falling in slow motion as he toppled backwards, his arms flailing in the air.

Dalton stepped forward and brought his ring hand up towards the body. The talisman was glowing brightly now, and he felt the power racing along its timeline as a connection was made to its deep past.

He saw a distortion in the space around Bergson, as the outline of a fearsome looking creature solidified around him, enveloping him with its phantom limbs.

46

AUGURS

[Citadel, Maelstrom.]

They waited at the gates of what Brother Valient called the 'Citadel'. It was a massive tower fortress made up of twelve tiers, each one stacked on top of the other, getting progressively smaller with each level until the final stage was nothing more than a spire.

Josh leaned on Caitlin, who was still dripping wet with seawater. She shivered and put her arm around him to pull him close. Their escape had been a narrow one, and both of them could still hear the screams of the passengers on the lower decks. It was a harrowing sound, filled with desperation and fear.

'You okay?' she whispered.

Josh nodded. 'Remind me about this next time I decide to go looking for my dad.'

'You weren't to know.'

'You nearly died.'

She put her head on his shoulder. 'My dad used to say "only worry about the ones you don't walk away from".'

'I don't think Fermi is my father,' Josh said thoughtfully. 'He didn't seem to know who I was.'

'Not at that point, no, but we'd jumped back three hundred years, and you can't be sure that he wasn't in the future.'

'I don't think I want him to be. He looked like he was pretty messed up.'

'Well, he's got something to do with it. That device he stuck in your leg was definitely for extracting your DNA. Maybe he had samples from other people?'

'Great, so I'm a test tube baby!'

'Does it really matter who your parents are? It's not like you can change it. They told me mine were dead for eight years, and now they look more like my older brother and sister.'

'Is it weird to have them back?'

Caitlin sighed. 'It's weird that they're the same age as when they disappeared. It's like it never happened.'

Josh thought about his mother and the life she was living now. He never wanted her to experience the pain of the world he'd known, although it was sad to think they would never talk again, never spend another evening shouting stupid answers at university challenge.

This was better, he told himself, even if it was all a little crazy.

'Who is he?' he whispered, watching Valient as he spoke to the guards, a pair of heavily armoured giants standing before a vicious-looking portcullis.

'I've no idea,' Caitlin whispered back. 'Mum mentioned something about Augurs. They're like a secret department dedicated to studying the Eschaton Cascade.'

'You've got a secret department for everything,' he joked.

'I guess we do,' she said with a chuckle. 'You spend so long being part of it that you start to think it's normal.'

Josh looked around at the enormous cavern. It was like the inside of a hollowed-out asteroid. 'Don't you think this place feels a bit like the maelstrom?'

Caitlin shivered again. 'A little.'

Valient had finished his negotiations with the guards and was beckoning them to join him.

'Can you walk?' she asked.

Josh tentatively put his weight on his injured leg and grunted. Valient had given him some kind of medicine when they first arrived, and the pain-numbing effect was better than a jug of tequila.

Caitlin held his hand as they walked over to the gate.

'Paradox,' he said with a slight bow. 'Please be so kind as to place your hand upon the Eschaton.' He pointed at the set of metal disks in the middle of the portcullis.

There were twelve concentric rings, each one made from a different kind of metal. At the centre was carved the Ouroboros, the snake eating its tail.

Josh shrugged at Caitlin and put his hand on the snake's head.

He felt history turn under his fingers as the twelve time-lines unfolded. The dials began to rotate independently of each other, back and forth, searching for their respective positions.

Josh could see the various chronologies weaving over and through each other, events branching and connecting simultaneously, making it impossible to focus on any one in particular. He allowed them to flow through him, glimpsing moments from each, but never enough to make any sense of what he was seeing. A ring locked into position with a click, then another, and like a complicated jigsaw puzzle, the pieces snapped into place.

When the final inner ring stopped moving, he heard Valient gasp. 'The twelfth!'

Josh took his hand away from the dial. He felt the familiar tingling sensation along his arm and pulling back the sleeve he found the fractal tattoo had returned.

The rings of the gate receded into the door, and the bolts withdrew.

'I cannot accompany you,' Valient said, bowing reverentially. 'I am an eleventh, and your path belongs to the twelfth.'

The gate parted, and a long corridor stretched out before them. It was colonnaded, like something from a Venetian palace.

The guards snapped to attention as he and Caitlin passed them, and Josh realised that the Ouroboros on their breastplates were zeros.

47

NIHIL

D alton was alone.

He had no idea where the rest of his team had gone or whether they were still alive. He'd lost count of the places and events he'd used to try to escape the Djinn, and wherever he went, it seemed to know exactly how to find him — no matter which direction he chose.

The ring had been useless against it. Whatever it was, nothing he commanded the Djinn to do had worked, and their weapons had no effect — it had been a disaster.

At first, the summoning seemed to have worked flawlessly. Bergson's body had convulsed as the Djinn had entered through his mouth and his limbs had flailed around as though it were putting on a new suit, but it had assumed control of the host quickly, and Dalton was sure that, just like the Wyrrm, Solomon's ring would command it.

And for a while, it seemed to be under his control.

While his men trained their guns on it, Dalton had

raised his hand and felt the power intensify as he walked towards it.

The Djinn didn't seem to notice his approach. It was too busy studying its new body, flexing its fingers and examining the muscles of its arms.

'Tell me your name, demon,' he commanded, feeling the energy flow through him.

Bergson's face twisted grotesquely as it raised its dark eyes towards him. Dalton thought he saw something move beneath the skin, a ripple of flesh as it slithered down into his neck.

With stilted steps, Bergson began to walk towards him.

The scientist's jaw opened slackly, and a terrible sound issued from the dark maw.

'I. Am. Nihil.'

Dalton smiled and pointed the ring directly at the Djinn. 'Nihil, I bind you to me.'

Thin figures materialised in the air around Bergson; spectral beings conjured up from the ring's past.

There was a hiss from deep within its throat.

Dalton had no idea what the beings were and tried desperately to search for a way to control them, but they stood as if awaiting a command he didn't know.

'What. Is. Your. Wish. Master?' the creature uttered in broken English, extending its arms towards him. The veins were shot through with black ink.

Dalton hesitated. There were so many things he had imagined would be possible with their power: eternal life, control of time, the obliteration of his enemies.

He was still contemplating his options when Mallary collapsed.

His lieutenant was kneeling on the floor coughing up a

thick, dark liquid, or to be more precise; he seemed to be inhaling it.

'Get up Mallary!' ordered Dalton.

But Mallary wasn't listening, and his body was beginning to shake. The veins in his neck were darkening as he struggled for breath.

Dalton looked at the others who were staring transfixed at the Djinn, their guns lowered.

'Be on your guard!' barked Dalton, looking at their blank faces. They all seemed to be in a trance.

He turned back to Bergson, and the creature had gained more control of its host's body.

'Your wish master?' it repeated with a leering grin and a mocking bow.

Dalton raised the ring again, but the ghosts and the feeling of power were fading.

'Release my men.'

Bergson raised his hand and let it drop.

The rest of Dalton's team fell to the ground like someone had cut the strings holding them up. He gave up on the ring and picked up one of their rifles and levelled it at the creature.

'Show me infinity,' he demanded.

Dalton watched the bullets leave the gun and fly towards their target. They moved through the air in slow motion as the final remnants of time ebbed away from the stasis field.

Forged from the metals of deadly weapons — each round had killed many times before — Dalton wanted to make sure they carried a payload of pain that could put down even the toughest Djinn.

But every one of them stopped before they reached the

creature, hanging in the air as it swatted them away like flies.

When the fallen men around him began to raise themselves awkwardly off the floor, he knew the mission was a disaster. Mallary was the first to stand, his eyes turning dark as another Djinn took possession of his body.

He dropped the gun and drew his sword. Dalton was surrounded by a host of infected men which only the talisman seemed to be holding back.

Bergson's Djinn was struggling to remain within the confines of its host body. The skin was darkening and cracking as it stepped forward towards him.

'Who are you?' it asked in a whispered hiss.

Dalton held up the ring, feeling the power slipping between his fingers.

'Nihil, I command you to obey me.'

The creature appeared to smile, the skin stretching until it split and the sharp bone of a jaw broke through, Bergson's face tearing in half as something alien emerged from his body.

'Behold! I am reborn!' it screamed as it sloughed off Bergson's body like a coat, its new skin like the carapace of a beetle, black and shiny.

Dalton dropped his sword and knelt down, his hands searching for anything he could use to jump out of the moment.

He'd tried to lose himself in the chaos. Just as Daedalus had described, 'wandering the lost paths of forgotten worlds'. He remembered thinking how amazing that sounded when he'd first read it, but in reality, it was tiring and filled with dangers of its own.

Running from one unstable world to the next, Dalton could find little in the way of refuge: avoiding falling buildings, violent storms and a hundred other kinds of danger and always with the sounds of the Djinn on his trail.

He cursed his ambition. He should have spent more time looking for the second book. Eddington had lied to him; the talisman was useless without the knowledge of how to wield it, making it nothing more than a relic from a bygone era.

Nihil was not a normal kind of Djinn, not what he was expecting at all.

He tried to take off the ring but it was stuck fast, and as he struggled with it twelve dark shapes appeared around him.

48

SURVIVORS

Josh and Caitlin were welcomed by two ageing nuns, who both dressed in white habits with the numerals XII embroidered in gold thread. They followed them to rooms decorated like something from a Moroccan Kasbah, draped in exotically woven tapestries, with a finely carved luxurious bed sitting in the centre covered in velvet cushions. The walls were punctuated with alcoves displaying an eclectic collection of astrological instruments.

A new set of clothes had been laid out on the bed, and a deep bath sat steaming in the next room.

'What is this place?' asked Josh, who was playing with an antique orrery, spinning the planets around the sun

'The Augur's headquarters I guess,' said Caitlin, laying back into the hot water.

'Are we under arrest?'

'For what?'

'I don't know. He said the Titanic was off-limits.'

'I've been thinking about him.'

'Valient?'

'Why was he checking the bodies?'

'Because he's a nutter?'

She laughed. 'I think they're all a bit crazy, but that's not what I meant.'

Josh's memory of the priest was a little messed up by the pain. 'Maybe he was searching for someone?'

'And who would've been on the Titanic that would've been of interest to the Augurs?'

'I have a feeling you're about to tell me.'

'Do you remember the hologram talking about dark matter?'

'The stuff he got from the maelstrom — that kept him alive?'

'Kind of. Dark matter makes up about eighty percent of the universe, except you can't see it, and astrophysicists believe it's there because of the effect it has on the observable universe. Anyway, there was a Dutch scientist on the Titanic called Jacobus Kapteyn, whose body was never recovered. He was the first to suggest its existence using stellar velocities.'

'And you think Valient was trying to find him?'

'Not sure, but I bet Fermi did.'

Josh walked into the bathroom. 'What does he need a Dutch scientist for?'

'Energy. Fermi's experiments require a massive amount of power. I think the further back he went the more he needed. He needed Kapteyn to survive so that he could continue his work on dark matter.'

'And that's got something to do with one of the Eschaton crises?' he asked, taking off his clothes and stepping into the hot water.

Caitlin frowned as he took up one end of the tub. 'Yeah, I think they're linked somehow.'

'Which one? Valient said he was from the eleventh.'

She sank lower into the water, entwining her legs with his. 'I think it's more like the eighth — *the discovery of a terrible power.*'

'So, how do we find this Kapteyn bloke?'

'My guess is that Fermi would have moved him to a research institute with other like-minded scientists, like Niels Bohr.'

'But surely the Augurs would have noticed?'

She nodded. 'Not if he inadvertently sank a ship full of people to hide what he'd done. The magnetic distortion from a fully functioning timesuit could easily have affected the Titanic's compasses. Put it on the wrong course.'

49

VIRUS

Lord Dee's expression turned grave as he examined Rufius.

'How long has he been like this?' he asked Alixia.

'At least two linear days. The Makepieces had the good sense to take him back into the maelstrom to arrest its progression, but I fear it may be too late.'

The founder nodded and placed the blanket back over the patient.

'I concur. This is no ordinary infection. I've not seen the likes of it for centuries.'

'From the maelstrom?'

'Many years ago,' he said and sighed. 'There was a case of a young Draconian by the name of Phillips who'd been struck down by a storm-kin during a minor breach in the Minoan. His timeline was nearly entirely corrupted.'

'But you found a cure?'

Dee shook his head. 'We were too late. There was nothing left to salvage.'

'So there is no hope?' Alixia asked despondently.

A white-gowned nurse appeared with a fresh poultice and applied it to Rufius' forehead.

'There's always hope, my dear Alixia. This place was built on that very principle.'

The sanatorium was housed in the outer wall of the third level of the Citadel. A series of clean, white marble rooms, the hospital was quiet and solemn. A cool breeze swept in through the arched windows that looked out over vistas of Italian valleys. The sound of waves crashing over rocks echoed from the seascape on the opposite side of the chamber.

'What is this place?' Alixia asked, taking in the different views.

'Somewhere I hoped we would never need,' the founder said, writing down a list of ingredients for the nurse. 'Let's join the others, as I'm sure they will all be asking the same questions.'

50

DISSONANCE

'What would you do if you could go back and change one thing?' Caitlin asked, pulling his arm around her.

Josh let the scent of her body fill his senses. His hand was dangerously close to one of her breasts, but he resisted the urge to caress it. There was some unspoken code that signalled when it was okay to do so, and he was pretty sure this was one of those 'just hold me' moments.

'Is this a trick question?'

'No. Seriously, what one thing would you change?'

He could think of a hundred things in a heartbeat, but none of them was quite as important as his mother, which he knew was pointless. No one could change her condition other than Fermi — and that timeline came at too high a price.

'Okay. So what if the colonel never went into the maelstrom? Never wrote the books of the Djinn. I think that one thing would pretty much fix this situation.'

She scoffed. 'What if you'd never given the tachyon to Fermi.'

'He stole it,' Josh corrected.

'Yeah, and changed the course of humanity.'

Josh went to pull his arm away, but she held onto it tightly.

'You have no idea what it was like,' he said.

'I do. You were trapped between two worlds. The one you'd grown up in and the new reality of the Order. It happens to us all; it's a kind of cognitive dissonance.'

'What's that?'

'Holding two opposing concepts in your head at the same time and believing both of them.'

'Like believing England could win the World Cup?'

She smiled. 'They have, twice.'

'Once. In 1966, my gran used to go on about it all the time.'

'And 1998, against France.'

'Not in my timeline. That I would remember.'

She lifted her head up to look at him; her eyes were sleepy. 'I keep forgetting you're from an alternate.'

'So what would you do?' asked Josh, changing the subject before she asked any more questions about her other self.

This was apparently the question she'd been waiting for. She took her time, chewing her bottom lip and pretending to contemplate the answer.

'Well there are many possibilities that come to mind, but the most likely is that I would have stopped my parents from leaving.'

'Makes sense.'

'Although I've no idea how. They were even more stubborn than me, and at ten-years-old, I'm not sure I would've been able to convince them.'

'But you can go back any time you want.'

She sighed. 'I have, many times, but there's nothing I can think of that would make them change their mind. I want to believe that they were doing it for me, and the only way to save me was to leave — yet there's another part that really wants them to admit it was a stupid mistake.'

He felt her body tense as she turned her head into the pillow, the small shudder in her shoulders as she cried.

'Cat, don't,' he whispered, 'they love you. I'm sure they wouldn't have done it if there was another way.'

'They left me!'

'At least you had them. I've never known my father. Can you imagine what that's like? To wonder every day who your dad was?'

'No,' she said sullenly, wiping her eyes.

'None of us had the life we wanted, or deserved, and we get what fate gave us — as my gran used to say. All we can do is make the best of it. Crying over what we never had is just a waste of good tears.'

'She sounds like a very wise woman.'

'Oh yeah. Maybe one day I'll let you meet her.'

She turned over and took his face in her hands. 'Really, you would?'

'Yeah. She'd love you to bits.'

She kissed him hard on the mouth in a way that signalled this was definitely not a 'just hold me' moment.

51

DECOMPRESSION

Da Recco, Lyra and the Makepieces were all sitting in the central area of level three. The rest of the floor was deserted, a grand spiral staircase in the centre winding up into the higher levels like a nautilus shell.

It was as solemn as a church. No one felt like talking. The journey from the temple had been a simple portal jump, which as far as they could work out had taken them somewhere deep inside the maelstrom. Thomas and Juliana had lots of questions for the Augur reception committee, but no one had given them any answers, especially about what the Citadel was for.

The medics had taken Rufius away immediately while the rest were instructed to wait in quarantine. They had no idea what they were being quarantined for, and the chamber they were escorted into was like an enormous decompression chamber.

'A decompression chamber for demons?' Lyra's voice echoed off the copper walls as the airtight door was closed behind them.

'Please do not be alarmed,' came a voice through a small metal speaker.

'Well, I wasn't until you said that,' muttered Juliana, taking her husband's hand.

Three hours later they were released and escorted to level three — no one was quite sure what the quarantine had actually achieved.

Everyone stood when Alixia and the founder came out of the ward.

Alixia's grave expression answered the question on everyone's minds.

'It's good to see you,' said the founder. 'From what Alixia has told me you've all taken great risks to bring Daedalus here, and for that, I am eternally grateful. He's in the best place, the only place in fact, that may be able to help him.'

The old man bade them take their seats and took out a clay pipe, lighting it with a long taper from one of the many candles that hung from the high ceiling.

'This is the Citadel, a place that I'm quite sure none of you has ever heard of.'

They all stared at him blankly.

'Good. It would be catastrophic if you had. The Citadel has been a secret for as long as the Order has been in existence.'

'Why?' Lyra asked the question everyone was thinking.

The founder smiled, and smoke drifted from the sides of his mouth.

'My dear Lyra,' the founder said benevolently, 'if only everyone was as direct as you. This is the headquarters of a shadow guild, created to observe our timeline for specific events, ones that couldn't necessarily be detected from within.'

'To watch us?' asked Thomas.

'To some extent, yes, but it's also a monitoring station hidden deep within the maelstrom.'

'Looking for signs of the Eschaton,' said Juliana.

The founder puffed on his pipe and blew out a large cloud of blue smoke. 'That is its primary objective. It has other duties, but they are of no consequence now. Suffice to say you are currently the guests of the honourable guild of Augurs.'

'I knew it!' blurted Thomas, turning to his wife, who simply glared at him.

'There are twelve levels to this establishment, each one dedicated to the study of one of the critical events required for an Eschaton Cascade. The members are specialists in their own branch of the theory and isolated from the others — none of them are allowed to share information with the other departments.'

Lyra looked confused. 'Why?'

'To stop any potential interaction between the crises,' answered Thomas.

The founder nodded. 'They operate in cells, insulating the other teams from any potential disaster.'

Lyra shrugged, looking none the wiser for the explanation. She picked up her tea and turned her attention to the biscuits.

'So who determines whether an Eschaton event is occurring?' asked Juliana.

'I do,' came the deep voice of a stranger.

The founder waved his pipe at the large figure — cloaked in long black robes with a forked white beard — who appeared on the central spiral staircase. 'May I introduce Michel de Nostredame, more commonly known as Nostradamus or the curator, and the only one allowed to walk the stairs.'

'And a bloody long way it is,' bellowed Nostradamus, walking over to shake the founder's hand. 'It is good to see you, my friend, although I doubt you're here out of choice, and who are these good people?'

'Friends,' replied the founder. 'Friends who need your help.'

'Well it seems to be a day for it,' Nostradamus said with a gleam in his eye. 'I have another two waiting up on twelfth.'

52

REUNION

Caitlin rushed into the arms of her parents when they appeared at the door. Josh was glad to see them too, but showed a little more reserve, looking past them for the colonel.

'Rufius is very ill,' explained the founder, taking Josh to one side. There were dark shadows beneath his blue eyes, and Josh could tell the old man was in grave danger. 'This place may be his only hope.'

Lyra came over and hugged Josh. 'He's not dead yet,' she whispered in his ear, before going to sit down with the rest of her family to listen to Caitlin's story.

Nostradamus and the founder went off to have a serious discussion, leaving Da Recco standing on his own, staring out of the unusual windows.

'How do they do this?' he said, pointing at the different views.

'I've no idea,' Josh admitted.

'Is it magic? Or maybe witchcraft? I think not,' he mused, touching the window frame.

'Probably better if you don't,' warned Josh. The scarring

on his arm was fading, but he could still feel the tingle of the burn.

'This world is *pazzo*. How do you know which is today and when is tomorrow?'

I don't, thought Josh, realising he had no idea what day it was. The colonel had warned him once that it would become harder to remember when you were, that it would seem less important.

'You just deal with the now, I guess.'

Da Recco nodded solemnly. 'I too.'

'Is the colonel bad?'

'Yes. He's in a coma.'

'Coma?'

'Si. The colonnello is forgetting his past, and without that, what is a man?'

Josh thought about all the times when he'd wished for a father, wondering what kind of life he was having, and what stories he'd tell of his adventures when they finally met. The colonel was the nearest he'd ever come to having a dad, and it was painful to think he might lose him. It wasn't a feeling he'd ever experienced before.

Da Recco seemed to sense his pain and put his hand on Josh's shoulder. 'It's going to be okay. This man will fix him.' He nodded at Nostradamus.

Josh wasn't so sure, there was something about this place that made him uncomfortable, but he couldn't put his finger on what it was.

'How bad is it?' the founder asked, lowering his voice.

Nostradamus gave him a rosary made of twelve beads, four of them had turned black. 'We've passed level four, and according to my latest intelligence two more will fall in the next day or so.'

The founder grimaced. 'It was worse than I feared.'

'We have lost touch with the third, too.'

'They've gone over to the Protectorate. Ravana has taken control of the Council.'

The curator nodded. 'This we know. My spies tell me her son has gone missing.'

'He concerns me the most. His obsession with the Djinn puts us all at risk.'

'The fifth floor are looking into it now. Have you spoken to Derado?'

'Not as yet,' the founder said, handing back the rosary. 'But, he's an honourable man and won't abandon his post.'

Nostradamus nodded. 'So, what ails your friend?'

'His timeline is being systemically corrupted — the only conclusion I can draw is that he's come into contact with dark energy.'

'Aetherium?'

'I need more time to be certain, but it bears all the hallmarks.'

'The eighth crisis,' Nostradamus mused, holding the bead between his fingers.

The founder grimaced. 'I may be wrong, but there are only so many ways to be certain, and all of them put his life in mortal danger,' he said, glancing over at Josh.

Nostradamus flicked the beads over his fingers, feeling each one with his thumb as they passed.

'The Paradox was not what I expected.'

Josh was trying to stop the Italian navigator from climbing out of one of the windows.

'But he may be exactly what we need.'

Nostradamus grunted. 'You're implying that we've grown too set in our ways.'

'We've become too comfortable. It's a flaw in the human condition, and the subtle, insidious nature of regularity leaves us unprepared for change.'

'Except you anticipated it,' Nostradamus said, looking around the room. 'You created the Citadel.'

The founder frowned. 'Even that may not be enough.'

53

RAVANA

Ravana paced the floor of the star chamber, her steps resounding across the tiles as the remaining heads of the guilds watched her.

'We have two problems,' she began, holding up two fingers of her left hand. 'The first lies with the Copernicans, whose inability to restart their computational engine is obviously a passive protest, but undermines our ability to determine the best course of action — this is being corrected as we speak.'

The Copernican grandmaster tried to stand and protest, but two Protectorate officers clamped their hands down on his shoulders, pinning him to his chair.

'Secondly,' Ravana continued, ignoring his complaints, 'it appears that my request for an increase in weapon production has fallen on deaf ears. Madame Bullmedrin, how exactly does the Antiquarian guild imagine we will defend ourselves when the tenth crisis arises?'

The Antiquarian grandmaster bowed her head, unable to look the Chief Inquisitor in the eye.

'Members of the council, this has to change. We're about

to face the worst threat to our existence, and our beloved founder has abandoned us — left us to face the consequences of his poor leadership. We must make ready with what little time we have left. Any disunity now threatens the future of the continuum and will be met with the most extreme punishment.'

She nodded to the guards, and the grandmasters were led out of the chamber.

Ravana was running low on patience, and this was the worst possible time for Dalton to disappear. Three days had passed since they'd argued and no one had seen him since. When he was a child, he could sulk for days, finding places to hide in the castle until his hunger got the better of him, but he'd grown out of that kind of behaviour, or rather his father had beaten it out of him.

His disobedience was an insult to her leadership, and she knew others would have noticed it too. Anger boiled under her cool exterior, but she couldn't let them see it affecting her. She had to be strong no matter how disappointed she was with him. It was something she'd learned to hide from the very first day they'd discovered he was a seer.

Ravana had always blamed her husband for his latent abilities, since her family could be traced back through many generations of noble Copernicans, including Malarant Eckhart— the man who designed the massive computing engine. It was a dark day when Dalton was born; no Eckhart had ever shown the slightest abnormality until then.

And now he was nowhere to be found.

· · ·

'Ma'am,' interrupted one of her guards. 'Inspector Sabien is here.'

'Send him in,' she ordered, fearing the worst. She straightened her uniform until there was no sign of a crease; it was a routine that helped her to remember who she had to be in front of her men.

Sabien was a handsome, strong man, one of the finest of her detective division. He strode across the chamber with purpose, holding the arm of a young red-headed Draconian.

'Chief Inquisitor,' Sabien greeted her, with a small bow of the head.

'Inspector, who do we have here?'

'This is Artificer Bentley, and he has information that I believe you alone will find of interest.'

Ravana took the hint and dismissed the guards.

'Bentley,' prompted Sabien when they had left, 'tell the Inquisitor what you told me.'

Bentley looked nervously at Ravana, and she could see that what he had to say was going to displease her, so she smiled. 'I promise I won't shoot the messenger.'

The young Draconian described the incident at the church. How Dalton had used him to open a Wyrrm bridge and taken a team into the maelstrom, how he had executed his father to force Bentley to help him.

Ravana listened intently, keeping her emotions in check beneath a mask of stoicism.

When Bentley finished, it seemed as if time had stopped. All the years of waiting for the news, like the mother of every seer that had ever been — knowing that one day the madness would come and take their child. It was the curse they all faced, and she'd already resigned herself to the fact that one day her son would finally kill himself.

'Thank you master Bentley,' she said. 'Inspector would you be so kind as to place him under arrest.'

'But —' Bentley protested.

'I can't have you telling everyone that my son has walked into the maelstrom, can I? There are many who would use that kind of information against me.'

Sabien nodded and clapped a pair of handcuffs on Bentley's wrists before marching him out of the chamber.

Now I must plan for the worst, thought Ravana.

54

DARK ENERGY

The founder finished his conversation with Nostradamus and walked over to Josh. Food arrived on simple wooden trays carried by monks with intricate tattoos. Da Recco made his excuses and left the two of them alone.

'What's with the tattoos?' asked Josh, watching them laying out the table.

'They're a form of almanac. Augurs believe so devoutly in their cause that they turn their own bodies into vestiges.'

'So each mark is made in a different time?'

'Exactly. Their bodies are a living embodiment of their missions.'

'They really believe this cascade is going to happen?'

'They do. Professor Eddington convinced me that we should set up this place to focus on exploring the various crises. We kept it secret from the rest of the Order so as to make their work as unbiased as possible. They have spent hundreds of years studying the finer details of the crisis scenarios and finding a way to stop it has become something of a religion to them.'

'I've seen what happens to this timeline,' Josh said with a sigh. 'In four hundred years there won't be much to save.'

'You have seen one version of the future. It doesn't have to be that way if we can avoid it, but tell me what you saw.'

They sat beside the window and Josh described what had happened when they went back to his mother's university, how he'd followed the stranger in the suit into the future and found Fermi's facility. The founder interrupted him to go over some of the smaller details, specifically about the power plant and how it had been built into the heart of a volcano. He seemed less interested in the cloning of Lenin but became very excited when Josh explained how he was being used to travel to key points in time.

'Can you remember exactly which points he was targeting?' the founder asked.

Josh shook his head. 'Not really, there were too many — Caitlin was paying more attention.'

The founder failed to hide his disappointment.

'Was it important?'

'Potentially. There has always been an issue trying to link the external factors of the Eschaton theory — Nostradamus has been looking for a single unifying thread that would explain how the cascade is triggered. I thought for a moment that your professor and his experiments might have held the key.'

'It wasn't really him; he was using Lenin. Somehow he was able to transfer his mind into Lenin's body, using this black stuff — he called it dark energy.'

The old man's eyes narrowed at the mention of the word.

'He was using dark energy?'

Josh nodded. 'He said it gave him extraordinary powers, but it was changing him — he wasn't human.'

'It's a hazardous substance; Rufius' condition is probably due to no more than a single drop of it.'

'Is he going to die?'

The founder placed his hand on Josh's shoulder. 'Not if I can help it.'

'Is he getting worse?' asked Josh, staring at the frail old man lying in bed.

Nostradamus consulted the colonel's notes. 'Yes, his timeline is slowly being broken down, corrupted by the dark energy — we call it aetherium.'

Josh realised that Lenin must have infected the colonel somehow when he knocked him out back at the university. 'How do we fix it?'

'It's not that easy. Reversing this kind of corruption will take a great deal of energy; a lifetime is a very tricky thing to put back together.'

'He's still in there,' said Lyra, clutching the colonel's hand. 'Waiting for his wife — she's pregnant.'

'I thought he lost her?' said Josh.

'He's holding on to his most precious moment,' said the founder, walking back into the room. He was carrying a small leather bag over one shoulder.

'Are you leaving?' asked Caitlin.

'No, you are, if we're going to save this man's life.'

'We can't go back to the continuum. The Protectorate has imposed martial law, and Dalton's already tried to kill us once!' protested Lyra.

The founder took the small box out of the bag and placed it on the table. They all recognised it immediately.

It was the Infinity Engine.

He opened the box, and they were surprised to see it

empty. 'I'm afraid there are far worse things than master Eckhart awaiting us.'

'Where is it?' Caitlin asked, staring at the empty case.

'It is safe, for now, but it's the only thing that can save him, and I need some of you to go back and retrieve it.'

'I'll go,' volunteered Josh without a second thought.

'No. I need you for another mission. I believe that the recovery of the engine is probably best left in the hands of the Makepieces.' He handed the box to Caitlin's parents. 'I take it your timeship can travel back beyond the datum point.'

Juliana nodded. 'It can go anywhere in the continuum. As long as we have an artefact to locate with.'

'For that, you will need to find a friend of mine.'

55

CAPTURE

The creature held him off the ground, razor-sharp talons gripping his throat. Dalton stared down into the many dark eyes and felt the alien mind probing his.

WHO ARE YOU?

The question appeared in his mind as it began to explore his timeline. The Nihil had none of the subtlety of a seer, and it raked over his life like a wolf devouring a kill, looking for some tasty morsel.

But Dalton was a master seer, and while it focused on pillaging his past, his mind skilfully delved into the creature's timeline.

The Nihil's chronology stretched far back into the distant past, its branches weaving across millions of years, creating a lattice more complicated than the continuum itself.

It was an epic history of conquest, shaped by the countless lives the creature had taken, every world it had destroyed. Dalton followed the roots of its devastation back into the maelstrom and beyond. Through the chaos and out into other timelines. As the scale of what this creature had experienced became clear, his mind struggled to cope with the wonder of it all. He witnessed so many alternate realities, some just like his own, while other civilisations were far more advanced than theirs — and all had fallen before the Nihil's forces.

He learned from the lips of the dying why they called themselves 'Nihil', they were annihilation incarnate, but it was just one of a thousand names. They were a legion of nightmares that existed beyond the physical dimensions. To them, time and space were nothing but rooms in a house, and they showed no mercy, decimating everything as they ravaged time in search of their goal. Dalton could feel the hunger within the creature, the burning need for something that was just beyond its grasp, gnawing at its soul, driving it forward in search of the one thing it needed to survive.

Aetherium.

They craved the dark energy but had no way to collect it, relying on others to refine it for them. Their need for it drove them into a frenzy, and that was their weakness, one that Dalton could use to his advantage.

Dalton felt the creature becoming aware of his presence and withdrew, leaving the Nihil studying the moment he'd first met the Nemesis.

WHO IS THIS?

It demanded, replaying the moment over and over again.

NO ONE.

Dalton responded.

HE IS NIHIL?

It asked in a way that wasn't entirely a question or a statement and opened Josh's timeline — which seemed to also expand in many different directions.

'I', Dalton struggled to speak, putting his hand to his

throat trying to loosen the claws that were sunk deep into his skin.

The creature tightened its grip further.

I CAN TAKE YOU TO HIM.

56

ARMAGEDDON GALLERY

The founder looked deep in thought when Josh arrived. He was standing in the middle of a small circular room, one that sat precariously at the very top of the spiral staircase, the highest point in the Citadel. The chamber had twelve arched doorways, each with a number on the keystone above it, and looked out on a different point in time. The tenth seemed to be on fire.

'They call this the Armageddon Gallery,' the founder explained. 'Each one of these is linked to the most likely event that could cause a crisis. Please take a seat,' he added, waving to a chair.

Josh did as he was told and sat on the only seat in the room.

The founder swept his arm around the walls. 'Nostradamus has spent many centuries studying all but one of the crises. Can you guess which one?'

Josh stared at each of the arched portals, trying to pick up any clues from their appearance. 'No.'

The founder laughed, walking over to the door with the Roman numeral 'I' above it.

'The first, strangely enough. No one has ever been able to identify the source of the Paradox. Not even I. Your existence has always been just a statistical probability on which everything else was based. Although there have been many theories, no one has ever proved how you came to exist.'

Josh looked down at his feet. 'You asked me to find my father, and I failed.'

'Oh, I wouldn't say that. You've opened up many new lines of enquiry. From what you and Caitlin have told me, this professor may well be the missing link — he's certainly experimenting with dangerous materials.'

Josh remembered the face of Fermi inside the glass tank, his eyes full of darkness, and wondered if he was nothing more than a science experiment. It worried him to think that he might be another one of the professor's clones.

'We can't go back there,' said Josh. 'Something went wrong. The whole thing was going to collapse.'

Nostradamus entered with Caitlin following behind.

'So shall we begin?' he asked the founder, coming to stand beside Josh.

The founder nodded, and Nostradamus walked to the second portal, which was marked with the Roman numeral II.

'As you know, twelve key crisis points have been identified within the Eschaton Cascade. We have divided these into four parts.'

'The first three,' he said, pointing to the arches on either side of him, 'you all know. Prophecy, Division and Insurgency. We refer to these as the primaries. Joshua, you are quite literally the first proof we've ever had of the first; the other two were very predictable outcomes based on your existence.'

Nostradamus shut the doors to the first three and walked to the number IV.

'The next section is more ambiguous. We have named these 'environmental', and they involve chronospheric abnormalities, temporal fluctuations and deviations in standard random.'

'Like the Wyrrm?' asked Caitlin.

Nostradamus smiled. 'Exactly, and the creature that you captured during your second mission was a prime example. My abnormalists were very impressed with that particular incident.' He closed the fourth door. 'Although they're still unsure as to how it will play a part in the crisis.'

He moved to the fifth door. 'Which brings us to the fifth crisis — "the awakening of the elder gods" and something that I should explain about the cascade. Many believe they don't occur in sequence, which is why we have always placed them on the round; it may well be the five is the trigger for four but has not occurred as yet — such is the nature of non-linear consequences.'

Caitlin saw the confusion in Josh's face and tried to explain. 'The crises are connected through quantum entanglement — they can happen at a distance and in different times,' she tried to explain.

'Like calling Australia?'

'Kind of. They don't occur one after the other, but they still affect each other.'

Nostradamus waited patiently for them to finish, and continued. 'From what you have told us it is quite possible that the future is interfering with past events, and up until now we could never identify any kind of pattern.'

Josh thought back to the analogue computer they stole

from the Romans. 'Rufius stopped an attempt to give the Romans a piece of advanced technology, and I witnessed a whole different timeline based on gunpowder being used at the Battle of Hastings in 1066.'

'Both of which were most likely initiated by your professor,' the founder observed as Nostradamus moved to the seventh door.

'Interventions from beyond the frontier,' the curator intoned. 'The details of what you saw in the future gives us a clue as to the source of the threat, but we still have no clear picture of what the final sequence will be.' He nodded at the last two doors.

They all looked at XI and XII, whose portals were dark.

'No one is to enter those scenarios until we know exactly where they lead.'

'So where do we begin?' asked Josh impatiently.

'What are they working on in the eighth?' asked Caitlin, staring through the door at a Nazi base carved out of the side of a mountain.

Nostradamus consulted his almanac. 'The eighth is investigating the Nazi Nuclear programme. There are signs that someone may be trying to help them develop an atomic bomb.'

'Are we going to try and find the scientist from the Titanic?' Josh whispered to Caitlin.

She sighed. 'Kapteyn. Yes.'

57

CEREBRIUM

[Richmond, England. Date: 11.580]

Alixia stepped out of the *Nautilus* onto the marble floor of the Copernican Cerebrium. She was wearing the traditional scarlet robes of the guild, with her black hair tied tightly back, as was the requirement for Copernican women.

The ceramic tiled rooms of the subterranean basement were a restricted area, dedicated to the processing of members who bequeathed their minds to the Order. One wall was lined with shelves of glass jars, each one containing a brain preserved in formaldehyde.

She grimaced at the overpowering smell of sandalwood and camphor. It reminded her of the cholera epidemic she'd witnessed as a child in Lisbon, the town's guards used it to hide the smell of decay and death, so much so that she had come to hate it as much as the odour it was trying to mask.

Juliana joined her and immediately covered her nose with her hand.

'Holy shit, what's that smell?'

'The dead,' replied Alixia.

'But this is a Copernican archive. They deal with numbers, not corpses.'

Alixia turned towards her. 'They also prepare their departed for the Intuit,' she said, walking along the rows of mortuary drawers and pulling one open.

Da Recco and Thomas — both wearing the robes of master statisticians — appeared from the ship and came over to join them.

They all gaped at the sight of the body within.

'What on earth have they done?' asked Juliana, looking at the body of Professor Eddington.

'Limited the threat of resistance,' said Alixia stoically. 'The Copernicans present the greatest threat to authority if their calculations don't agree with the Protectorate plans.'

'So they executed him?'

'It would appear so,' Alixia said, closing the drawer.

They walked silently along the avenues of minds until they reached a central elevator shaft.

'Engineering is three floors up and two over,' Juliana said, pulling back the metal shutters.

'How do you know?'

'The chief is an old friend of mine from the institute. If I know him, he'll have crawled inside a bottle by now, better if we go in bearing gifts.'

58

BRIEFING

'The eighth have lost a few members recently, so they're likely to be a little tetchy,' warned Nostradamus, ushering Josh and Caitlin to their seats in an auditorium filled with Augurs dressed in Nazi uniforms.

'Permission to speak sir?' said a young man, raising his hand in the row behind Josh.

'Yes, Brother Bartholomew.'

The man stood up, cleared his throat and addressed the room in a polite German accent.

'I believe I speak for all of us when I ask — who are these people?'

'Quite right,' agreed the curator. 'Your work has been a closely guarded secret for so long it would seem strange to share it.' He turned to Josh and Caitlin. 'Our rules forbid us from sharing knowledge with another team, but in this case, I believe we can make an exception. Bartholomew, this is the Paradox — Joshua Jones,' he said pointing at Josh, 'and this,' he added with equal sincerity, 'is Caitlin Makepiece — who has some new information for us.'

Caitlin stood up and cleared her throat. 'During a recent

mission, we learned that someone might be altering the development of quantum research. We have reason to believe that Kapteyn may have been abducted and is working with the German Nuclear Research programme.'

There was a collective intake of breath from the crowd, followed by half-whispered conversations that Josh couldn't quite catch.

'Now, they're merely joining as observers,' Nostradamus added, raising his voice over the hubbub.

Josh realised they seemed to be more interested in Caitlin than him, a fact not lost on her as she started to blush.

Nostradamus turned his attention to Bartholomew, who was still standing. 'Perhaps, brother, you would like to brief our guests on the current situation of the eighth crisis?'

The young man nodded and stepped down onto the floor.

'We have been plotting the rise of the atomic age. Since many believe the eighth predicts the use of nuclear warfare, we have concentrated on the latter half of the twentieth century. Our previous mission was to study Oppenheimer and the Los Alamos laboratory.'

'The Manhattan project?' asked Caitlin.

Bartholomew nodded. 'Yes. The development of the atomic bomb.'

'And quantum tunnelling.'

He looked impressed. 'Indeed.'

Josh always felt a small twinge of pride when they realised how smart Caitlin was. He, on the other hand, had no idea what they were talking about.

'We recently detected a slight fluctuation in the time-line,' continued Bartholomew. 'There are signs that

Germany may be closer to developing their own fission bomb than was originally speculated.'

'But that didn't happen!' Josh interrupted.

Everyone smiled politely.

'Nor will it if we do our job correctly,' said Nostradamus, joining Bartholomew on the floor once more. 'If someone is manipulating the past to their advantage, we must understand how, and ascertain how it could escalate in the future. A crisis doesn't just appear out of thin air.'

Bartholomew motioned to someone at the back of the auditorium, and a black and white film flickered into life on the screen behind him. It was grainy footage from an old newsreel showing a group of German generals being taken around a scientific institute by a team of bespectacled, white-coated scientists.

'The year is 11.944 and Uranverein, the Nazi uranium programme is close to a testable weapon.'

The camera focused in on four men. 'This is Kurt Diebner, Abraham Esau, Walther Gerlach, and Erich Schumann,' — he pointed at each one in turn — 'the lead scientists on the project and the current focus of our investigation. Schumann in particular.'

The film ended with a flicker, and a photograph of Schumann's case file appeared in its place.

'He was born in Potsdam, Brandenburg and went to study under Max Planck at the Humboldt University, from where he went on to become an extraordinarius professor of experimental and theoretical physics at the University of Berlin. In 11.933 he joined the Nazi party.'

The image was replaced with a propaganda film of one of Hitler's massive rallies, thousands of soldiers marching in ranks ahead of tank divisions and missile launchers.

'In 11.934 he was commissioned by the German army to research nuclear energy.'

Bartholomew waved his hand and the light from the projector faded.

'Based on our latest calculations there is an eighty-three-point-four percent probability that he has been adjusted.'

'Adjusted?' asked Caitlin.

'A term we use for individuals who've been given knowledge from the future.'

'By what means?'

Nostradamus took over from Bartholomew. 'We don't know for sure. The last team that was sent in have gone dark — we've heard nothing from them in over a week — protocol dictates we send in a recovery team.'

Caitlin didn't reply. She seemed lost in her thoughts.

'What happens if Schumann has been adjusted?' asked Josh.

'A war to end all wars,' replied Bartholomew. 'The Third Reich would use their weapons to obliterate the Allied forces. The US would respond in kind and Hiroshima would be nothing more than a side-show compared to the devastation that followed.'

'So, if you would like to get changed,' Nostradamus said, waving at a door to his left, 'we would like to be on our way.'

59

CHIEF MACKENZIE

Chief MacKenzie sat with his feet up on his desk and cradled his tin cup, debating whether to pour himself another Cognac. It was a Remy Martin Black Pearl Louis XIII — worth a small fortune in the linear world, and something he'd been saving for special occasions.

Professor Eddington had presented it to him as part of his twenty-fifth anniversary, along with a gold tachyon, which he cherished, keeping it safely locked away in the velvet-lined presentation box in his drawer for the last four years.

One year away from retirement, he thought. One year, and he would have been bored out of his mind playing golf and restoring antique steam engines with all the other grumpy old farts.

He took the bottle and pulled the fancy fleur-de-lis stopper out with his teeth, pouring a large measure into the tin cup. It probably deserved a cut glass tumbler, but such delicate things tended to get broken in his workshop. He rolled the amber liquid around the bottom of the enamelled cup before knocking it back in one go.

MacKenzie chuckled to himself. He was celebrating a minor victory. He could still picture Ravana's face: her cheeks burning with rage at the news that the Infinity Engine was missing.

She would never guess where it was; the founder was too canny. He'd been careful to plan for just this kind of scenario.

A polite tap on the door broke his reverie.

'Enter,' he called out, putting down the cup and taking a steel spanner from his workbench. Everyone on his detail had left for the day, so whoever wanted to speak to him wasn't going to be from engineering.

The door swung back to reveal a group of Copernicans headed up by Juliana Makepiece, a woman he hadn't seen or heard from in over ten years.

'Hello George,' she said through a wry smile, and holding up a bottle of sixty-two-year-old Dalmore whisky. 'I wondered if you fancied a drink, for old times?'

The chief looked surprised. 'T'were only twelve bottles ever made,' he said, putting down the spanner and walking over to inspect the label. 'Is this what you've been doing? Hunting down vintage whiskies?'

She shrugged. 'Amongst other things. I've also got a twenty-five-year-old Pure Pot Still Whiskey from Nun's Island — unopened.'

MacKenzie's eyes widened, and he searched around for some extra cups. 'Will your friends be staying?'

'Oh, I think you're going to want to join us,' she smiled and tapped something on her wrist.

Suddenly, a pressure door appeared in the wall on the other side of the room.

'So you finally built her?' he said.

'Oh yes,' Juliana replied proudly, spinning the brass wheel. 'Although I've still got a few concerns about the rudder that I could use your help with. But that can wait until later. We've more important things to discuss.'

60

DRESSING

'What's the matter?' asked Josh, buttoning up the black jacket of his Gestapo uniform.

Caitlin was frowning at herself in the mirror. She was wearing the dark grey uniform of a nurse, austere and practical, with a starched white apron decorated with a golden swastika.

'Just once I would like to go in as an officer, or a doctor. Something that wasn't so bloody far down the pecking order.'

Josh knew she wasn't expecting an answer, but couldn't help himself.

'Nurses are important.'

'I know, but you're missing the point. Travelling back into history isn't very empowering for a woman.'

'What about Elizabeth or Victoria? They were pretty powerful.'

'I'm not sure I can go on a mission as the Queen of England.'

'Oh, I don't know, I reckon you could pull it off.'

She smiled and helped him with his buttons. 'You, on

the other hand, look every bit the Aryan officer. Are you sure there isn't any Nordic blood in your family?'

'No idea, as mum never talked about it. Gran couldn't remember what day it was, let alone who her parents were, and the jury's still out on my dad.'

'Maybe we should go back and visit them when they were younger. I'd like to meet her.'

'Yeah, if we get through this.'

She kissed him. 'When we get through this.'

'So you think Fermi passed something on to Schumann?'

Caitlin frowned. 'No, I think they're looking at the wrong man, right time though.'

'I'm still not sure why he's doing it.'

She raised an eyebrow and took a deep breath. 'He's using their collective brains to help him improve his technology. Every discovery they make is one less for him, and the beauty is that he can keep going back and improving it. It does mean that he wasn't able to reverse engineer the tachyon — which is good news for you.'

'You're never going to forget that are you?'

'The fact that you gave away a quantum device to a quantum physicist? No, probably not.'

'I didn't give it away. I was out cold when he took it.'

She folded her arms across her chest. 'So we still haven't discussed why you were there? We said there would be no more secrets.'

Josh had run out of excuses. 'To steal some chemicals — for drugs.'

Caitlin looked genuinely shocked. 'You were a drug dealer?'

'No! A driver, that's all — Lenin was into drugs.'

'Lenin the clone?'

'Yeah, I still don't understand how he ended up there. It's a long story —'

There was a knock at the door.

'We're leaving in five,' warned Bartholomew.

Caitlin turned to Josh and took his face in her hands. 'Whatever it is, just promise me you'll always tell me the truth — I can't stand the thought of you hiding stuff from me. We have to trust each other.'

He pulled her close. 'I will,' he whispered, 'when this is over, I promise I'll tell you everything.'

61

HEADBOLT

Thomas was having trouble believing what he was hearing.

'You shut down the whole thing?' he repeated with a chuckle.

The chief's eyes gleamed as he took another slug of whisky. 'Sent everyone home. The boilers will be as cold as a polar bear's nuts by now.'

'Or Ravana's heart!' joked Thomas.

They all laughed, even Alixia, who had worn a permanent frown since they'd started this mission.

Juliana opened the Nun's Island Whiskey and filled MacKenzie's glass. 'We need your help George,' she said, sitting down opposite him.

They were in the galley of the *Nautilus*. It had taken them over an hour to satisfy the Chief's fascination with the ship, and she'd only managed to keep him out of the engine room by promising to show him the plans and let him drive later.

'Any friend of headbolt is a friend of mine!' he said with a toast. 'May your screws always turn clockwise!'

'Headbolt?' said Thomas to his wife.

'Long story,' she replied with a frown. 'I'll tell you later'.

'We've been instructed by the founder to recover the Infinity Engine,' said Alixia, getting right to the point.

The chief looked taken aback by her directness.

'Have you indeed?' he asked, seeming to sober up quickly. 'And how exactly can I help you with that?'

'By telling us where it is hidden?' Alixia replied.

'And you think I know where it is?'

'You are cautious, that is to be expected, but we don't have time for games. The founder gave us something to prove you can trust us.'

Juliana produced the carved wooden box.

The chief picked it up and examined it. 'A fair copy, there's no doubt it could be mistaken for the reliquary.'

'The founder also told us that you would have a key — a locket — something personal he left with you.'

The chief nodded, tapping his pocket. 'Aye, He did, and I'll take you there, but it'll cost you more than a bottle of whisky. I want to drive this beautiful ship.'

62

HEISENBERG

[Nuclear Research Station, Haigerloch, Germany.
Date:11.944]

The canteen was deserted when they appeared. The researchers of the eighth had done their job well, carefully selecting an entry point that would attract the least amount of attention. It was early morning, and the clock on the grey wall was showing just after two. The night shift wasn't particularly hungry, and if the lingering smell of cabbage was anything to go by, Josh could understand why.

'What are we looking for?' he asked in German, opening some of the metal lockers that lined one side of the room and picking up the fleeting memories of the technicians who worked there.

'Something to get us close to Schumann,' replied Bartholomew, pulling out a Geiger counter which started clicking immediately. 'This is a prototype reactor, built by his lead scientist, Heisenberg, and his team. They were secretly trying to create nuclear material.'

'For a nuclear warhead?' asked Caitlin.

'Eventually,' Bartholomew said, sweeping the device around the room.

'Schumann had Heisenberg's group moved out of Berlin because of the bombing,' added one of his colleagues. 'The allied forces knew that there was something under development and hit anything that looked slightly industrial.'

'Radiation levels are minimal,' Bartholomew said, tapping the dial. 'Let's go and check the main chamber.'

'Is this even safe?' asked Josh as he disappeared through the door.

They followed Bartholomew halfway down a long tunnel that looked like it had been carved out of the rock by hand. Metal doors were set back into the walls at regular intervals; like pressure doors from a ship, they had a central locking wheel and a small glass porthole.

Caitlin looked into one and stepped back, her face white as a sheet.

'What?'

'Don't look,' she warned, walking away.

Josh moved closer to the glass.

'I warned you.'

The figure inside the room was hardly human, its blistered body covered with large open sores all over its pale skin. It was blindly shuffling around the room like a zombie.

'What happened to him?'

'Radiation sickness,' she replied, looking into another cell. 'I'm guessing they've been using slave labour as part of their experiment.'

'He's one of ours,' said Bartholomew gravely, looking through the porthole.

.   .   .

The reactor sat in the middle of a vast chamber. A large iron sphere surrounded by metal cylinders with wires and pipes winding out across the floor.

Bartholomew's men had already taken out the guards who lay unconscious on the floor, their arms and legs bound together and their mouths gagged. Killing them wasn't an option he'd explained before they left; this mission was to have a zero impact on the timeline.

'Levels at thirty millisieverts and rising,' reported one of the team, holding up the Geiger counter.

'We have less than thirty minutes,' warned Bartholomew, 'let's get this over with.'

The others began to scour the room, rifling through documents and journals looking for anything that directly referred to Schumann.

'What happened to them after the war?' asked Caitlin, as she walked around the reactor.

'Operation ALSOS — in 11.945 the allies seized anything to do with the Nazi nuclear weapon project, including materials and personnel. Most were caught at Hechingen and shipped off to England.'

'Why?'

'To keep it out of the hands of the Russians. It was ground-breaking technology, and they all wanted a piece of it.'

'And Schumann?'

'That depends on the outcome. In this timeline he's ridiculed as an incompetent, in another alternate he's a hero whose weapon brings the western world to its knees before the Third Reich.'

'And how do we make sure that doesn't happen?' asked Josh.

'We find the reason and protect it.'

One of the team handed Bartholomew a well-thumbed journal, which he began to flick through. 'It appears that Heisenberg has made more progress than he's been reporting to his boss.' He held up the page for them to see. 'These calculations go far beyond the formula for Nuclear fission. They're the basis of quantum mechanics, so whatever Heisenberg was developing it was more than a nuclear weapon.'

'Forty millisieverts,' intoned one of the team.

'We need to go,' Bartholomew said, moving to put the journal into his rucksack.

'Aren't you going to follow it?' Josh asked, putting his hand on the book.

Bartholomew shook his head. 'We recover the evidence. There's a whole department back at base who need to analyse it and determine the best course of action.'

'I don't think we have time for that,' Josh said, opening its timeline.

'But the protocol dictates...'

63

AHNENERBE

Josh put Heisenberg's journal down and looked out of the window. It was winter, and the view of the snow-topped Alps took his breath away. The steep-sided valley was covered in a blanket of white, and it was like looking at one of those Christmas cards his Gran used to send his mum.

'Hohenwerfen Castle,' Caitlin said, looking up at the heraldic symbols above the baronial fireplace. 'This once belonged to the Hapsburgs.'

Josh's breath clouded the window pane, and as he wiped it clean he could feel the age of the lead latticework that held the stained glass in place; the smell of the solder as they sealed them in the panes flowed all the way back to the eleventh century.

The castle was quiet, almost too quiet. It was hard to believe that just a few floors below him a garrison of SS soldiers were busy polishing their jackboots.

Heisenberg had converted the medieval room into his

personal study and Caitlin was busy examining the black-boards that were lined along the wall at the far end. They were covered in chalk formulae, hastily scrawled into every available inch of the green-black slate.

Josh wasn't surprised to find that Bartholomew's team hadn't followed them; they would stay on mission. Schumann was still the primary target, and the Augurs would focus on their original objective. He was impressed by their sense of duty; they were like an ultra-religious version of the SAS.

'This is inspired!' gushed Caitlin, tapping the board.

'All his own work?' asked Josh, the white squiggles reminding him too much of the painful maths lessons he'd endured at school. He loved numbers, but algebra and dyslexia did not mix well.

She traced her finger over the chalk marks. 'Well, he certainly wrote it all. Whether someone was helping him, it's hard to tell.'

'What does it say?'

'I'm not an expert, but you can see he's using his theory of quantum matrices to map how the physical properties of particles evolve over time.' She pointed to a bunch of symbols.

'Obviously,' agreed Josh, squinting at the tiny lines. 'So what's he trying to prove?'

'It's not nuclear fission, that's for sure. This is closer to Schrödinger's wave formulation.'

Josh was totally lost. He loved that Caitlin was so smart, so knowledgeable, but sometimes it made him wonder if she might think he was a bit thick.

'Yeah, I must have missed that lesson.'

She laughed. 'You don't have to be good at everything,'

she said, taking his hand. 'Do you want me to explain it to you?'

'No, just work out what we need to do so we can leave,' he said, and shivered. 'This place reminds me of Dracula's castle.'

She nodded and went back to the blackboard.

Josh wandered around the rest of the room, picking up random items of Heisenberg's and browsing their timelines.

'What's Ahnenerbe?' he asked Caitlin, flicking through a book.

'An elite SS research unit that was trying to validate Hitler's theory of an ancient Aryan race by using scientific methods,' she answered, without taking her eyes off the formula. 'He called them the "founders of culture". They were supposed to be looking for evidence of German racial superiority through archaeology among other things.'

Josh looked along the shelves. 'Well, Heisenberg has collected quite a few books about it.'

Caitlin wasn't paying him much attention, too busy studying a complicated equation on the last board – her eyebrows furrowing in the usual way.

Josh picked up an official-looking letter that was signed by Himmler and browsed its timeline.

'Cat?' he whispered. 'We need to go.'

'Shh! I've nearly got it.'

'The thing in the cave, it's not a nuclear reactor.'

'This equation,' she said, drawing her finger across a part of one line. 'He shouldn't know this. It's the quantum excitation of the Higgs field, and wasn't proposed until 11.960s and even then it took another forty years to prove.'

'Cat!'

'What?' she snapped.

'The thing in the cave isn't a reactor.'

'Can't you see I'm trying to work out what he was really doing?'

'That he was building a time machine?'

She looked confused. 'How do you know?'

Josh held up the letter. 'Because I've just seen the demonstration!'

64

EL PRESIDENTE

S itting in the red leather pilot seat, Chief MacKenzie pored over the brass controls of the *Nautilus,* admiring the fine detail and craftsmanship of the navigation system.

'Well?' asked Juliana.

'It's not your rudder. The trim's off by two degrees in the bow plane, and you need to replace the journal bearing on the second generator, but my god lass, she truly is a beauty.'

Juliana glowed with pride. 'I've had a lot of time to perfect her.'

'Thought we'd lost you for good.'

Her smile faded. 'So did we. It was only Marcus' plan that saved us.'

'I've heard nowt about him since that farce with the Eschaton presentation. Did he go back to wandering the lost paths?'

She shook her head. 'I've no idea. He's always been one to follow his own trail.'

'Do you still have it? His plan?'

Juliana looked towards her husband who was staring out of the viewport. 'Thomas is obsessed with it, and has hundreds of variations on the original, but they all come back to the same endpoint.'

'The end of times?'

'Yes, Thomas is convinced the only way to make a difference is to introduce the Paradox, but he can't work out exactly how it will change the outcome.'

'Sometimes you just have to put your trust in fate.'

'Ha! Don't let the Institute of Engineers hear you say that — you'll get expelled!'

The chief chuckled. 'I doubt it. I'm the bloody president.'

'What? How the hell did you manage that?'

'Everyone else died, or retired,' he said with a tinge of sadness. 'It's not like the old days. You'd hardly recognise it.'

'No more Christmas parties?'

'Oh, we still have those. We managed to get chucked out of Goldsmith's Hall last time.'

Juliana smiled. 'Does Newton still do the speech about the apple?'

'Every year and Davey does the trick with helium.'

'Still pisses Faraday off?'

The chief nodded.

She laughed at the memory of the two scientists nearly coming to blows. 'Never gets old.'

'Never. Now shall we see if we can find this damn engine.' He reset the dials on the main control desk and pulled a series of levers. The lights dimmed slightly as the generators kicked.

'You may want to go and sort out number two.'

'On it, El Presidente,' said Juliana with a mock salute.

65

TIME MACHINE

The cave was packed full of SS officers, all eagerly awaiting the start of the demonstration. Standing at the centre of them, looking impatiently at his watch, was Heinrich Himmler.

Heisenberg looked stressed as he oversaw the final preparations of his experiment. There was a constant hum of power from the reactor, the vibrations so intense that Josh could feel it through the soles of his boots.

Arranged in a circle at one end of the chamber were twelve black obelisks. Standing at over two metres tall, each one was covered in ancient runes and connected to the reactor by thick, industrial cables which were making them vibrate ever so slightly.

Caitlin was standing behind the lead shielding with the other nurses, while Josh had found a radiation suit that looked more like something from Star Wars, and had made his way into a group of technicians collected close to the circle.

'The search for our ancestors is nearly over,' said

Himmler to his officers. 'Soon we shall know the true heritage of our forefathers.'

Heisenberg took his cue from Himmler and stepped into the circle. 'This will be a momentous day for the Reich. To conquer time and prove to the world that we are truly an Aryan race! For this demonstration, I have chosen one of our primary archaeological sites, Bohuslän, twelve hundred years before Christ.' He nodded to his assistant, who pulled a lever and the low whine of the reactor changed pitch. 'We will require over a million kilowatts of energy to create the temporal field,' he shouted over the noise of the device. 'I suggest you all take refuge behind the screens.'

Heisenberg placed a padded helmet over his head and turned towards a group of soldiers, motioning them to come forward with one gloved hand.

Josh watched through his half-fogged visor as three men strode out into the circle.

They were all blonde, athletic-looking specimens in white vests and shorts, which they proceeded to remove once they were in the centre. Their bodies were taught and muscled, like Greek gods, and each one of them stood proudly in the glare of the spotlights displaying the swastika tattooed over their hearts.

Josh could see the others watching eagerly from behind the shields. Many of the nurses were taking it in turns to stare through the glass slits at the naked men. There was a tiny pang of jealousy as he wondered if Caitlin was one of them.

Heisenberg signalled to his team, and the thrum of the reactor shifted pitch. Everyone felt the surge of power as the energy poured through the obelisks and out into the circle. A bubble of distortion materialised between the three men, expanding quickly to envelop them. They became distorted inside the ball of flux, like a hall of mirrors, their limbs elongating as their heads seem to twist on impossibly long necks.

There was no sound other than the high-pitched whine of the reactor.

Then they were gone.

Nothing remained of the men, other than the faint impression of footprints on the dusty floor.

The reactor began to wind down, and Heisenberg took off his helmet, his hair sticking limply to his head.

'Very impressive,' said Himmler, stepping out from behind the lead screen, 'but how do we know it worked?'

Heisenberg pulled off his gloves. Josh could see his hands were shaking as he pointed to the crowd behind Himmler. 'I believe Herr Wirth should be able to confirm its success.'

An older man stepped out from the crowd, wearing a tweed suit that reminded Josh of a stereotypical university professor.

The archaeologist cleared his throat with a subtle cough. 'The men were given a straightforward brief. As we're all aware, this is not an exact science and a one-way mission at best.'

Wirth took out a series of photographs from a leather briefcase and showed them to Himmler.

'These were taken on my last visit to Bohuslän,' he began, pointing at the images of cave art. 'At the time there was no evidence to suggest that they were anything more than bronze-age petroglyphs.'

Himmler's face was a mask of concentration as he studied the black and white photos, and then slowly a smile broke across his face.

'You are a genius, Herr Heisenberg,' he crowed loudly,

showing each of the other officers the photograph. 'Do you see? There in the carvings. It's them. The swastika.'

The other SS officers each took their turn to look at the image, nodding and congratulating their commander.

Josh removed his helmet and moved around through the group until he could see for himself.

There in the photograph were the simple rock drawings of three elongated men, each one with the Nazi symbol carved into their chests.

'We should go,' Caitlin whispered in his ear.

66

SNOWBALL

[Date: -654,000,000]

'When are we exactly?' asked Alixia, looking out through the observation window onto a sheet of snow and ice.

'Minus six-point-three-three to the eleventh,' Juliana said, consulting the dials.

'Wow!' exclaimed Thomas, looking out across the bleak white expanse. 'Six hundred and fifty-million years ago? That's snowball earth territory!'

'Snowball?'

'The Marinoan glaciation. The entire earth surface is covered in ice.'

'How on earth did the founder get a vestige back this far?' Lyra wondered aloud.

The chief climbed up from the engine room, his face smeared with grease.

'That's your bearing fixed.'

Juliana nodded her appreciation.

He took in the view from the window. 'I see we've arrived.'

'What exactly are we supposed to do back here?' Alixia asked the engineer as he wiped his hands.

'You wanted to know where the founder hid the engine and I've brought you to it.' He nodded at the icy landscape beyond the glass. 'He put it out of most members' reach.'

'He can travel back this far?' blurted Thomas.

The chief shrugged, holding up the founder's locket. 'His range is virtually infinite. The temporal location contained in this vestige would only be accessible to someone with a ship like this or an infinite.'

'And he's the only one,' Thomas mused. 'Very clever.'

'Indeed,' agreed the chief. 'Now, assuming you've cold weather gear, I suggest we get out there and recover the device before your friend gets any worse.'

67

CAVE ART

[Bohuslän, Sweden. Date: 11.936]

Josh and Caitlin looked down from the top of the rock outcropping, their shadows matching the elongated figures of stick men carved into the stone plateau below — they were exactly like the ones from the photograph. The swastika was unmistakable.

'We're not supposed to use naturals,' complained Caitlin.

'We don't have much choice,' said Josh. 'We can hardly let the Third Reich go back fifteen-hundred years and start some kind of Aryan super race.'

'You don't know for sure that they did.'

The German archaeologist Wirth and the rest of his expedition were busy taking photographs further down the valley. For some crazy reason, they had brought a musicologist called Fritz Bose who was making recordings on something called a magnetophon.

Josh had to improvise, using the timeline from the photograph to get them back to the point when it was taken.

It was an impulsive decision, one he didn't really have time to discuss with Caitlin, and she wasn't particularly happy about it.

'We should've gone back and told the founder about the time machine,' she insisted, unpacking their travel robes.

'Isn't there another crisis about time machines?'

'Yes, the eleventh. So we can be pretty sure that these two are related.'

'Which means there's going to be another team dealing with this already,' Josh said smugly.

Caitlin didn't look convinced. 'I doubt it. They're not making the same kind of connections as we are — it's like they're too scared to think outside the box.'

'Do you think Fermi came back to give Heisenberg the information he needed?'

Caitlin's lips pursed as she considered the idea. 'That would explain how he managed to overcome the gravitational quantisation issue —'

'Just so I'm clear on this,' Josh interrupted. 'Do you guys actually know how to build a time machine?'

Caitlin laughed. 'Belsarus spent years trying to. There are a hundred different theories and thousands of books on the subject, but no, we don't know how to build a time machine. All we know, is that if someone does, it will potentially cause the end of time as we know it.'

'Potentially?'

'Sim puts it at about ninety-four point-two percent.'

'That's pretty much a sure thing then.'

'Pretty much.'

'And you still think I started it?'

'Yup.'

. . .

Caitlin knelt down and touched one of the figures. The rock was weather-beaten and smooth, but she could still sense the latent timelines stored deep within it. She saw fierce-looking men with primitive flint tools chipping away at the stone while a shaman stood over them with a firebrand, chanting.

'It's some kind of ritual,' she said, taking her hand away from the stone.

'Maybe they sacrificed the blonde gods to Odin.'

'I don't think so.' She looked distracted as if something was bothering her.

'What is it? Are we going to jump or not?'

'There was something familiar about their shaman.'

'Like you know him?' Josh asked, sounding surprised.

She shook her head. 'No, but he looked a hell of a lot like my dad.'

68

ICE AGE

The ice pack was vast. Millions of years of snow lay undisturbed, compressed into a thick blanket by the weight of layer upon layer of snow-fall.

There was only one set of footprints to follow, which without the specific date would have been lost in a matter of hours.

The team from the *Nautilus* tramped slowly across the glittering white plain. Clothed in thick sealskin coats lined with fur and bound together by ropes, they blindly followed in the footsteps of the chief. Moving like old men hunched against the biting wind, they made their way across the tundra.

The temperature made it impossible to speak, and they'd wrapped scarves around their faces to prevent their lips from freezing which were now strung with white pearls of condensation. Snow goggles reduced the glare off the ice but made it difficult to tell them apart.

The chief led the party, sinking his poles into the fresh powder in front of him as he followed the imprints left by the founder, his snow-shoes obliterating his master's tracks as they turned over the loose top layer.

Alixia, Thomas and Da Recco followed behind him, Juliana opting to stay with the ship. She was concerned the freezing conditions would drain the batteries too quickly and wanted to monitor their levels in case she needed to take it back into the maelstrom.

After a couple of hours of slow, laborious progress the party made it to the cave entrance.

Hidden beneath a precipice of ice carved out by the wind, the entrance glistened with long icicles that reminded Da Recco of a dragon's mouth as he passed underneath them.

Sheltered from the icy chill, they pulled off their thick mittens and shook the snow from their headgear.

'That's the coldest I've ever been,' said Da Recco through blue lips and chattering teeth, 'and I've been to Scotland.'

'I would say minus eighty degrees centigrade at least,' suggested Thomas to Da Recco, whose blank expression told him that he had no clue what a centigrade was, leaving Thomas wondering what they used for temperature readings back in the fourteenth century.

'So where exactly are we?' asked Alixia.

The chief chuckled. 'The Himalayas, about four kilometres north of where the temple will stand in six hundred and fifty-million years.'

They looked around the cave. The walls were covered in a slick layer of water and lichen.

'The first signs of life,' said Alixia, touching the small plants tenderly. 'The Cambrian explosion begins.'

'In about a hundred million years from now,' corrected

the chief, stamping his feet on the floor. 'Now where's that damn engine?'

At the far end of the cave was an opening, a crude arch that led further into the mountain. Shedding their heavy coats and snowshoes, they filed through into the cavern beyond.

'Geothermal?' wondered Thomas as the air warmed their faces.

'Temporal flux,' Alixia whispered, studying the inside of the chamber.

The rock around them looked as if it had been intricately carved into strange geometric patterns, but when she examined them closely it was obvious the fractal-like formations could only have occurred naturally.

Floating in the centre of the cavern was a sphere of iridescent blue light, surrounded in a halo of energy that swirled over its surface like oil on water.

'Beautiful,' said Da Recco, moving towards it.

'Wait!' ordered Alixia, stopping him in his tracks. 'We have no idea what physical contact with the engine will do,' she added, pointing to the transformation of the cave walls.

Thomas took out the box the founder had given them. 'How is that going to fit in here?'

The chief chuckled, taking the wooden container from him. 'It's bigger on the inside.'

They all held their breath as MacKenzie approached the glowing light. Walking into its sphere of influence he seemed to grow younger, his bald head sprouting hair and his body tightening — growing stronger and fitter.

'Mio Dio!' gasped Da Recco.

'Time dilation,' whispered Thomas. 'He's just regressed thirty years.'

The chief opened the lid of the box and reached out to the sphere. It seemed to shrink in his hand as he held it and in that instant, they all saw his expression change. He turned to them, his eyes dark pools of infinite black, and a moment of ecstasy passed across his face.

Everyone felt the effects of time slowing; seconds turned into minutes that stretched into hours before suddenly it was gone, and the engine was inside the box, and a fragile old man stood where the younger one had been.

'How long was I gone?' he asked, his hands shaking as he held the case.

'Too long,' replied Alixia, taking the box from him and handing it to Thomas.

'It was wonderful,' he muttered, his skin mottling as he continued to age.

'Did you know?'

MacKenzie nodded, smiling at something over her shoulder, something none of the others could see. She watched his eyes whiten with cataracts.

'I saw everything.'

His skin had become paper-like and transparent, and his fingers swollen and deformed as arthritis twisted them.

'Tell the founder the Nihil are coming.'

He collapsed to the floor, his desiccated body turning to a pile of ashes where he knelt.

Alixia collapsed into Da Recco's arms.

'We have to leave now!' cried Thomas.

69

SHAMAN

[Bohuslän, Sweden. Date: 8.500]

The night sky was dark and full of stars.

They'd travelled back three and a half thousand years in the blink of an eye, and appeared in the middle of winter with a biting cold wind that sliced through their travel robes without mercy.

'We need to find some shelter until morning,' Caitlin said, nodding to a cave halfway up the rock face.

Josh remembered the last time he'd been in a cave with her; he'd inadvertently pulled her into the Mesolithic while trying to escape from a Monad. Back then it had seemed like the right thing to do, and she'd teased him about what they got up to for weeks afterwards. This was another time and another Caitlin, although it was becoming harder to tell them apart now, the differences between them blurring. He realised she'd stopped asking questions about her other self.

'Yeah. It's freezing,' he said, shivering and blowing on his hands.

. . .

Luckily, the cave was unoccupied. Josh went out to scavenge wood to make a fire, and while he was gone Caitlin scouted around for something to eat. There was some strange looking fungus growing in the back of the cave, but she opted for the mushrooms growing near the entrance.

'Are you sure they're not magic mushrooms?' Josh asked when he got back with an armful of kindling.

Caitlin smiled and began threading them onto a thin twig. 'They're Chanterelles. Wild ones are the best.'

She showed Josh how to light the kindling with flint, taking great pleasure in his failure to get anything to ignite.

'So you and your dad used to come back here?' he asked as they warmed themselves in front of the fire.

'Way further back than this. This is positively recent compared to where we used to go.'

When he was younger, before his mum became ill, Josh used to imagine what it would be like to have a dad who took you on adventures. There were the grand expeditions that he would plan in intricate detail, expeditions that involved going away for the whole summer, like the ones Caitlin went on, and then there were the simple day trips, to the zoo or a football match — nothing too extravagant, but still moments he felt he was missing.

There were a few times, early on, when he'd been invited along to other boy's birthday outings. They had given him a sense of what it should have been like: loads of six-year-old kids high on fizzy drinks charging around a network of foam-covered climbing frames while their dads hung out at the bar comparing fantasy football teams, but it wasn't really what he'd had in mind.

'Do you ever wonder what he would've looked like?'
'Who?'

'Your dad,' she said, smiling. 'Remember, I can read you like a book.'

'No, not for a long time.'

'When my parents disappeared, I used to see them in crowds, but they were always much older. It's weird when you're thirteen — you think everyone over thirty is ancient.'

'When my mum first got sick, I was looked after by my Gran, and Mrs B, who used to live next door. Now she was properly ancient.'

Caitlin pulled a kebab out of the fire and blew on it to cool the mushrooms down. 'Like over forty?'

Josh laughed. 'More like ninety I think. She would still chat up any bloke that passed near her front door.'

Caitlin tasted one and handed another to Josh. 'I guess you would say my grandfather was a bit more traditional. He did his best, and I loved him to bits, but it was a relief when he left me with Alixia — going shopping with her was a revelation.'

Josh thought of all the times he'd been to the charity shop for his mother when her agoraphobia got so bad that she refused to leave the flat. With the clothes he could afford, he was glad his friends never got to see her.

'We didn't have a lot of money,' he said. 'There were things I had to do just to keep the lights on.'

'Is that why you did those things with Lenin?'

He nodded. 'I did what I had to do to survive. Not bad stuff, but not strictly legal either.'

'Like what?' She shuffled closer until their hips were touching.

'Stealing cars mostly,' he said, idly picking up a branch and throwing it onto the fire.

'And?'

'I broke into a few places, mostly sheds, and then there was the Colonel's place.'

'You broke into his house?'

'I needed three grand or Lenin was going to take the TV and anything else that wasn't nailed down.'

'Why did you owe him so much money?'

Josh sighed. 'Because dope helped with mum's spasms. MS is a terrible disease and cannabis can relieve the symptoms. Except she wouldn't go to the doctor to get it, so I had to buy it.'

'And Lenin was your dealer?'

Josh nodded. *He was way more than that*, he thought.

'Lenin ran the Ghost Squad, and they controlled most of our estate. Me and him go back a long way.'

Caitlin pulled another row of mushrooms off the fire and waved them around in the air. The smell was delicious, and Josh made a grab for one, but she moved it out of his reach.

'You'll burn your tongue. Have you always been so impatient?'

'Always,' he said, grabbing her around the waist. 'Now give me food, woman.'

Later, when they were lying in the makeshift bed she'd made from their clothes, Caitlin asked, 'So how did Lenin end up in the future?'

Josh was half asleep, thinking about whether they could just hang out here for a few days and forget about all the Eschaton stuff. He knew everyone was expecting him to pull some kind of rabbit out of a hat, but he didn't have a clue what he was supposed to do. He wasn't even sure how he got the job in the first place, and the thought of all that responsibility was beginning to stress him out.

'I don't know. I think he was working for the professor. We broke into Fermi's lab at the university — that was when I lost the tachyon. I think he paid Lenin to find me, and when they couldn't he kidnapped my mum.' Josh intentionally left out the part where Lenin shot Caitlin and the terrible choice he'd had to make about Gossy.

'Shit,' she said, putting her arm across him. 'He sounds like a real nasty bastard.'

Josh lifted his arm so she could put her head on his chest. 'I thought I'd left that behind, but it seems fate has other ideas.'

She sucked air in through her teeth. 'Don't let Sim hear you use that word.'

'I know, his face goes all pinched like he's bitten into a lemon,' Josh said, pulling a grim expression.

Caitlin laughed. 'That's it exactly.'

She kissed him. 'You're such an enigma, Joshua Jones.'

'Is that good?' he asked with a cheeky smile.

She twisted around until she was on top of him. 'Oh, it's more than good.'

Josh woke before the dawn. The fire was low, nothing more than warm embers glowing in the half-light. Caitlin slept soundly in his arms, and he could feel her chest rising and falling against him.

Figures moved in the shadows, furtively staying out of the light. Josh held his breath and listened as their soft feet padded across the stone floor. He thought about waking Cat, but she would make too much noise, and he didn't need that. What he needed was a weapon, but there was nothing but the half-burned branches and a few rocks.

There was a scraping sound like metal on rock, and two half-naked warriors came out of the night, their eyes wild, bronze blades raised above their heads.

Josh pushed Caitlin behind him and reached for a fire-brand, bringing it up to block the first attack and jabbing the glowing end into the man's belly. The second held back as the first howled with pain. Josh bent his knees, dropping his centre of gravity.

Behind him, Caitlin complained about being woken up and pulled the clothes over her. The first warrior was getting to his feet and Josh's branch was cooling. He knew it probably wouldn't survive another blow.

He heard more footsteps behind the others.

Then a crazy man ran into the cave shouting loudly and dropped something into the fire that flared up like a firework, and the two Neolithic thugs turned and fled.

The shaman crouched down on the other side of the fire, putting his hands out to warm them. He was dressed in a cloak of fur and feathers, his hair matted and wild like he'd slept in a bush — he looked like a feral version of Caitlin's dad.

'You took your time,' he said in English. His dark eyes shone out from a deeply lined face that was covered in runes. 'Which crisis are you from?' he asked, throwing more wood onto the fire.

The new logs hissed and popped as they caught, finally waking Caitlin.

'Dad?' she said, covering herself with a robe.

'Caitlin?' the Shaman replied, looking surprised.

'It's not your father,' Josh told her.

'No,' the stranger agreed. 'I'm Marcus, his brother — which means you must be the Paradox.'

'Josh,' insisted Josh, quickly pulling on the trousers of his union suit.

Marcus Makepiece picked up one of the short swords they'd dropped. 'They've been watching you since you arrived. Local boys, kind of proto-Vikings, probably would have killed you and taken Caitlin for breeding stock.'

Caitlin slipped on Josh's shirt. 'Breeding stock?'

'Or sacrifice. They won't be back tonight. They think I've got a direct line to their gods.' He held up the palm of his hand, which had a crude circle of rays with an eye in the centre. 'They're mostly sun-worshippers, with a few pagan fertility rites thrown in for good measure.'

He took out a flat loaf from a small animal-hide pouch and handed it to her.

She broke the crusty bread in half and gave some to Josh. 'Dad never really talked about you.'

Marcus laughed. 'I'm not surprised. We've never really got on.'

'What are you doing here?' Caitlin asked, taking a small bite of the food.

'Same as you; following the eleventh crisis.'

'No, we were on the eighth.'

Marcus thought for a moment. 'Isn't that the discovery of a terrible power?'

Caitlin nodded. 'Heisenberg used a nuclear reactor to create a time machine and start the Aryan race.'

'Ha. They're so bloody arrogant, but I guess that does explain the three blondes that turned up last month. Don't worry, the master race has already been taken care of.'

Neither Josh nor Caitlin wanted to know how.

'So we have convergence — that's not a good sign,' Marcus continued.

'Convergence?'

He threw back his feather cloak and sat down crossed-legged on the floor. They could see that his arms and legs were also covered in tattoos.

'When crises overlap or intersect. I've been studying them for a long time, but this is the first I've heard that they were converging.'

'I thought you lot were just dedicated to one crisis?' asked Josh.

'My lot?'

'Augurs.'

Marcus shook his wild hair, threw his head back and laughed. 'I'm not an Augur,' he said when he caught his breath.

'What are you then?'

'Once, a long time ago, I was a Dreadnought, but now I think of myself as an Anthropologist: I study languages and ancient cultures. I'm also the one that proposed the Eschaton Cascade — although no one took me seriously.' He sighed. 'I calculated the end of times, and they laughed at me.'

'Well, they're not laughing now. The founder created an entire guild to study your work,' said Caitlin, poking the fire with a stick.

'The Citadel. Yes, I've heard of it. Our paths cross now and then — they seem a little highly-strung.'

'It's become a religion to them. They're obsessed with understanding how to stop it.'

Marcus laughed. 'You can't stop it. It's inevitable, like night following day. All we can do is prepare for the twelfth and hope the Paradox survives.'

'Me?' Josh asked.

'Both of you, actually. Caitlin is as important to this as you. Which reminds me,' he said, looking at her, 'I must go back and tell your parents they have to leave you.'

Caitlin's cheeks flushed. 'So, it was you — that night in the kitchen?'

'It will be — now I've met you,' said Marcus, staring deep into the fire. 'There are so many variables to consider, but one thing was clear in every scenario that I ran. You would never meet the Paradox if you remained with your parents, and without you, he won't have the strength to achieve his destiny.'

Caitlin glared at him, finding no words to express the pain she was feeling.

'What exactly is my destiny?' asked Josh. 'Since you mention it.'

The shaman leaned back and spread out his arms, his eyes glazing over as he spoke. 'There are many roads to choose from, and it is your fate to find the right one.'

'So basically, you can't tell me.'

Marcus shook his head. 'All I know is that your future path is entwined with hers.'

'Maybe we should go,' Caitlin suggested, putting one hand on Josh's shoulder.

'No,' Josh replied through clenched teeth, shrugging off her hand. 'I want to know why — why me? What the hell did I do to deserve this?'

Marcus snapped out of his trance and got to his feet. He was over six feet tall, and the shadows he threw across the cave walls were full of menace.

'I cannot tell you because I don't know. I'm not a seer, just a Draconian that saw the light.' He pulled open his cloak to reveal the twelve symbols of the Eschaton tattooed across his hairless chest. 'Whatever the reason for your existence, it's nothing more than an abstract set of probabilities to me. Whatever you do will be shaped by everything that has already happened. You're the sum of your life experiences, and you should trust yourself — certainly more than anyone else, including the Order.'

Caitlin sighed. 'The Order is falling apart.'

'And especially not the founder,' Marcus added.

'What?' snapped Josh.

'There was a mission, back in the time of Solomon. I found an out-of-place artefact — the Antiquarians call them talismans — it showed me things, visions of the crises to come, and the founder was there.' Marcus pointed at the end of the map on his chest. 'I'm not entirely sure what part he plays, but he's a significant factor.'

With that, he moved his fingers across the tattoos on his arms and vanished.

Caitlin sat staring into the fire while Josh thought about what Marcus had said. Neither felt like talking, so they watched the flames, both lost in their thoughts.

'I don't trust him,' said Josh eventually.

'I don't think we have to.'

'It's not like we know him — how do we know he discovered the Eschaton?'

'He convinced my parents,' she said, pulling on her robes. 'They owe me an explanation.'

She turned towards him and held out his shirt. 'Are you coming?'

70

THE GRAND SEER

Ravana paced impatiently around her office like a caged tigress. She wasn't accustomed to waiting for anyone, let alone the ridiculous fool of a Grand Seer, and every minute that passed made her hate him even more.

Dalton had been missing for over three days now, and it was growing increasingly unlikely that she would ever see him again. Her only hope was that the crazy old buffoon had some way of reaching him.

There had been many times when she'd wished he'd never been born. The product of a loveless marriage, arranged by her parents before she was twelve, Dalton was a burden from the day he came mewling into the world.

From the very beginning, he was spoiled. At first, by his grandparents, aristocrats who refused to leave their pre-unified Prussia. Ravana was treated like nothing more than a wet nurse by her in-laws, and all their love and compassion went to their only heir — and so they created a monster.

Their son, her husband Valtin, was no better. A bully with sadomasochistic tendencies, she did her best to protect

Dalton from his explosive outbursts, but as Dalton grew older, his father's rages got worse.

She'd always known it would end badly. The day of the accident had been a long time in the making, and when Dalton had returned smothered in his father's blood, she'd wept, not for her husband, but for her son, who had done the one thing Ravana never had dared to do herself.

Without a knock, the office door opened, and Edward Kelly strolled in. He was dressed in his usual eccentric manner: a cloak of ravens' feathers fluttered from his shoulders, a jerkin of black studded leather and a pair of long black boots. She couldn't help but notice that he'd painted his nails purple.

How has it come to this? Ravana said to herself, forcing her mouth into a welcoming smile. 'Grand Seer, thank you for your time. Please, take a seat.'

'What are your thoughts on the Eschaton crisis?' she asked as Kelly made himself comfortable.

Kelly pretended to hold up a set of cards as if he were playing bridge. 'A game of three hands — you are holding the clubs, but not aces, and the jack has gone missing.'

His riddles drove Ravana to distraction, and nothing was ever simple with the Grand Seer, but she could make some sense of his words.

'Does Lord Dee have a better suit?' she asked.

Kelly's eyes widened slightly as if he hadn't expected her to play along.

'He has the King of diamonds — although still a little rough around the edges.'

'And the third hand?'

He folded the imaginary cards away and produced a real

ace from his pocket. 'Belongs to a demon. It bids for hearts, but its own is as black as spades.'

Ravana was struggling to make sense of the last part when Kelly lifted one finger.

'And don't neglect the dragons. They will be needed sooner than you think.'

'There's an attack coming?'

'Perhaps. A ruff at least, but one should never rely on a trick — play your best hand before the coup en passant.' He waved his hand, and the card disappeared.

Kelly stood up to leave, buckling his feather cloak back onto his shoulders with a golden clasp of two intertwining snakes.

'Wait. My son — the jack. Is he still alive? How can I reach him?'

The seer's eyes glazed as they rolled back into his head, the whites staring at her like a blind man. His fingers made small movements in the air as if he were playing some unseen musical instrument.

When he spoke, his voice was thin and distant. 'Your son is changing suit. What returns may not be a card you wish to play.'

'I need to know.'

His eyes returned to normal. 'Look to the past. He will be like a Phoenix, reborn in fire.'

71

DEBRIEFING

The eighth mission team were clustered around the blackboard, taking it in turns to add their own opinions to the algorithm. Josh and Caitlin watched them argue over the rights and wrongs of their plan, and like squabbling children, no one seemed to be able to agree on what happened.

'Will everybody sit down!' ordered Nostradamus as he entered the auditorium.

They dutifully took their seats, leaving the board covered in a confusing set of random notes and rubbings-out.

'Does one of you want to tell me what happened?' the old man said, staring directly at Bartholomew.

'It was my fault,' admitted Josh, standing up. 'I disobeyed orders.'

Nostradamus seemed a little disgruntled by the interruption. Josh could see he wanted to make an example of Bartholomew and hadn't expected anyone else to step in and take the blame.

'While I appreciate your honesty master Jones, I would

prefer to hear what the senior officer on the mission has to say about it.'

As Josh retook his seat, Bartholomew stood to attention and cleared his throat.

'We entered the facility at two hundred hours as planned. Team alpha swept the room for contacts and neutralised the guard by two-ten. Team Beta detected significant radiation and traced the source to a prototype nuclear reactor in the main chamber. Evidence suggested it had been recently used.'

'He's not going to mention the victims,' Caitlin whispered to Josh.

'Radiation exposure was set at a maximum of thirty minutes, and both teams proceeded to search the main chamber for material of interest. There was a considerable number of items, all were scanned and documented, and a chain of custody record and research label have been assigned to each and are currently being processed.'

Nostradamus nodded. 'All very commendable brother, but tell me, when did you realise that Schumann was not the one that had been adjusted?'

Bartholomew turned towards Josh. 'Not until after the Heisenberg journal was returned.'

'They weren't going to follow it up!' protested Caitlin, getting to her feet.

'Our guests took it upon themselves to deviate from standard procedure: Jones and Makepiece stole the journal and went off-mission to investigate Heisenberg.'

Nostradamus' face looked as if he was chewing a wasp.

'And I'm grateful that they did! I think we can all learn a lesson from their initiative — the information they have given the eleventh has significantly improved the chances of stalling the development of the time machine.'

Humiliated, Bartholomew sat back down.

'We have no idea how these crises will develop. It is imperative that we remain open to these kinds of deviations. Time does not travel in straight lines. You two, with me.' He gestured to Josh and Caitlin to follow him and left.

Without another word, Nostradamus guided them down the spiral staircase and into a sub-basement.

It appeared to be a storage facility. They walked along a gantry suspended from the ceiling high above the thousands of items of unused equipment and crates stacked up in neat rows.

'Our storehouses rival those of the Antiquarians,' noted Nostradamus. 'Although most of it has yet to be processed.'

They arrived at a vault door, with a sentry posted outside. The man had the kind of stare that could freeze your blood. Josh got the impression they would never have been allowed to get this close if it hadn't been for Nostradamus.

There were a number of clicking sounds as if the combinations of a hundred locks were all being opened at the same time, and the door slid back.

The Nautilus was suspended in dry dock when they entered the hangar. Josh and Caitlin both marvelled at the size of the ship. Having never seen it from the outside, it was hard to appreciate the beauty of the craft her parents had created.

She was long and sleek, her knife-blade hull made from copper sheets riveted together. The engines along her aft were like jet engines from a 747; their paint stripped back to reveal a shining pair of silver turbines. Along the side, her father had painted her name in large copperplate letters, below which a team of engineers were bolting on a very serious-looking set of cannons.

'Your father's idea,' said her mother, who was coming up the gangplank to meet them. 'Time cannons. He's been talking to Methuselah about some type of temporal phase induction.'

They were huge barrels, each one nearly ten metres long and almost a meter wide. Josh was about to ask what kind of bullet it would fire when Juliana beat him to it.

'Direct energy weapons are not my speciality, but at least it means we don't have to store a ton of high explosives on board.'

They met her father in the galley, where he was brewing tea and making Welsh cakes on the griddle. Caitlin hugged him tightly. It was still a novelty to have them back, and she found it hard not to burst into tears every time she saw them.

Josh was relieved to learn they'd managed to retrieve the Infinity Engine, but Caitlin was sad to hear that Chief Mackenzie had sacrificed himself.

'He was a good man,' said Juliana mournfully. 'They don't make them like him any more.'

'Broke the mould,' agreed Thomas.

'Where is the founder?' asked Caitlin.

'He's taken the Infinity Engine up to Rufius,' her father answered.

'And the others?'

'Lyra hasn't left his bedside, and Alixia has returned to Draconian HQ. Da Recco is around here somewhere.'

Caitlin closed the main door and spun the locking wheel. 'We need to talk in private.'

'You met him?' Caitlin's mother said in disbelief.

'An earlier version.' Caitlin pouted. 'Before he persuaded you to leave me.'

'Ah,' said her father. 'The Shaman.'

'That was the trouble with Marcus, always got too involved in the epoch and lost all his sense of perspective,' added her mother.

Caitlin glowered. 'He said that it would make me strong enough to survive the future.'

'Did he now?' said her father. 'What exactly —'

Juliana interrupted. 'We've talked about this, Cat. His predictions were very compelling.'

Caitlin folded her arms. 'And what exactly made him the expert?'

Her father stepped in. 'Your uncle was one of the most dedicated Dreadnoughts I've ever known. But when Marcus came back from the Solomon mission, something had changed in him. Then he just disappeared for years, and we'd pretty much given him up for dead until he showed up that night.'

'What was the Solomon mission?' asked Caitlin.

Thomas shrugged. 'No idea. Top secret. Marcus had a thing for dark operations.'

'Like the SAS?' asked Josh.

'I guess so. Whatever it was, he never spoke about where he went or what he did, but that was nothing unusual. He'd always been a bit of an odd fish.'

'Where is he now?' asked Caitlin.

Her father shrugged. 'He was there at the breach, working with Jaeger's team on a new equipment test. He got pulled into the maelstrom with the rest of us. I don't know what happened to him after that. We've never found any other survivors,' Thomas added with a sigh. 'Until, of course, you two showed up. Just as Marcus predicted in the fourth crisis.'

'We need to find out what happened on this Solomon mission,' insisted Caitlin. 'I want to know what he saw that caused all this.'

'I don't know how that will help,' her mother said, trying to reassure her. 'The path we're on seems to be following the course he predicted.'

Caitlin stood up, her face flushed with anger. 'But don't you want to know why mother? Do we have to follow it blindly? Shouldn't we be doing everything in our power to change it?'

'Don't you think we've thought about that?' her mother snapped. 'Every single day since we left you. There's no way to know whether we'll make it worse.'

'I don't think it could be much worse, do you?' Caitlin shouted, her eyes glowering. 'You're all so scared of screwing up that you can't see that could be the exact reason it's going to happen.'

She stormed out before she said something worse.

'Wait for me!' said Josh, going after her.

Thomas caught up with Josh and stopped him. 'Best to let her go,' he whispered. 'Makepiece women tend to need to break things when they get like this.'

'I heard that,' said Juliana.

72

CURING THE COLONEL

Lyra looked exhausted when Josh walked through the door, as she hadn't left the colonel's side since they'd arrived at the Citadel.

'Good luck,' she said, hugging him as she left.

The founder was sitting on the other side of the bed, the casket of the Infinity Engine lying in his lap.

'This will require all of your focus,' he said, standing up and putting the box on the old man's chest.

'Before we begin, I need to teach you how to protect yourself from the time dilation effects of the engine. It's a complex meme that's easier if I intuit.'

'What do you want me to do?' asked Josh nervously, standing at the end of the bed.

The founder put his thumbs on Josh's temples and opened his mind. He felt the intuit establish between them and the memories of how to manipulate the engine flooded in.

Once it was complete, he motioned to Josh to sit on the opposite side of the bed and placed the colonel's hand inside the box.

'The aetherium has corrupted his timeline, and we need to reassemble it; a billion fragmented moments scattered across the continuum. For that, I will need to channel the power of the engine, and you will act as its lodestone, attracting the relevant threads and weaving them back into a cohesive pattern.'

'But I don't know everything about his life.'

'You're the Paradox. It means you have an inherent ability to know the right path to take. Trust your instincts, Josh, and let them guide you.'

Josh felt like a ten-year-old again, feeling the adrenaline rush as he got into the driver's seat of his first car. The founder motioned for him to sit on the opposite side of the bed, then took his left hand.

'Lyra tells me that he's holding on to the time he found out his wife was pregnant. I suggest you begin there. Use it as a springboard into his past.'

Josh placed his right hand on the colonel's forehead. His skin was so deathly cold and clammy it felt more like wax. Closing his eyes, he let his mind drift into the old man's timeline, or what was left of it.

He found himself in a storm of ash, tiny fragments of moments whirling around him in a chaotic cloud of disconnected events, shifting like black sand through his mind as he searched for some sign of the colonel's old life.

Then, just as Lyra had described, Josh glimpsed the faint glow of a distant sun. He felt the founder squeeze his hand tighter as he tried to move his mind towards it, but some invisible force was resisting him, trying to hold him back.

'Let the engine do the work,' the founder whispered. 'Feel its energy flow through you.'

As he spoke, a prickling sensation wound its way up Josh's arm, as if someone had injected ice into his veins. Josh felt the rush he used to get from driving at a hundred miles an hour in the middle of the night — like he was unstoppable.

He swept the chaos aside and the moment glowed brightly before him, and nothing had the power to stop him from entering it.

'I've found him,' he said through clenched teeth.

The colonel was sitting in the waiting room of a Victorian hospital reading The Times newspaper. Lyra had told Josh that this event was like a panic room, or a bomb shelter, somewhere that you would instinctively go to when your life was in danger, a place of safety to wait until the threat had passed. In the case of time travellers, it usually meant jumping back into your most treasured moment.

Josh could hear the muffled voice of Doctor Crooke in the consulting room.

'It's our first,' the colonel said proudly, looking up from the paper.

Josh forced himself to smile. There were so many things that went wrong in his friend's life after this point it was no surprise that the colonel retreated to this moment.

'Is your wife joining you?' the colonel asked politely, putting down the paper.

'Soon,' Josh lied, buying himself some time while he tried to think of the best way to break the news.

'Good. Well, sit yourself down, before you fall down. You look half asleep boy! They say you should make the most of it while you can; not much rest when the little 'un comes!'

Although they were safe within this interval, Josh could

already sense paths that would ultimately lead to her death, strands of time rebuilding from this moment as the organising influence of the Infinity Engine began to take effect.

'When did you first meet?' Josh asked, trying to ignore the lines of inevitability.

'Now let me think,' the colonel mused.

Josh saw new lines spiralling out towards the past. He watched the events connecting, mapping a path to their beginning, like pieces of a four-dimensional puzzle snapping back together.

'It was at the end of the first English Civil War. I was on a mission, serving under Sir Thomas Fairfax for the Parliamentarians. She was a Royalist, daughter of Sir Francis Throckmorton, and a Catholic to boot.'

As the past was reconstructed, Josh could see other minor moments being restored, like the roots of a tree, branching off in all directions.

He drew on the power the founder was channelling into him and pushed himself down the timeline, strengthening and accelerating the healing as he followed it back.

73

LADY ANNE

[Warwick, England. Date: 11.646]

The colonel was dressed in the red coat of a musketeer with a bandolier of twelve cartridges slung over one shoulder and a sword belt over the other. He carried a heavy-looking matchlock musket and looked rather young with his short hair and lack of beard.

She was a lady, or at least the daughter of one. Fairfax's detachment had surrounded their estate, Coughton Court, a grand Tudor house set in the Warwickshire countryside.

Once they had overcome the local militia, the company commander lost control of his men, who began to ransack the mansion: plundering the house of all its silver and plate, as well as harassing the women and killing any man that got in their way.

The colonel left the musket at the door and moved swiftly through the house, avoiding the pillaging, until he reached the upper floor and opened a secret panel that led up into the tower.

Because of his connection with the engine, Josh intuitively knew it was an old priest hole from the days of the Catholic purges of James I, when his Secretary of State, the infamous Robert Cecil, hunted down any practising Catholic priest.

'Come no further,' said a woman's voice from the shadows.

'I mean you no harm my lady,' replied the colonel calmly.

'I beg to differ,' she said, coming forward and holding a rapier out before her. A tremor ran down the blade as it glinted in the candlelight. She was stunning, even with the cobwebs caught in her hair — Josh could see that the colonel was batting well out of his league.

The colonel held up his hands in surrender.

'I have orders to remove you from this place.'

'To the tower no doubt?' she said mournfully. 'I know what is to come.'

The colonel smiled, taking off his bandolier and his sword belt. 'I don't think you would believe me if I told you.'

He stepped forward, letting the tip of her blade press into his chest. 'You are Anne, the granddaughter of John Throckmorton, cousin of Sir Frances, the conspirator?'

Her jaw lifted defiantly, and her eyes narrowed. 'I am.'

The colonel pointed to her necklace. 'And that, I believe, is a family heirloom?'

Her fingers went instinctively to the silver chain around her beautiful pale neck.

'As is this sword,' she said, pushing the blade into his coat. 'They are all we have left.'

The colonel took off one of his gauntlets and touched the blade. 'A fine weapon, one I have no intention of taking from you, but I do need you to take me to him.'

'Sir Frances? His body is in the family vault. Which I'm quite sure is being desecrated as we speak.'

'You misunderstand.' He grasped the blade tightly, blood seeping through his fingers as he opened its chronology.

Josh watched as more paths coalesced around the colonel's timeline, connections coming together into a series of incidents until the route that he took Lady Anne shone out like a lit fuse amongst the dark mass of lost moments.

74

CHOICES

[Warwick, England. Date: 11.583]

The priest was on his knees in the cramped room when the colonel and Anne appeared. If he had any doubt about his faith, it was doubled by their sudden arrival.

While the cleric cowered on his knees, the colonel took the sword out of her shaking hand. She was still getting over the shock of travelling back sixty-five years.

Josh looked back at the trail they'd created. There was a structure now, a rudimentary spine running through the colonel's timeline with smaller, subsidiary events collecting around it as his history fell back into place.

'How?' asked Anne.

'There's no time for that now,' said the colonel calmly, taking out his almanac and checking his tachyon.

'What year is this?' he growled at the priest.

'Year of our Lord, fifteen eighty-three.'

'Where is Sir Francis?' he barked.

'In the library,' stuttered the priest, 'with his brother.'

Josh realised that the colonel's uniform was gone, leaving him in the travel robes he wore beneath. His wife-to-be, on the other hand, was wearing nothing but her necklace.

The colonel turned the sword on the quivering cleric. 'Padre, I'm afraid we need to borrow your cassock.'

The library room came together like pieces from a jigsaw, the books, the furniture and wall hangings snapping into place. Two men were sipping wine when the colonel burst in.

Thomas rose, his sword drawn, ready to strike. Sir Francis remained seated, a large pile of letters on the desk before him.

'Gentlemen,' the colonel said calmly, 'stay your swords. I am not here for you.'

'Who are you?' demanded the younger man.

The colonel turned to Anne. 'My lady, may I introduce your grandfather's cousins, Sir Francis and Thomas, both of whom are plotting to assassinate her majesty Queen Elizabeth and replace her with Mary.'

Anne's eyes were wide, her hand gripping the necklace.

'What kind of devilry is this?' bellowed Thomas, raising his sword once more. 'You're working for Walsingham!'

'She wears the pendant,' interrupted his brother Francis. 'Calm yourself, Thomas, let the man speak.'

The colonel paused for a moment as if not sure what to do next.

Josh realised that time had stopped; something was wrong with the stream of energy from the founder.

He broke his connection with the colonel and looked up at Lord Dee, who looked worried.

'Something wrong?'

'The men in that room were plotting to assassinate Elizabeth I. The documents on the desk incriminate half the English nobility, those with Catholic sympathies. They're linked to a spy, Bernardino de Mendoza, the Spanish Ambassador and Mary Queen of Scots.'

'Yeah,' Josh said and looked at the colonel. 'So, I'm guessing he's there to stop them?'

The founder nodded. 'He was, and in doing so condemned Francis to death.'

'And?'

'The ambassador was thrown out of the country, and the Spanish were not welcomed back into Court until after Elizabeth's death.'

'Doesn't sound like a big problem.'

'The lack of diplomatic parlay was a precursor to the Gunpowder plot.'

'Which was stopped.'

'Perhaps it shouldn't be.'

'You want to change history?'

'Many think that it may have led to a very different England, one who's conquests and empire building would have been subject to the Catholic Church and unified under Rome. It would effectively have reduced the tension in medieval Europe — and stalled the sixth crisis.'

'Which was?'

'The escalation of conflicts.'

'I don't see how that will change anything.'

'Let us see,' he said, placing his hand back on the Infinity Engine.

. . .

'Why shouldn't I tell them that it failed?' whispered Anne, while the two brothers hastily packed away their documents.

'Because there are rules,' the colonel explained. 'Ones that cannot be broken without dire consequences.'

'But they're my kin.'

'Who are plotting to bring down the Queen of England.'

She crossed her arms. 'And would have done so if not for some informant.'

'It had to be done,' the colonel said quietly. 'The consequences of a Catholic revolution would have led to the most terrible civil war. Much worse than the one we have just left.'

Her eyes narrowed. 'It was you, wasn't it? Who are you?'

'My name is Rufius Westinghouse, and I am a Watchman.'

'And what exactly do you watch?' she asked sarcastically.

'Time, my Lady. I guard the future.'

In any other circumstance, Josh thought, she would probably have called him insane or had him burned at the stake — but he could see that she wasn't afraid of Rufius, more intrigued.

She nodded towards the men. 'So they are to die then?'

'Walsingham already has them under surveillance, so the best I can do is save some of their accomplices. My mission was to collect the documents and report on the movements of the Jacobite rebels.'

'Then why bring me here?'

'I couldn't leave you to those animals — it was the only honourable thing to do.'

Her expression softened. 'Then may I ask what you intend to do with me?'

As the colonel considered his answer, Josh felt the timeline splitting. They had reached a nexus point, and whatever decision the old man was about to make was a critical one.

Two paths stretched out before him, one that led to marriage, the other to an altogether different future. This was an alternate in which his friend would never suffer the heartache and loss that Josh had witnessed, but where he would never meet another like Anne and spend the rest of his days as a confirmed bachelor.

Josh hesitated, waiting for the colonel to decide — as did Anne. The connections to their life together were beginning to fade as he contemplated the options.

'The documents,' said Sir Francis, handing over the leather satchel to Rufius.

The branches of time multiplied around him as the colonel held the heavy package in his hands, weighing the consequences of his next decision. Finally, he threw the bag to Francis' brother. 'Thomas, I think you should courier them to Philip directly.'

'But what about Mendoza?' protested Thomas.

'He will be sent home shortly. It would be best if you were out of the country when that happens.'

Anne nodded her thanks.

The other paths disappeared, and their life together solidified. Josh could see all of the next ten years fall into place, leading up to the painful events that would end it.

'Is there no hope?' Sir Francis asked after Thomas had left.

'None,' the colonel said sternly. 'Prepare yourself, and may God be with you.'

[London, England. Date: 11.605]

The undercroft beneath the House of Lords was dark and damp. Josh watched the colonel and Anne, now dressed in the travelling robes of the Order, as they moved through the basement tunnels towards the cache of gunpowder.

'He's taken her with him!' Josh whispered to the founder.

'His judgement is impaired, and his emotions are getting the better of him. Can you see how the lines bifurcate in the next few hours? This is the point where the plot is either foiled or succeeds.'

Josh scanned the lattice of lines that were forming out of the black miasma. 'Not very well. There's too much interference.'

'Move further back, see if you can find the source of the virus, and then we should be able to get a clearer picture.'

Reluctantly, Josh left the gunpowder plot weaving back down through the years until he came to a massive dark cluster. It was a hard, crystallised structure that encased a weak glow of some critical event.

'What is that?' he asked, sharing the vision with the founder.

'Apparently, it's the day I discovered him.'

When Josh drew closer to the dark structure, he was overwhelmed by the despair emanating from it. The feeling of dread reminded him of the Djinn he'd destroyed in the maelstrom.

The cluster bristled with malice, as though it was carved from pure evil, filled with the terror and doubt that crept into his thoughts on the long, sleepless nights of his childhood.

'It thrives on fear,' the founder whispered. 'You must overcome your self-doubt.'

Easier said than done, thought Josh.

He'd spent most of the last five years struggling to survive in a world that wanted to break him. Whether it was the daily challenge of caring for his sick mother, getting through school, or staying out of prison, he never knew if he was doing the right thing — and the truth was Josh didn't think he had.

Lenin had always preyed on this weakness, using it to make Josh question himself — keeping him down. He could feel the years of pent-up frustration turning into rage as he blamed himself for letting it happen. Everything from Lenin, his mother's MS, the kids that teased him about his dyslexia — all the crap that he'd put up with ignited a fire within him and the power of the Infinity Engine enhanced it.

He embraced the temporal energy, letting the countless possibilities flow through him, forging a connection between him and the continuum that made him feel invincible. Suddenly, his mind was no longer restrained by the laws of time, and the physical reality around him fell away as the infinite stretched out before him.

The river of time wound away into the past, just like he'd seen in the colonel's observatory, except now Josh could see how far back it went, the engine increasing his range, allowing him to look back millions of years.

He left the flow, drifting out into the maelstrom, and realised that it was not the only timeline. Far off in the distance, he saw that there were others, like a forest of thin twisting trees. Glowing against the dark background of the maelstrom were hundreds of other continuums, some much smaller, others old and wiry or blackened and dying.

And there, stretching out from one distant dead chronology, was the founder's timeline.

Confused, Josh returned to the colonel's life and focused his energy on the darkness that encased it.

When his mind touched the outer shell, he felt the effect of the dark energy, and it was so negative and empty, and filled with desolation.

Josh attacked the emptiness with light, burning out the darkness with his anger, and as he did he realised it wasn't rage at all, but a love of life — everything he'd worked for, everything he fought to protect was because he wanted to make a better life — for him, for his mother, and most of all, for Caitlin.

As Josh took his hand away from the colonel, he could see the colour already returning to his cheeks.

He turned to the founder. 'Who are you?'

Lord Dee looked exhausted. He placed the case on the side table and rubbed his neck. 'Do you know why I founded the Order?'

'To protect the future?'

The founder stood up and walked over to one of the windows. 'But from what exactly?'

Josh thought about what he'd seen in Fermi's facility and the devastating effect his obsession with technology had on the planet. 'I guess from ourselves. We seem to be pretty good at messing things up.'

'True. You're a particularly self-destructive species, but that isn't the reason. The future is like a delicate flower, an orchid, that must be nurtured and attended constantly, to ensure that we don't repeat the mistakes of the past.'

'Like wars?'

He shook his head. 'I speak of another past, from another continuum.'

'How many are there?'

The founder held up his hands. 'The Egyptians have a phrase for large numbers; they say it's "too many to count".'

'So, why did you leave?'

'I had no choice. I am the last survivor of my time. We were once very similar to yours, a thriving civilisation with highly advanced culture and technologies. Our scientists were some of the finest minds I have ever encountered, comparable to those of Einstein and Hawking. We'd developed to a point that some in this timeline would call a 'Singularity', placing us a few hundred years ahead of where you are now.'

The founder's eyes grew sad and his voice sombre.

'My quantum division had discovered new forms of energy in the universe, and we were on the verge of limitless power, releasing us from the reliance on dwindling supply of fossil fuels. And then the Nihil came.'

'Nihil?'

'They have many names, and we came to learn them all. They were from the maelstrom, a race of beings that fed on aetherium, dark energy, and my experiments attracted them — they decimated our world, collapsed the entire timeline — our entire history, as well as billions of lives, were lost.'

'But you escaped?'

'I did,' he said sadly, 'though it cost me dearly. I was working on a prototype of the Infinity Engine before they arrived, and I used it to create an escape route — into this universe. I've been trapped here ever since.'

'And you think they're coming for us? Is that what the Eschaton is?'

The founder stared directly into Josh's eyes.

'They're drawn to aetherium, something I have been trying to ensure was never discovered in the future of this timeline, but one that I believe you've already seen.'

'Why are you telling me?'

'Because if you are the Nemesis, then someone created you to help us defeat the Nihil. You may be the only hope this timeline has of survival.'

75

COPPER SCROLL

Since each level of the Citadel was sealed off, every floor had its own refectory, and the third's looked like it had been borrowed from one of the colleges at Oxford. He hadn't seen Lord Dee since they'd cured the colonel and Josh had spent most of the last few days with Lyra, helping her to care for the old man. Caitlin appeared at meal times but was so obsessed with finding out more about the Solomon mission that they had hardly seen each other, and when they did, he never seemed to be able to get a word in edgeways.

'How's the colonel?' asked Caitlin, sitting down opposite him with a tray of food.

'He's on the mend. Where have you been all day?'

She grinned like a Cheshire cat. 'Guess what I found on the fifth floor.'

'A swimming pool?'

'They have a library completely dedicated to the Templars.'

'How are they involved in the fifth crisis?'

There was a fire in her eyes, and she looked at him with

the kind of intensity she always got when she was trying to solve a problem. 'It's to do with awakening the elder gods — the fifths believe that the Templars discovered a treasure. They've infiltrated the brotherhood, but haven't found anything significant. I think it's got to be linked to what Marcus found.'

'Because the first Templars were stationed in the ruins of Solomon's Temple?'

Caitlin looked impressed. 'You've studied them too?'

He nodded. The stories of the crusader knights had helped him through some of the worst nights of his mother's illness. 'Jacques de Molay, the Holy Grail, Saladin.'

She laughed. 'But you know it wasn't about the cup of Christ, right?'

'Yeah. I'm not a complete idiot. They were protecting a bloodline.'

Again she laughed. 'Not the Da Vinci Code, please tell me you don't believe that?'

Josh shrugged. 'So, what do you think it was then?'

'Gold. Or treasure maps, at least.'

'Maps?'

'Copper scrolls. You know they found all those jars full of scrolls in a cave?'

Josh nodded, it was a bonus question once on University Challenge. 'Dead Sea Scrolls.'

'One of them was a list, locations of caches of treasure. When the temple was being ransacked by Nebuchadnezzar, Solomon's treasure was broken up and hidden. The Augurs on the fifth are doing some kind of audit, trying to trace all of the artefacts.'

'And you think they're looking for something in particular?' asked Josh, pushing his plate to one side.

She smiled. 'Remember Marcus said he found an out-of-place object?'

'Like the computer thing in Greece?'

She looked at him with a puzzled expression, and Josh realised she was never there. 'Never mind. Wrong timeline. Carry on.'

She leaned in closer as if sharing a secret. 'Do you know what Solomon's mines were?'

He leaned in and stared into her beautiful green eyes. 'Big holes in the ground?'

She shook her head and sat back. 'The Antiquarians believe that Solomon's treasure wasn't mined at all, but came from the tombs of dead Pharaohs. There's a theory that Solomon and his father were actually the last of the Egyptian Kings who occupied one half of Egypt and held the other half to ransom. It would explain where his fabled fortune came from.'

'And what did they find in the tombs?'

'No one knows. The treasure has been lost, and after the Great Breach, the whole period was quarantined. The Antiquarians haven't been allowed in to catalogue any of it.'

Josh crossed his arms. He knew where this was leading. 'And when exactly was this?'

'Twenty-second dynasty — around 9.100.'

'Nine hundred BC?'

She nodded. 'I think we have to go back there.'

'Via the Templars?'

'The Augurs have already infiltrated their order during the second crusade, so we can see if they've discovered the scroll and use it to get back to Solomon.'

Josh grinned. 'I should have known you'd already have a plan.'

76

DALTON-JINN

D alton couldn't feel his body. The Nihil had immersed him in a tank filled with black oil. It dissolved his robes and clung to his skin, pouring into every orifice and making him fight for breath. The liquid wasn't inert but alive, and he felt it move through his body like a thousand bees racing through his veins.

I can survive this, he told himself. *I just need to control the fear.*

As he focussed on the liquid, he felt the trace of a time-line that had once been a sentient being. Whatever primor-dial state it had been reduced to, there were still remnants of a past, and he clung to that and let himself fall under the surface.

Holding his breath, he opened his eyes, feeling the sting of the vitriol against his corneas. Somewhere within the distorted abstract of a chronology was its beginning. His mind searched desperately for a sign of an origin, and as his lungs began to ache, he found it.

· · ·

The Nihil was once a noble race. Hundreds of millions of years ago they had lived like other beings, sharing a planet with another sentient life form known simply as the 'Omni' — it was a symbiotic relationship, one unable to survive without the other. The Nihil were the warriors and the builders, while the Omni were more cerebral. Their scientists were the first to learn how to discover and harness the power of aetherium, and everyone was ecstatic at its potential.

But there were factions within the Nihil that saw a greater use for the dark energy: there were constant threats to their world, and the army demanded better weapons and stronger soldiers, all of which aetherium could easily deliver.

The wise Omni knew the dangers of misusing the power and refused to allow the Nihil unfettered access to their resources.

So the Nihil took it by force, and in the process destroyed the delicate balance between the two races, ending their civilisation.

What remained of the Nihil had roamed the timelines ever since, like a nomadic race of hunters, searching for refined aetherium. They were wraiths, the dark energy transforming their physical bodies into non-linear, multi-dimensional entities — they were virtually immortal.

And Dalton saw how he could become one.

He rose from the dark liquid, the talisman still glowing on his hand, his body covered in dark, slick oil.

The Nihil stood around his tank, their bodies freed of the mortal shells reverting into strange and hideous forms that were the stuff of nightmares.

'I am Nihil,' Dalton declared, his body beginning to undergo the transformation.

77

FIFTH DOOR

Josh hefted the crusader sword from one hand to the other, feeling the weight of it pull on the muscles of his forearms. It was a finely-balanced weapon, one that could break a bone or pierce armour plate. He could feel the history of it; this was a Knight's blade, one that had drawn blood at the capture of Edessa and the Siege of Damascus.

'Do you actually know how to use it?' Caitlin asked, strapping a dagger onto the inside of her thigh.

'Aye M'Lady,' he said, swinging the blade through an impressive series of arcs. 'Nostradamus insisted I went through the intuit training for the fifth.'

'Me too,' she said. 'Except women don't get to fight,' she added grumpily, smoothing down the long grey habit. 'Don't see how being a nun is going to help.'

Josh smiled at her. 'I don't know, looks kind of sexy.'

She pouted. 'Really, we're about to go back into the crusades, one of the most brutal periods in recent history, and that's all you can think about?'

He sheathed the sword in its scabbard and pulled her close.

'So, what were the other options?'

'You know full well. Whore or serving wench, which were virtually the same thing.'

Josh put his hand behind her neck and kissed her gently on the mouth.

'I've missed you,' he whispered as his lips moved to her ear, making her shudder.

'I've been right here,' she purred.

'You've had your nose stuck in a book.'

She pushed him away. 'I need to understand what's going on. Don't you see how important this is?'

Josh was going to tell her about what he'd learned from the founder, but something stopped him. 'Totally, but it's like you shut yourself away when you do this. I feel like a spare wheel.'

Caitlin bit her bottom lip and played with her necklace. 'You hate books. I just assumed you wouldn't want to spend all your time in the library.'

Josh pulled her close once more. 'I don't, but you're not the only one with ideas about how this is going to play out. I learned something about the founder too.'

'What?'

'Marcus might be right about him. He's not what he seems.'

Nostradamus knocked at the door. 'When you two are quite finished.'

The fifth level of the Citadel was modelled in the style of a Norman castle. Men and women in medieval robes strode along the stone-carved cloisters like servants on urgent errands.

'I have to say I was quite surprised by your request,' said

Nostradamus, leading Josh, Caitlin and Lyra through the flag-stoned corridors. 'One of our reconnaissance teams had reported increased activity around the Templar base, but nothing that would warrant an intervention.'

Caitlin glanced guiltily at Josh. 'Let's just call it a hunch.'

Nostradamus looked puzzled. 'A hunch? I would never have believed a Scriptorian would ever use such a word.'

'Probably spent too much time around me,' joked Josh.

'Hmm, well I know better than to doubt the intuition of the Paradox.' Nostradamus stopped at a door marked '11.120'. Josh counted at least five other similar portals, all marked with the Templar cross.

'Just before the second crusade,' noted Lyra, who'd chosen to dress like a serving girl.

They were joined by three heavily armed 'protectors', all of whom looked very capable of defending themselves. Nostradamus had insisted they take bodyguards, reminding them that they'd lost four teams in this period and he wouldn't be responsible for losing another.

The men had hard, scarred faces and massively muscled arms under their chain mail, like steroid-enhanced gym bunnies, and they made Josh feel slightly inadequate standing next to them. He was nearly six-feet tall, and they all looked down on him.

'Remember you're going into a war zone,' warned the curator, like an over-protective parent. 'The city of Jerusalem may be under Christian control, but the surrounding area — "Outremer" as they call it — is a lawless place where many pilgrims have been slaughtered on their way to the holy city.'

'What scenario is the local team currently working on?'

Nostradamus took out his almanac, which was very different from the standard issue they were used to. The book had a dial with twelve symbols on the cover, and he turned to the fifth before he opened it.

'Their last report was filed two days ago. Apparently, the Templars have discovered a tomb in the ruins of Solomon's temple — there's a seventy-four percent probability that it contains treasure and the team were going to investigate.'

'Sure it's not the Grail?' whispered Josh to Caitlin.

Caitlin stuck out her tongue.

'Wait!' called a voice from down the corridor.

Nostradamus rolled his eyes. 'Brother Geoffroy, where the devil have you been?'

Geoffroy was a short, round man with a broad face and rosy cheeks. He was dressed like a Cistercian monk, his hair cut in a tonsure, and he was carrying a large pack on his back that refused to stay in one place as he ran.

'I had to collect a few herbs,' he said, bending over double and panting.

'May I introduce your medic, Geoffroy Fitzstephen. He has many fine qualities, timekeeping unfortunately is not one of them.'

'Ironic, really, considering,' the monk wheezed, waving his hand. 'Please don't let me delay you any further.'

Nostradamus nodded, and one of the bodyguards opened the door.

The view of the desert city beyond took their breath away, as did the wave of heat that washed over their faces.

Their guards were through the door without another word.

'Quickly!' urged Nostradamus, 'before the portal is detected.'

[Jerusalem. Date: 11.120]

The narrow streets of the old city smelled of intoxicating spices, herbs and sun-baked ground all underlined with a faint odour of shit and body odour. The proximity of so many unwashed people assaulted every one of Josh's senses as he marched through them, reminding him of the harsh reality of a past with no real sanitation or personal hygiene. The roads were full of pilgrims, wealthy merchants and their entourages of mercenaries and servants, all clothed in luxurious silks, parading past the few remaining stalls of the market traders who'd chosen to remain.

Massive walls towered over them, built to protect the holiest of cities, its watchtowers draped with the flags of the current occupying forces of Baldwin II, King of Jerusalem.

They followed the general flow of traffic as it wove through the streets towards the centre of the city and Temple Mount. Even in the shadow of the wall, the heat of the midday sun was intense. Josh was wearing three layers of armour: padded chausses, a long mail shirt and a surcoat, all of which made him appreciate how strong the knights would have to be to fight in these conditions. His throat was parched after ten minutes of walking, and the waterskin he carried was half empty by the time they reached the entrance to the Temple.

There was a steady stream of visitors flowing through the open gates. The Templar guards were vigilant, but stood back and let the westerners enter without question. They were fierce-looking men, each holding a spear and a shield with the red cross emblazoned on it. They saluted Josh as he passed as if he were a brother knight.

'Where are the rest of the Templars?' Caitlin asked Geoffroy in Latin as they walked into the inner courtyard.

'In a wing of the Royal Palace,' he said, nodding towards the mosque-like building that stood across the square from them. Caitlin could see it was well guarded. 'Hugues de Payens is their commanding officer. He persuaded the Patriarch and King Baldwin to let them use the temple ruins.'

The three bodyguards spread out around them as they walked across the square, their hands never leaving the pommels of their swords as if they expected trouble even within the safety of the compound. Josh, Caitlin and Lyra followed Geoffroy across to the temple entrance where the medic produced a scroll with a wax seal of two knights riding on one horse — the symbol of the Templar order.

While the guards opened and read the scroll, Lyra turned to Caitlin and whispered something in her ear. Caitlin looked concerned and whispered something back.

'What's the matter?' asked Josh.

'Something's not right,' whispered Caitlin. 'She says this place is filled with evil spirits.'

The guards didn't seem convinced by the document and were asking Geoffroy questions in French. They kept looking over at him and their protection team as if not convinced that they were other members of their order. Geoffroy stood his ground and mentioned something about being sent by Bernard of Clairvaux, then took out a hefty purse of coins, which seemed to have the desired effect on their suspicions.

Jacques De Molay, grandmaster of the Templar order, sat opposite them on an ornate chair that looked more like a throne. Geoffroy had explained that he was the Senior Augur coordinating the joint operation between the fifth and sixth, and he seemed very annoyed at being pulled out of his own mission two hundred years ahead of their current location. Sitting on either side of him like chastised schoolboys were André de Montbard and Godfrey de Saint-Omer, two Augurs of the fifth.

'Nostradamus knows better than to interfere in an active mission,' he said gruffly. 'Especially one as complicated as this.'

'The fifth has discovered something unusual,' said Geoffroy. 'We've been sent to investigate.'

'Solomon's treasure?' De Molay sneered, looking suspiciously at Josh and Caitlin. 'I wondered how long it would take the Antiquarians to start sniffing around.'

'We're not Antiquarians,' snapped Caitlin.

De Molay raised an eyebrow. 'You're not Augurs either.'

'No,' interrupted Geoffroy, 'but I am, and I have the authority of the curator himself. You're to show them every courtesy.'

'And what exactly do you require?'

'Access to the site,' replied Caitlin.

'To what end?'

'To assess the impact on the fifth Eschaton crisis — why else?' said Geoffroy.

'My men tell me that they're nothing but old stone jars. I fail to see how that constitutes an intervention?'

'Did you find any treasure?' asked Josh.

De Molay looked at Montbard. 'The fifth's current mission objective is to trace long-lost artefacts. The Templar's excavation of the tomb is purely for archaeological research.'

'Not just an army of warrior monks bent on slaughtering Muslims then?' scoffed Lyra.

'That is why the sixth are here, to study the roots of conflict in this area, but before you start judging us, you should know that Saladin is also a member of the sixth too.'

Lyra looked abashed.

'There is no easy way to manipulate the violence of this era. Men died in great numbers and calculating a peaceful outcome would require a legion of Copernicans. Our primary objective is to study the impact on the future.'

Josh thought of all the news stories about the troubles in the Middle East and wondered how much worse it could possibly get.

'In the short term, Guy of Lusignan will lose Jerusalem by 11.187, assuming they're still defeated at Hattin. Then Saladin can focus on stabilising the region,' he explained.

'Good luck with that,' scoffed Josh.

'When are you from?' asked De Molay.

'The present.'

'Then you know exactly the crisis we're trying to reduce.'

'Are you not bothered about the treasure?' Caitlin asked in disbelief.

De Molay laughed. 'I have three hundred years of political turmoil to manage. Do you really think I care whether there's some magical artefact in the tomb?'

'Not magic, but potentially evidence of an out-of-place object — the fifth may have stumbled upon something very rare. While looking for gold, no doubt.'

Montbard and Saint-Omer avoided her gaze, confirming what she already suspected.

'Gold has its uses here,' De Molay replied. 'As for your investigation — you have my consent. Although I will be logging an official complaint with Nostradamus.' He turned to Geoffroy. 'You can tell him that we will hold the city for as long as it takes to clear the area. In the meantime,' he said, standing up, 'I have to get back to my own era — Philip is about to accuse the Templars of heresy, and we all know how that ends.'

As they entered the cool shade of the temple, the guards closed the doors behind them with a resounding boom.

The air was still, and the only sound was the clatter of swords against chain mail as they walked down the dark, sandstone passage. Lyra looked around nervously as they went, staring into the shadows and flinching at the slightest sound.

'Lyra! Pack it in. You're freaking me out!' hissed Caitlin.

Geoffroy overheard her. 'What's the problem?'

'Lyra's seeing ghosts,' joked Josh.

The monk chuckled. 'I'm not surprised, this temple has seen more than its fair share of conflict in the last thousand years. Some parts of it go back to the time of Solomon and King David.'

'Not that,' said Lyra, shaking her head. 'Something else.'

Geoffroy's eyes narrowed. 'What kind of something?'

She waved her hands around in the air. 'Bad vibrations, like a fly trapped in a spider's web.'

Geoffroy took off his crucifix and pulled out a small metal rod from inside it.

'What's that?' asked Josh as the monk held it out in front of him.

'Divination rod.'

'Are you trying to find water?' mocked Caitlin.

'No, time eddies. If there's a temporal fluctuation in here, this will pick it up.'

. . .

They reached the excavation site. Wooden gibbets had been used to lift the stone slabs away with block and tackle, and the underlying rock had been cut away. The edges showed the crude marks of pick axes where the men had hacked their way through to the chamber below.

Geoffroy crouched over the hole, his divination rod vibrating in his hand.

'I can't see anything,' he said, staring down into the crypt.

One of the bodyguards drew his sword and stepped onto the makeshift wooden ladder, while another lit an oil lamp on one of the torches and threw it down into the darkness.

They watched as the small clay pot smashed on the floor below, igniting the oil as it spread out in a flaming pool across the stone floor.

Lyra was muttering to herself and wringing her hands.

'What is it?' Caitlin asked her.

'Something bad,' was all she would say.

Josh saw the bodies in the flickering light of the fire, like broken dolls, the Templars lay scattered across the floor of the crypt, still holding their swords. But there was no sign of what killed them.

The guard descended cautiously and worked his way around the edge of the fire, stopping to examine each of the bodies in turn.

'They're Augurs,' he said, 'and they're not dead — just concussed.'

The other two guards went next and confirmed that it was safe before allowing the rest of them down, all except Lyra who refused to go anywhere near the hole.

Geoffroy took out an assortment of medieval medical

supplies from his pack: salves and potion bottles were uncorked and applied to deep wounds and purple bruises.

'Where is your commanding officer?' Josh heard one of the guards ask a recovering soldier.

His reply was weak, but they all heard it.

'Taken.'

Caitlin was helping Geoffroy, so Josh took one of the unbroken oil lamps and went off to survey the rest of the tomb.

There was a small collection of clay jars stacked at one end of the room. Each bore the runes of an ancient language written around a sealed lid. It reminded Josh of the jar that the colonel had used on the Strzyga — the one that had contained a Monad.

'What are they?' asked Josh as Caitlin came over to join him.

'Canopic jars. Egyptian funeral goods, for storing the internal organs, but they should have heads on them: a falcon for the intestines, baboon for the lungs, a jackal for the stomach — these are weird — I don't recognise the glyphs either.'

Josh looked around the chamber. 'And there's no mummy.'

'This wasn't a tomb. I think it was something else.' She pointed to the walls, which were covered with hieroglyphic inscriptions carved into the sandstone.

The symbols meant nothing to Josh, although he thought they looked a lot like the ones in the temple Dalton had tried to sacrifice them in.

Caitlin stood back and ran her fingers through her hair.

'These are more like containment jars, like the ones the Xenos use for trapping monads, but the symbols could be Akkadian or Babylonian.'

She went over to one of the jars that was laying on its side in the middle of the floor.

'I think they opened it and let something out,' she said, reaching inside the jar and carefully pulling out a copper tube.

'Copper scroll?' asked Josh.

Caitlin carefully unrolled the thin foil. It was a delicate leaf of beaten copper on which someone had inscribed rows of symbols.

'This is more like Mishnaic Hebrew,' said Caitlin, a little puzzled. 'They're locations.'

'Don't!' warned one of the injured men. 'It's cursed!'

Caitlin ignored him. As she read the text, Josh felt the hairs on the back of his neck stand on end as the temperature in the chamber dropped dramatically.

Caitlin was oblivious, her lips forming silent words as she concentrated on the translation.

A sudden wind rose in the stillness, fanning the oil fire and driving the flames up until they formed themselves into a creature.

'Cat,' whispered Josh.

'There's so much here,' she murmured, lost in the details of the scroll, unaware of what was taking shape in the fire.

As he watched, the beast grew several more heads and many limbs, which it used to strike out at the dumbstruck guards, cutting through their weak attempts to defend themselves.

'Caitlin!' shouted Josh, as the men fell.

Geoffroy was bravely trying to drag the fallen out of its reach when he caught a side-swipe from one of the fiery limbs and went flying across the floor.

'Abaddon!' shouted Lyra, suddenly dropping through the ceiling and landing in a crouch like a superhero.

The creature's body went rigid, the flames frozen in mid-air.

'Who names me?' spoke a chorus of voices.

'I do!' replied Lyra, standing and stepping forward into the pool of light made by his fire. She had something in her hands. Josh couldn't see clearly, but it looked like a small idol.

The glow within Abaddon flickered and waned as if the fuel was running low. 'I have many names,' it answered in a harsh, rasping voice. 'You are the first to bind me to one. What is thy wish, mistress?'

'Pick up the jar,' Caitlin whispered to Josh. 'Lyra's going to need it.'

Josh took the jar and moved behind the creature.

'I need you to leave,' said Lyra, holding up the idol.

Other forms appeared around her like an ethereal horde of guardian angels, except these were nothing like any angels Josh had ever imagined — they were terrifying.

'Those are not your powers to command, girl,' it cackled. 'Jedidiah has lost the ring, and all the lords of terror are free.'

'No more, demon,' Lyra said, making a sign in the air and the ghosts launched themselves at the fire demon.

The symbol hung in the air in front of Lyra, reminding Josh of what the colonel had done in the maelstrom when they were fighting the Djinn.

'Put it down in front of her,' Caitlin growled at Josh through clenched teeth. 'She's losing him.'

The ghosts were tearing at the fire demon, pulling it apart as it struggled to set itself free.

Lyra said something in a strange language and dropped the small idol into the jar. The Djinn was dragged along into it, and Caitlin stepped in quickly to seal the lid.

. . .

'What exactly was that?' asked Josh, after they'd made doubly sure the jar was sealed. The guards were helping the injured out of the chamber.

'Abaddon, one of the angels of the abyss,' Lyra said casually, helping Geoffroy to dress his wounds.

'Fire Djinn,' Caitlin said, raising an eyebrow. 'We don't believe in Angels.'

'You don't,' replied Lyra under her breath.

Caitlin ignored her. 'I'm more interested in the weird ghosts you pulled out of the idol.'

'Guardians, from the talisman.' Lyra raised her voice on the last word to give it greater emphasis.

Josh spoke to Lyra as if she were a five-year-old. 'The little statue you were holding? The talisman. Where did you get it?'

Lyra smiled. 'It told me where to find it. Upstairs in the temple. It was calling to me — that's what was disturbing my karma.'

'And you knew what it was?' asked Josh.

'Sim told me about them. He had to find one for Eddington. They're special, really ancient vestiges from way back — minus a million or more.'

'And they give you power over the Djinn?'

'The spirit guardians have fought the Djinn before, a long, long time ago. They know how to deal with them.'

'So you were just channelling ancient spirits?'

Lyra shrugged. 'I guess so. I wasn't really in my body at the time.'

Caitlin gave up. Much as she loved her adopted sister, there were times when her inability to speak like a rational human being drove her insane.

'So who trapped all these Djinn and left them down here?' she asked herself, looking at the collection of jars.

Josh scratched his head. 'Solomon I guess — maybe that's what your uncle saw?'

Caitlin shook her head.

'This has something to do with it,' she said, waving the copper scroll in his face. 'It's a list of over sixty locations of temple treasure. Thousands of lost ancient artefacts — an Antiquarian's wet dream. I think we need to trace it back to the origin.'

'But what if we walk into another Djinn? That thing nearly killed Geoffroy!'

'Not even close,' quipped the medic, as Lyra helped him get to his feet.

'Send a message to Sim,' Caitlin said to her sister, 'he'll know what to do.'

[Jerusalem. Date: 9.065]

The temple of Solomon was still under construction when they appeared. Wooden scaffolding enclosed the tall columns that lined the sides of the grand hall. Each one was being intricately carved with hieroglyphics and geometric shapes.

They hardly recognised Marcus standing at the top of the stairs, next to the empty throne. He was dressed as an Egyptian priest, with his head shaved and glyphs painted over his bald skull. Josh thought he looked younger than the last time they'd seen him.

'Who dares defile the temple of the King?' Caitlin's uncle demanded in Coptic — something that Josh understood even though he'd never intuited it. The Infinity Engine was still helping him somehow.

'Marcus?' Caitlin replied, unsure if the man would recognise them.

'Are thou servants of Hemsut?' he asked, pulling back his sleeve to show the Ouroboros tattoo, the mark of the Order.

Caitlin looked confused for a moment, and then her eyes widened. 'The goddess of fate. Yes,' she replied, showing her tattoo.

'And destiny,' Marcus corrected her and smiled.

They heard the voices of the workman returning, and he pulled them into an alcove.

'Who are you?'

'I'm Caitlin, and we're kind of related, or at least we will be one day.'

His eyes narrowed as he studied her face. 'Tom's child? Well, you certainly have your father's eyes, but you haven't been born yet, and in my timeline, he's only just met your mother. What are you doing here?'

'I need to know about this mission.'

He frowned. 'It's top secret. How the hell did you find out about it?'

'You've been sent to find the talismans, haven't you? The ones that Solomon collected?'

There was a moment when she thought he was going to deny it, but then she saw a flicker of acquiescence in his eye.

The carpenters and stone masons were complaining about their lunch while they collected their tools from the benches and made their way to the scaffolds. Marcus looked at them both and sighed.

'You're in way over your head, and I haven't got time to take you back and sort this out. Solomon has gathered an extraordinary collection of artefacts, yes. Even some that I would call out-of-place. I don't know for sure how he came by all of them, but the ones I've seen have very unusual powers. His subjects think he's been gifted them by God, and from what I've seen they're the nearest thing to magic. But they're dangerous — they can manipulate time in ways I've never imagined. I would say they constitute the most serious threat to the continuum since the discovery of the maelstrom.'

78

NINTH LEGION

[Haslemere, Surrey. Date: 12.018]

G illian sat patiently in her car waiting for the lights to change. The engine purred quietly, and the man on the radio was waxing lyrical about the unusual period of fine weather they were having. The summer had been a long time coming, and she was anxious to get back and plant the boot full of shrubs she'd just bought from the local garden centre before the sun got too high.

The dashboard clock read 9:59 and the streets had emptied after the usual madness of the school run.

The traffic lights seemed to be taking forever to change. They were temporary ones, the kind that workmen put up when they're digging the road. She could easily pull around and get on her way, but she wasn't that kind of driver — not in seventy-three years had she ever broken the law.

Finally, the red changed to amber and Gillian's hand moved down to the gear stick to put it into drive when the engine made a strange whine and died.

'Bugger,' she muttered, turning the keys in the ignition

and looking in her rear-view mirror to apologise to the driver behind her.

Her hand froze on the keys as she went to restart the car.

Standing behind her was an entire cohort of Roman soldiers — the ninth legion. She recognised the standard from the talk a local historian had given at her WI meeting only two months ago.

The hard faces of the legionnaires looked even more menacing as they surrounded her car.

Assuming it was a re-enactment society, she smiled politely and waited for them to pass. Which they duly did, marching on through the junction.

The engine came back to life after they had disappeared around the bend, but Gillian thought better than to follow them. Something didn't feel right about the way they looked at her, and her instincts were generally very good about people.

As she took a deep breath to slow her pulse, the lights returned to red, so she took it as a sign and put the car back in park and reached for a packet of mints.

A light tap on the window made her jump.

A police officer was standing beside the car, signalling to her to wind down the window — which she did with the push of a button.

'Good morning madam,' he said with a smile. 'Would you mind stepping out of the vehicle?'

As she got out of the car, she realised he was wearing a rather antique looking uniform, as if he'd just stepped out of the nineteen-fifties.

He pulled out a strange-looking notebook.

'Your name and date of birth?'

She told him.

'Address?'

Without thinking she rattled off her address including postcode.

'Thank you,' he said with another smile.

She wanted to ask whether they were following the legionnaires, but before she got the chance, two other officers appeared from behind the car and joined him.

'They've shifted again,' one said to the other, showing him his notebook and grimacing.

'Bollocks,' the first said, turning back to Gillian.

'My apologies ma'am. Would you mind looking at this for a second?'

He held up a beautiful old watch. She loved antiques, and this one looked as if it were late seventeenth century. One curious thing about it was that the hands seemed to be moving backwards.

'It's ten o'clock and time for the news with ...' came the voice over the radio.

The lights turned green, and Gillian put the car into drive and moved off. It was going to be another hot day, and those peonies weren't going to plant themselves.

79

WAR ROOMS

Sim was busy working on the progression of the Eschaton Cascade. The algorithm was spread out over four giant blackboards, which were covered in equations and temporal formulae.

Grandmaster Derado had asked him to form a think-tank to analyse the information that was coming in from the various Draconians stationed out in the field.

Sim had managed to recruit a group of statisticians and a stochastic professor who was hiding out in the twelfth century, and they'd spent the last few weeks analysing data and complaining about how much easier this would be if they had a difference engine.

Sim had tried his best to appease them, but it was a thankless task. He quite liked doing it the old-fashioned way, with a slide rule and a blackboard — there was some-thing quaintly satisfying about going back to basics, and after a few days they stopped moaning and got down to business.

'What do we have on the thirty-third iteration?' one of

the older actuaries asked, holding up a page of calculations. 'I'm getting coefficient deviation that's out of range.'

'That's because you're supposed to be working on the thirty-first,' said one of the others, rolling up a scrap of paper and throwing it at his colleague. 'Norman's on the thirty-third.' They all laughed, except for Norman, who'd fallen asleep in the corner. Sim knew they were all working long hours, and the strain was beginning to tell on them.

They were tracking reports of over twenty anomalies in the last two days. As predicted in the fourth crisis, something was happening to the fabric of space-time; it was being stressed to breaking point. Grandmaster Derado had asked Sim's team to calculate potential weak points in the chronosphere, so he could deploy his Dreadnoughts to shore up any breaches before they escalated.

But it was becoming too difficult to manage.

They'd been allocated the Dreadnought 'War Room', which had a large map of time etched into the slate surface of the boardroom table. Without the benefit of the Infinity Engine, this had become the nearest thing they had to a continuum, and there were insignia of the various detachments placed at strategic points along its length to indicate their deployment.

A capsule arrived down the pneumatic tube, and Astor took out the memo from inside and read it.

Everyone had stopped their work and waited to hear the latest report. The capsules never brought good news, and they were coming more frequently with every day that passed.

'Roman legion seen in Haslemere, 12.018,' he summarised, taking a pen and scribbling 'Ninth Legion' on a note before sticking it on the relevant part of the timeline. 'And reports of a fire Djinn in Jerusalem, 11.120.'

'A fire Djinn? Who's on the eleventh?'

'Norman,' said one of the others with a snigger.

'Let him sleep,' Sim ordered, 'I'll take this one.' He sat down at his desk and sharpened his pencil. 'Has anyone seen where I put my copy of Britannica 1100?'

'Norman's using it as a pillow,' Astor replied.

'Very funny.'

'No, he really is,' insisted Astor.

80

DANGEROUS MYTHS

Nostradamus sat quietly listening to their report, his inscrutable expression hardly changing throughout Caitlin's monologue, one that she was careful to exclude any mention of the Solomon mission or her uncle's warnings.

'Did De Molay mention the projected success of his mission?' he asked when she'd finished.

Caitlin shook her head. 'No, but that's not the point. They released a Djinn in a heavily populated area, and the repercussions could have been catastrophic.'

The curator nodded. 'Indeed. It was most fortunate that you were there to stop it,' he said through a knowing smile.

'You knew?'

The curator held up his hand, and the scribe taking down the details of the meeting put down her quill and placed her hands over her ears.

'Let's say, off the record, that we knew it was very likely that it might occur.' He stood up and went to close the door on the fifth portal. 'That the talisman Lyra discovered was one of their unofficial objectives.'

'Of course it was,' said Caitlin.

Nostradamus opened his hands. 'Officially there are no such things as talismans. The Antiquarians will deny such an artefact exists. The founder has forbidden any documentation of such a find. Talismans are a dangerous myth that, should they be found to exist, could escalate the crisis dramatically if they were to fall into the wrong hands,' he said, and winked.

'But —'

The curator nodded to the scribe, who picked up her quill and began to take notes once more.

'Let us concentrate our efforts on the Eschaton, and since we don't have an endless supply of Augurs to chase down every last anomaly, I suggest we look into the next crisis — number seven.'

Caitlin bit her lip in frustration. Josh could see the colour rising in her cheeks, and turned to the seventh door.

'What happens in seven?'

'Interventions.'

81

INTERVENTIONS

[London. Date: 11.664]

Her men stood uneasily at the edge of the temporal field, their guns trained on the swirling void where the altar should have been.

Ravana stared into the maelstrom, trying to imagine what it would be like to walk into the chaos — knowing that her son had done precisely that.

'What happens now?' she asked the Grand Seer.

'Wondrous things,' he said, staring wild-eyed into the vortex.

'You have no idea do you?'

'Not a clue.'

There were very few moments in her life that Ravana thought of as milestones: marrying into the most powerful family in Germany was one, giving birth was another, even the death of her husband perhaps, but none of them compared to the apprehension she felt now as she faced the swirling aperture that stood before her.

One of the Protectorate officers was edging nervously

towards the portal. A rope was lashed around his waist. The others looked on stoically, all secretly relieved they hadn't been chosen.

'How do you know he's still alive?'

'I don't,' said Kelly. 'The miserable have no other medicine but hope.'

Ravana turned to him. 'You told me you could find him.'

'I have seen no comets.'

'Enough with your riddles,' she snapped. 'Is he coming or not?'

The officer disappeared into the aperture, and the rope snaked in behind him. Everyone held their breath, waiting for a reaction from the void.

Suddenly, the line tightened as though a fish were caught on the end of it. The men struggled to hold the cord as it thrashed back and forth before going slack once more.

They frantically wound the rope back in, everyone expecting to find nothing more than a severed end. When the intact empty loop appeared they all looked to one other with confusion and fear in their eyes.

'Witchcraft!' declared Kelly, waving his hand in the air. 'There's magic in the web of it!'

'Nonsense!' Ravana said, turning towards one of her officers. 'Give me the skull.'

The man removed the rune-covered skull from its silk bag and handed it to her.

'Dalton always said that Daedalus would show us the way.'

Holding it out before her, she walked towards the aperture. The sigils began to glow with an iridescent hue as she drew closer.

The Grand Seer took a piece of chalk from his pocket and hastily drew a small circle around himself, embellishing it with arcane symbols and glyphs while whispering some unintelligible incantation under his breath.

As she stood on the brink of the precipice, ribbons of energy began to leech off the surface of the skull, like gas escaping from a punctured balloon, the tendrils winding around each other as they were sucked into the vortex.

Ravana used both hands to steady her grip as a ghostly outline of a man's face materialised around the bone. He was an old man with pale eyes that stared directly at her, his mouth moving as if saying something, but she couldn't hear.

Cold numbed her fingers, gradually working its way along her forearms, yet she refused to yield. Like frostbite, the burning raced along her nerves, turning her arms to lead, but she held on, knowing this was the only chance she would ever have of reaching her son.

'Where is he?' she hissed through gritted teeth.

Other shapes were beginning to form around the skull. The malformed limbs of creatures twisted and curled like the snakes of Medusa as they writhed out from the portal.

'Ravana!' she heard Kelly try to warn her as the Djinn began to manifest, but it was too late; she'd felt a connection with Daedalus' timeline and her mind leapt into it.

The world around her disappeared as the darkness reached out and took her.

She calmed herself, knowing that in reality, she was still standing in the middle of a church in 11.664 — if Ravana concentrated hard she could still feel the floor underneath her feet.

Daedalus' skull was shining brightly in her hand, like a beacon, the line of his life spreading out like glowing ribbon into the infinite void. She followed it back through time; the skull had been lost for millions of years, sleeping below the earth while the world turned. She felt the aeons pass as the ice came and went. No one had ever travelled this far into pre-history — it was a time before the age of man, and her own laws forbade anyone from going there.

Even though Ravana knew she was still within the continuum, she could feel the hostility of the maelstrom around her, waiting just beyond the shadows.

Reavers would always speak about the maelstrom as if it were the place beyond death, the stygian land of no return. Even her husband, the most rational man she'd ever met, had an unfounded fear of what awaited him in the afterlife.

But not her. Ravana had always known, with scientific certainty, that the logical antithesis of order must be chaos.

She located the point where Daedalus had entered the continuum, the moment when his head at least had appeared out of the maelstrom and into standard linear time. The skull was now fully fleshed, a bearded man in his fifties sitting between her hands, still talking animatedly to someone she couldn't see or hear.

'Where is my son?' she asked him again.

Daedalus formed words, but they remained as mute as before.

She found herself standing in a rock-strewn desert, vast purple mountains rising like broken teeth along the horizon. It was barren, with no vegetation, only a harsh, dry wind driving stinging sand across the dunes.

The head was too heavy to hold now. She placed the skull on the ground and stood back as time continued to reverse around it.

His head seemed to grow a neck and shoulders until a

man rose from the ground before her. A dark shape flick-ered into existence beside him, a colossal creature with black armour and a great scythe of a sword.

The blade was slicing upwards through Daedalus' neck, sealing the awful wound, as his execution played out back-wards before her eyes.

There was a brilliant white flash as an aperture appeared in mid-air and Daedalus reversed onto his feet and ran backwards towards it.

He was trying to escape, Ravana thought.

His executioner stepped back through the portal, but before it disappeared, she caught sight of his face, or rather the wicked smile that sat upon it.

It was Dalton.

A detachment of heavily armed Dreadnoughts appeared out of thin air, surrounding the Protectorate officers, who imme-diately surrendered their weapons and were moved out of the firing line.

Grandmaster Derado, in full battle armour, made his way through his men to the Grand Seer, who was kneeling inside a chalk circle as if in prayer.

'How long has she been in there?' Derado demanded, staring at the figure of Ravana shrouded in layers of dark, swirling energy.

'Longer than I would like,' Kelly replied gravely.

Derado stared into the spinning vortex, his eyes narrowing as he studied the chaos within. He turned to his lieutenant. 'The Wyrrm is holding a bridge open, and we need to shut it down. Get the civilians to safety and reini-tialise the stasis fields.'

The officer nodded and began to relay the orders to the

others. Within a matter of minutes, the church was cleared of all non-essential personnel, and the artificers were busily repairing the stasis units.

Derado put on his helmet, activated his temporal shielding and walked slowly into the centre of the circle. Ravana had become a pale ghost of her former self, old and haggard from prolonged exposure to the maelstrom. But she was smiling, and tears were running down her cheeks; whatever she was experiencing seemed at least to be making her happy.

'Do you want us to disrupt the connection?' asked one of the technicians through the comms system.

'Do we know when she is?'

'Negative. The readings are off the scale.'

Derado looked into her glazed eyes and sighed. 'Leave her. I doubt anyone will thank us for bringing her back anyway.'

'But the council?'

'I will explain to the council. Let's focus on locking this down before anything serious comes through.'

He walked back out of the breach and took off his helmet. 'Bentley!'

'Yes sir,' Bentley said, stepping forward.

'Well done son.' Derado slapped him on the shoulder. 'You've just stopped the seventh crisis.'

Bentley winced in pain as his commander took his hand away. 'Still giving you trouble?' he asked.

Bentley nodded. 'Nothing that won't mend.'

He couldn't explain why Sabien had helped him escape from Ravana's cells, but the things he'd witnessed in there would stay with him for years. The medics said his injuries were going to take weeks to heal, but it was worth it to see the old witch sealed in with what was left of Daedalus' skull. They were both too dangerous to be allowed to survive.

Bentley looked over to where Darkling's body lay. 'What happens now?' Bentley asked.

'We bury our dead and regroup. It's time to see if we can rebuild the Order.'

82

VIKING

The colonel was sat by one of the more dramatic windows when Josh came to visit him the next day.

He was staring out at the stormy seascape, lost in the power of the waves as they crashed against the granite cliffs.

'Hey,' Josh said as he sat down on the bench beside him, 'how are you doing?'

The old man looked around at him, his eyes taking a moment to focus. 'Joshua, it's good to see you.'

There were so many things Josh wanted to discuss with him, but he could see the weariness in his eyes; the aetherium had nearly destroyed his past, and it looked as if he had been reliving it ever since Josh put it back together.

'You saved my life,' he said with a sigh. 'Although there are definitely some parts I would have chosen to leave out.'

'Yeah, sorry about that.'

He smiled. 'It's not your fault. Without the sadness, we would never have the joy — as my mother used to say.'

It was the first time he'd ever spoken about his mother, and for some reason, Josh couldn't imagine the colonel as a child.

'When were you born?'

'10.875. In Jórvík or York, as you would call it. Back then it was part of Danelaw under the control of the Vikings.'

Josh laughed. 'You're a Viking? That explains a lot!'

The colonel raised a fist. 'Careful boy, I'm not that weak.'

'Okay, okay.' Josh held up his hands. 'So who discovered you?'

'I was one of the first,' the colonel began proudly. 'Back in the days before the Order existed, we were just a disorganised bunch of clans using our talents for our own ends. It was a lawless time, every man for himself. No one cared too much about changing the world or protecting the future. We were totally wild and incredibly selfish.'

Josh had never thought about a time before the Order existed. It seemed to him like it had always been. 'And the founder changed that?'

The colonel nodded. 'He walked into the town like a Shaman with his followers in tow, talking of the dangers that lay ahead — the usual oracle stuff we do to ingratiate ourselves with the locals. Next thing I know one of his acolytes, Dolovir, had singled me out and was asking if I wanted to join them — the rest is history.'

'The founder told me something after we saved you.'

'Did he now.'

'That he's not from this continuum.'

'Oh that. Well, we've all got our little secrets. I've never held it against him.'

'You knew?'

The colonel sighed. 'I've known him for nigh on eight hundred years, and there aren't many secrets left when you get past a hundred — not that he remembers me of course.'

'And the Nihil?'

'Never heard of them.'

'The founder never told you about the Nihil?'

The colonel shrugged. 'Are they bad?'

'I don't know,' said Josh thoughtfully. 'He said they feed off aetherium, the stuff that you were infected with.'

'Then they've got terrible taste. So where is the founder now?'

'I haven't seen him since we cured you.'

The colonel stood up and swayed a little. 'Have you told anyone else about this?'

Josh shook his head.

'Good, keep it between us for now. Djinn are bad enough, and I'd rather not start spreading fear amongst the ranks with stories of even more dangerous creatures. Now, let's see if we can find him.'

83

FUNDAMENTAL TRUTHS

Grandmaster Derado flexed his toes as he stood in the centre of the Star Chamber surrounded by what was left of the Order. It was an old trick that his father had taught him when forced to stand for long periods of sentry duty, stopping his legs from cramping. The meeting had been in session for over an hour, and still, members were arriving.

He needed them all before he could begin; he didn't want to have to say this twice.

A quick scan of the seats told him what he most feared, that the Copernicans had suffered the worst under the rule of the Eschaton Division and those that had come numbered less than fifty. He was hoping more had chosen to disappear into the dark niches of the past and would take some coaxing to come out of hiding.

The Antiquarians and Scriptorians appeared to have survived the coup far better, and from his reports, Derado knew that some of them might have even collaborated with Dalton. There was no time for recriminations; for now, he needed them all to put aside their differences and work together.

Finally, the chamber fell silent, and he found himself the centre of attention.

'Ravana is dead,' he began, watching their faces as the news sank in, 'as is her son, we believe. The Protectorate has been relieved of all their duties.'

A general buzz swept around the auditorium, so the grandmaster had to raise his voice over the swell of chatter.

'I will report the facts as they stand. Both the Nemesis and the founder are still missing, and my sources tell me that the crises of the Eschaton Cascade are in progress.'

He took out a musket as the noise levels increased, and fired it into the air. The shock of the gunshot silenced the chamber.

'Please let me finish,' he requested, putting the gun away. 'The end of times may be upon us, or it may not. As our Copernican colleagues would agree, this is merely a hypothesis, and as with all theories, there is an element of uncertainty. No one knows what it will be that collapses the timeline, but the founder was prepared — while you were busy mocking the prediction, he formed a shadow guild, a secret one known only to a select few. Created to study the crises — they are known as 'Augurs' — and as I speak they're risking their lives to try and contain the cascade.'

Some of the audience nodded as if Derado were confirming a theory that they'd known all along.

'For too long now the divisions between us have made us vulnerable. We have become blinded by our theories until they were more important than the reality we were studying. The continuum is nothing more than a story we tell ourselves to bring order to chaos, a lie we choose to believe. This must end, there are only two fundamental truths that matter right now.' He raised his clenched fist and lifted one finger. 'One: We are stronger when we stand together. Two: The future has not yet been written. As we face the darkest time in our history, it is our duty to stand against the oncoming tide, to hold back the chaos, for are we not the Oblivion Order?'

The audience were on their feet now, their fists raised, cheering him on.

'Together as one!'

The chamber erupted as everyone rose to their feet and called out, 'As one.'

Derado turned to the Grand Seer whose eyes were full of tears.

'So, now the war begins, Master Seer. Tell me, do you know where the founder is?'

'In hell,' Kelly said grimly.

84

CONFLAGRATO

'Where is the founder?' demanded Caitlin as she stormed into the Armageddon gallery.

Nostradamus was sitting in the centre of the room staring at the world beyond the tenth door, a glass of red wine in one hand and a half-empty bottle in the other.

'Conflagrato,' he slurred, raising his glass to the fiery scene.

Caitlin looked through the arch; the whole of London was ablaze. The Thames was a ribbon of orange winding through a blackened sky.

'The Great Fire,' said Nostradamus,

'And the rest of the tenth?'

'They're all in there. God help them.'

Caitlin went to take a step into the portal.

'Wait!' ordered Nostradamus, putting the bottle down and getting up from his chair. 'If you're going to follow him in there you will need the correct equipment.'

· · ·

He closed the tenth door and turned the key anti-clockwise. When he opened it again, they saw a room full of strange-looking leather suits hung from the brass rails, glistening, as if they were drying from the rain.

'Wet suits,' explained Nostradamus.

'What?'

'Fire armour. Designed to reduce the heat of the blaze. There are also breathing masks and fire-resistant gloves. Should protect you from all but the hottest parts of the inferno.'

She walked into the changing room.

'Are you going in alone?' asked the curator.

'No she's not,' Josh said, walking into the gallery with the colonel close behind.

'I wondered when you'd get here,' said Caitlin, pulling a suit from the rail.

'You can't go in there alone,' the colonel agreed.

Caitlin smiled. 'Nice to see you back on your feet, but I'm going to have enough to deal with without having to wait for you two to keep up.'

'Do you have any idea what you're doing?' asked Josh.

'Following the founder.'

'Because?'

'Because he hasn't stopped the eighth,' Caitlin said and pointed at the open door.

'Why not?' Josh asked Nostradamus.

The curator looked sheepish. 'We were instructed to keep it open.'

'But we've proved it's been altered, and it's connected to four of the other crises, including the eleventh!'

Nostradamus shrugged in a way that said it wasn't his job to question his boss.

'Then I'm coming with you,' insisted Josh.

'So am I,' added the colonel.

'No, you're not,' Josh and Caitlin said in unison.

The colonel ignored both of them and started putting on a suit.

Once they'd all managed to struggle into their fire armour, Nostradamus switched the door back to the view of the inferno.

Caitlin stared through the tenth portal. 'Wouldn't it be wiser to go back to before the fire started?'

Nostradamus winced. 'We tried that. Twice.'

'And you couldn't stop it?'

'They're not allowed to,' interrupted the colonel. 'The fire has to take place. The only thing they can do is try to contain it.'

'And find the Djinn that started it,' added Nostradamus.

'The Djinn?'

'The tenth has data that proves this event was caused by a fire demon. The founder has gone in to help them.'

85

INFERNO

J osh could feel the heat from the blaze through the layers of water as it steamed off his armour. It was an odd sensation as it ran inside and outside of his suit, soaking his underclothes, and moving around felt like running in wet pyjamas.

Strong winds whipped the flames, sweeping the fire across the roofs of the old wooden tenements. Their upper stories had been built out so far as to be nearly touching their opposite number on the other side of the street. Screams echoed down the cluttered alleyways as a sea of people clutching their most precious possessions flooded through the narrow passages and out into the plaza. No one noticed the strangers as they stood in the shadows of St. Pauls Cathedral, whose wooden scaffolding was already alight.

The area around the church was full of discarded hand-carts and heaps of furniture that people had brought there for safety but abandoned when the fire reached it.

'Where are we going?' shouted Josh, touching helmets with Caitlin to help conduct the sound.

'East,' Caitlin replied, pointing towards the heart of the fire. 'We need to get closer to the start.'

'And then?'

'Move back to Sunday.'

They ducked as the stones from the roof exploded above them, firing shrapnel in all directions and sending glowing orange fireballs of molten metal into the ground around them.

'The lead's melting,' the colonel said, looking up at the liquid running down the walls.

He pulled Caitlin clear as a lump of masonry crashed into the ground where they had been standing.

'We go now,' he said, putting his face-plate to hers.

She nodded and ran into the crowd.

86

UNDER FIRE

[Ascension Island, Atlantic. Date: 11.927]

S im walked into Derado's private office and closed the
door. The grandmaster was lost in the details of his
latest report and hardly seemed to notice his entrance.

'Grandmaster.' Sim's tone was formal but insistent.

'Simeon now is not the best of times.'

'There will never be a good time to tell you this, sir.'

Derado looked up from his document and took off his
glasses. 'I assume you have something more important than
my despatches, master De Freis?'

Sim nodded and took a deep breath.

'There are significant signs that a Djinn attack is likely to
occur in the next few hours, and my best guess is that it will
actualise during the Great Fire of London, 11.666.'

'The fire? I've seen no mention of it in my reports.'

Sim shook his head. 'It's not in them. My sister, Lyra,
sent me a message about a fire Djinn being captured in
11.120. It made me think about the tenth crisis, the crossing

of the Djinn, and the more I looked into it, the more it made sense. Fire is hard to defend against — they're going to come under cover of the inferno.'

87

EAST INDIA COMPANY

There was nothing but a human tide of hysteria and chaos facing them as they made their way through the streets. The fire crews and their equipment couldn't navigate against the traffic and had resorted to carrying barrels of explosives by hand. Detonations shook the ground every few minutes as another house was demolished to create a firebreak.

Their progress was slowed further by having to avoid the patrols of Coldstream guards arresting anyone who looked foreign. A paranoia gripped the city as rumours of fires being started by foreign saboteurs had made everyone suspicious.

So they hid in burning buildings. Walking into fire went against everything Josh's survival instinct was telling him to do, and just like learning to swim, he had to conquer the primal fear of drowning, or in this case burning, to death. While the suit did a great job of holding back the heat — Josh couldn't help but wonder how long it would last.

The nearer they got to their destination the more intense the inferno became; the streets were scorched, and anything flammable was vaporised to ash. Walls of stone buildings glowed amber as the heat cracked them, and there was nothing left of the wooden floors above.

It was hard to breathe, the cooling system within the suit struggling with the intense heat. Josh followed Caitlin and the colonel as they made their way down what was left of Leadenhall Street.

When they reached the crumbling ruin of the building, it was a relief to see each one of them touch the wall and disappear.

[London. Date: Sunday, 2nd September, 11.666]

The founder was hard to recognise through the misty visor of the fire suit. Josh pulled off the helmet and sucked in a long, cool breath, coughing as his lungs cleared themselves.

They'd gone back to the night it had started, and there was an eerie calm to the city that evening, a stillness that gave no hint of the catastrophe to come. But somewhere a few miles to the East, a baker was trying to raise the alarm about his house catching fire.

'What's he doing?' Josh asked the colonel as they watched from an alley on the other side of the street.

'Waiting.'

The founder was stood staring up at the grand wooden house like a jilted lover waiting to catch sight of his mistress.

'Whose house is it?' asked Josh. It was an impressive wooden building, with a fresco of sailing ships painted across the square gable of the upper floor and the silhouettes of a sailor and two dolphins standing along the roof against the evening sky.

'It's the headquarters of the East India Company,' the colonel replied.

. . .

They stayed out of sight until the founder disappeared inside and then followed him in.

The house was dark, the occupants either asleep or away for the night. The colonel took out his tachyon and shone it along the corridor, letting the light play off the gilt frames of paintings. A proud fleet of ships lined the walls, each one bearing the company colours.

'What's he come here for?' Josh whispered.

A board creaked above their heads, someone's footstep on the floor above.

They froze, straining their ears for any sound.

'I don't know,' the colonel said under his breath, 'but I don't think it's got anything to do with the fire. By this time the East India Company had gone from state-sponsored pirates to a global trading company that rivalled the Dutch — but it was mostly spice, silks and dyes — nothing useful.'

They moved towards the staircase as they heard the scraping of a heavy box being dragged across the floor.

The upstairs room was just like the colonel's cabinet of curiosities.

The founder was kneeling beside a large trunk, rummaging through the contents and utterly oblivious to their presence.

'Master?' whispered Caitlin.

'Miss Makepiece,' he greeted her without looking up. 'I don't suppose you have seen any Anunnaki, small figurines about six inches high?'

'No sir.'

'They were a present from the Mughal Emperor Nur-uddin Salim Jahangir. Supposedly for James I, but I believe his emissary, Sir Thomas Roe, kept them for himself on the orders of the Company.'

'What do they do?' asked Josh.

The founder looked up over the lid of the trunk. 'Insightful as ever, Master Jones. As I'm sure you've worked out by now, this isn't an Eschaton crisis. I believe this is something far more dangerous — a Nihil attack.'

'The Nihil aren't part of the Eschaton Cascade?' asked Josh.

'They are a significant threat considering the weakened state of the timeline.'

'And the Anunnaki?'

'A very potent defence in the right hands.' He pulled out a mahogany casket. 'Ahh. Now, this looks more promising.'

'You really believe that a Sumerian myth can help us?' Caitlin didn't sound convinced.

He opened the casket and took a tiny figurine from its velvet-lined interior. 'These are ancient artefacts that go back further than the Sumerians. To a time when the Djinn was a constant threat.'

'It's a talisman.'

The founder's eyes narrowed. 'Where did you hear about that?'

Caitlin smiled. 'From uncle Marcus.'

'Marcus Makepiece. Now there's a name I haven't heard in a very long time.'

The founder took out another two figurines and placed them inside his cloak. 'The Solomon mission was not our finest hour. I assume he told you not to trust me?'

'He did.'

'Understandable,' the founder agreed, standing up. 'It would've been hard not to blame me. Can this wait?'

'No, I don't think it can.'

The founder sighed and sat down on a chair by the fire. Its embers were glowing faintly, and he stoked them with a metal poker.

'Sit. This is going to take a while.'

88

STORIES OF KINGS

'Solomon was an interesting king. Although there was little historical record it was clear he had access to great wealth — his father was buried in a silver sarcophagus. The Antiquarians were adamant that he was levying taxes on the people of Upper Egypt, where the tombs of the last Pharaohs of Egypt were buried.'

'The Valley of the Kings,' said Caitlin.

'Yes, there were reports of vast caches of grave goods being plundered, but the treasures were never found in any great number. It was as if they disappeared.'

'Perhaps he was a collector?'

The founder shook his head. 'He had a Greek mercenary army to pay and a Phoenician navy, so any remaining items were probably stolen by the Babylonians when they eventually invaded Tanis in 9.400.'

'Six hundred BC,' explained Caitlin as Josh started counting on his fingers.

'The Solomon mission was supposed to go back and index the treasures. Trace them back to their origin and help us map the early dynasties of the Old Kingdom and the First Intermediate Period.'

'Not the second?'

The founder winced at the name. 'At the time we had no idea what would happen in the Early Dynastic, as there wasn't enough data to go back that far. The plan was to use what Carter had found in the tomb of Tutankhamen as a starting point and weave our way up to Solomon.'

'Why?' asked Josh.

The founder shifted uncomfortably. 'There were stories, potentially apocryphal ones, that spoke of Solomon being given certain powers over demons. The Scriptorians had noted certain unusual details in some of the narratives that pointed towards a breach, but more unusual was the fact that Solomon seemed to have the power to contain them. Since he was not a member of the Order, we had to assume he had access to unusual weapons.'

'What kind of weapons?' asked Josh. He'd been losing interest up until that point; it was beginning to sound too much like a history lesson.

The founder smiled. 'Ancient ones. Things that had been buried for aeons. We assumed he must have found them amongst the treasures of the dead kings.'

'Out-of-place objects,' added Caitlin.

'Indeed. There have been cases were items have surfaced from antediluvian times. We call them talismans. They are very rare, and the Antiquarians have documented just six in the last twelve millennia. Some of them believe they are the relics of an elder race, but they do have a tendency for the dramatic.'

'And Solomon had one?'

The founder nodded. 'He seems to have acquired a ring.

A very powerful temporal vestige. We only discovered quite how powerful after the first team disappeared.'

'Uncle Marcus?'

'He was part of the rescue team. They say it changed your uncle, that he had visions and what he saw sent him off the rails.'

'What can this ring do?' asked Caitlin.

'It has roots in the primordial, so one can only assume it harnesses chaos fields.'

Josh stared into the fire. 'Dark energy.'

The founder's eyes widened slightly. 'That is one theory, yes.'

'What happened to the ring?'

'Marcus refused to tell us. Everyone involved in the mission took voluntary redaction or the long walk.'

Josh looked confused. 'Long walk?'

'Early retirement into pre-history,' the colonel explained. 'Although no one usually takes voluntary redaction.'

'There are members of that particular mission who would beg to differ.'

'So why does Marcus blame you?'

The founder sighed. 'I was the one who signed the order to seal the mission. Disavowing the members of the first team and essentially leaving them to their fate.'

'But they were already dead?'

'No, not dead, trapped. Solomon banished them into the abyss — the maelstrom.'

'You abandoned them?'

'The alternative was worse. They were supposed to bury the ring before certain parties became aware of it.'

'Like Dalton.'

'And others like him. The books of the Djinn are nothing

but instruction manuals compared to a talisman.' He held up a statuette. 'These have the power to summon incredibly ancient forces, amongst other things.'

Caitlin took it from him. 'So they can help protect us?'

'They possess latent energies within them that can be used to hold back the storm-kin, yes.'

Josh thought back to the charms Sohguerin had used during the fight against the monads back in the castle at Gisors. She had called them something.

'Godheads.'

The founder looked impressed. 'Indeed. The remnants of deities would be one way to describe them. 'Where did you learn that master Jones?'

'Something I picked up,' Josh said, shrugging. 'Fighting monads.'

For once Caitlin was speechless.

'Can I suggest we continue this discussion later?' the founder asked, getting up out of the chair.

'What are you going to do now?' Caitlin asked.

'I think this fire is nothing but a blind for something more sinister. This is more than just the crossing of the Djinn — I believe the Nihil are coming.'

89

ANUNNAKI

The fire was raging across the city, turning the ash-filled sky a dirty orange. There was nothing left of East India House now but blackened timbers, while many of the other buildings on Leadenhall Street had been reduced to piles of rubble.

'Where do we go?' asked Caitlin, as the founder stood in the middle of the street watching the swirling pillars of smoke.

He took one of the Anunnaki figures from his cloak and held it above his head.

'The wind is from the east, but the fire travels along other lines. We need to locate the breach and stop the Djinn before they destroy the entire city.'

The founder turned slowly around, using the figurine like a sensor, scanning for a signal. He stopped when it began to glow. 'To the river!' he said, putting out his hand.

.   .   .

They appeared in the middle of a firestorm. A massive Djinn that looked like a cross between a Chinese dragon and an octopus was hurling fireballs at a beleaguered team of Augurs and Dreadnoughts who were taking shelter behind a ramshackle barricade of stone and rubble. The unit was commanded by Grandmaster Derado himself.

'Master Derado? What the devil are you doing here?' asked the founder.

'The breach is five hundred metres beyond the beast. I've sent two artificers back to close it, but we've had no word from them.'

The founder put his head up over the parapet and then ducked back down as another ball of flame scudded off the top of the barricade, singeing his hair.

'I have something that may help,' he said, holding up the Anunnaki.

'I was hoping you were going to say that,' said Derado with obvious relief.

'Get your men back six hours or so. I will endeavour to send this beast back to where it came from and meet you there.'

He turned to Caitlin and Josh. 'I suggest you go with Master Derado.'

'Not a chance,' uttered Josh.

Caitlin shook her head, and the colonel was already loading up a gunsabre.

One by one, Derado's men disappeared. The creature roared as the founder moved out from behind the shelter and held the figurine in front of him. The noise was so loud that the ground beneath their feet trembled and Josh found himself covering his ears.

They stayed behind the barricade and watched the old man walk defiantly down the street towards the beast. He was whispering something as he walked and the Anunnaki's timelines wove around his arm like tame serpents

Waves of fire poured over the founder with no effect — the Anunnaki seemed to be creating some kind of force field around him.

The Djinn focused all of its energy on the glowing figure, blasting the ground that he walked on until the cobblestones glowed white.

The founder took a jar from another pocket and calmly placed it before the massive creature. He raised his voice, and they could hear a commanding tone but no real words. The limbs of the beast thrashed against the walls of the buildings around it, smashing them to pieces like a child's toy.

The founder's body seemed to lose cohesion, flickering in and out of existence as he channelled the power of the ancient artefact. Lines of energy leapt from his arms, trapping the demon, binding it to him and drawing it towards the small jar.

Josh watched open-mouthed as the Djinn seemed to collapse in on itself. The founder's voice changed pitch and outlines of other beings shimmered around the demon. They were tall, with elongated bodies, like life-size versions of the Anunnaki, inhuman and unworldly — the spirits closed around the creature and absorbed it, taking it into the clay jar, which the founder quickly sealed.

Exactly like the ones in Solomon's temple, Josh noted.

The founder looked exhausted when he returned to the barricade, carrying the jar. 'We need to move back to the breach,' he said, handing Caitlin the idol. 'You may need this.'

'Aren't you coming?' she asked, handling the figurine with a new respect.

The old man nodded. 'There will be more at the breach, and I can only hold one at a time. Do you think you can manage it?'

Caitlin probed the timeline of the artefact, finding that it stretched far beyond anything she'd ever experienced before. 'I think so.'

Josh was looking at her like a child who'd missed out on his Christmas present.

'What?'

90

THE BRIDGE

[Six hours earlier]

The Djinn broke through the barricade and swept down the street, igniting everything in their path.

'We need to blow the bridge!' screamed one of Derado's men.

Josh looked at the portal shimmering within the flames and the trail of destruction around them and wondered whether anything was going to survive this.

'You mean the breach?' asked Caitlin.

'No, the bridge,' he said, pointing to the structure spanning the Thames covered in seven-story houses. 'To stop the fire spreading to the south bank.'

The officer chose a few of the most able-bodied men and grabbed a handcart full of dynamite. The air was full of burning embers, and Josh thought it was a brave man who'd stand anywhere near such an explosive cargo — let alone push it down the street.

The founder went ahead of them holding the Anunnaki statue out before him.

'We need to try and keep them within the walls,' he said to Caitlin.

The Roman walls had acted like a firebreak for the first two days, but the Mayor's decision to close the gates to force the inhabitants to fight the fire had meant they were all trapped inside.

'When is the Duke of York coming?' asked Caitlin.

'Not for another six hours.'

The Djinn slowed as they came within the influence of the founder and the Anunnaki.

'How long will it hold them?' Caitlin asked, staring wide-eyed at the fire demons. Their leader was a magnificent specimen, with a tall and sinuous body of flame, and as he walked up the street like a nightmarish spectre, everything he touched turned to cinders.

'Long enough to get the civilians through the gates.'

'How many more gates are there?' Josh asked.

'Eight,' Derado said, joining them. 'My men have two under control, and the Augurs are working on a third.'

'We're not going to be able to save them all.'

'I never thought we would,' said the founder. 'Just save as many as we can; they've never been able to count the dead.'

'Why?'

'Fire was so hot it vaporised bone,' explained Caitlin.

The Djinn came to a halt before them. Josh could make out three distinct shapes — each one looked capable of taking them on its own.

91

NEMESIS

The first Djinn approached them, its eyes dark and full of malice. As it got closer, they could see that beneath the halo of fire its body was covered in vicious shards of bone. Razor sharp and stained with dark blood, the blades extended out like swords from its many arms. Josh counted at least six pairs, but it was difficult to be sure as they were constantly moving.

Behind it, the other two held their ground. They were smaller and more disfigured than their leader, each with bloated bellies that glowed as they belched fire.

The founder was tiring, his arms shaking as he held the Anunnaki before the demon; the fire seemed to be drawn to it, ribbons of flame flying towards the talisman, like so many moths to a candle.

The figurine was beginning to glow white hot again, and the ghostly spirit forms appeared around it.

'Caitlin, go forward and hold the others back,' the founder ordered.

She glanced nervously at Josh before making her way along the burning street. He could tell she was worried and fought back the urge to follow her. Josh had no idea how he'd be able to help and was pretty sure she would've hated the idea that she needed it.

Some of Derado's men were preparing to trap the Djinn the founder was holding, but it was proving hard to lock down. Josh could see the tremor in the old man's hands as he focused on keeping it in check.

A team of Dreadnoughts were following Caitlin up the street towards the smaller Djinn, who were throwing everything they could at the founder. Enormous balls of fire detonated against the shield that he'd created. Josh watched the flames wash over the invisible sphere, entirely engulfing him in fire.

Smoke and ash filled the air, like a black snow-storm, and it was becoming harder to see Caitlin clearly as Josh moved out from behind the defences to try to get a better view.

'Get back!' barked Derado, who was helping two young artificers set up a complicated-looking breaching device. They'd both taken off their helmets.

Josh recognised the red hair of his friend.

'Bentley?' Josh shouted, taking off his helmet.

'Josh?' Bentley said, looking around for him.

There were a million things he wanted to say, but there was no time. Josh could see from the strain on Bentley's face that the battle was not going well.

'Fifteen seconds,' warned Bentley's accomplice.

'Check,' Bentley responded, his concentration returning to the work at hand.

Josh turned back to the Djinn. He'd had enough of standing around; it was time to get involved.

· · ·

The Dreadnoughts couldn't contain the Djinn, and the founder was on his knees. Josh walked into the sphere and placed his hand reassuringly on the old man's shoulder before stepping out into the fire, knowing why he hadn't been given an idol.

These Djinn were too powerful for the Anunnaki, its bindings being broken as quickly as they were made, but Josh didn't care — he had seen the colonel take on hundreds of these creatures with nothing but a book.

All he had needed was a name.

The founder collapsed, and the holding fields dropped with him.

A scream burst from the demon's chest as it broke free, its whole being seeming to swell with power as it was released.

Josh stood calmly before it and waited for the attack.

As it touched him, he felt the cold, icy darkness again, just like the time in the maelstrom. He was like poison to them, and the moment they connected the Djinn realised it had lost.

Josh saw the creature's eyes grow dark as it fought to free itself, but it didn't stand a chance. The halo of flames flickered and died as its body crystallised and then shattered into a million ebony fragments.

Josh had no time to celebrate. He could see the team ahead were struggling to hold the other two Djinn. Caitlin was standing in the middle of a ring of fire as they tried to incinerate her.

Bentley and the rest of the Dreadnoughts rushed passed Josh, heading towards the breach. With the Djinn distracted it was their only chance to shut it down. Bentley moved like a soldier now, no more the bumbling, overweight blue falcon, but a well-drilled lean, mean, fighting machine.

Caitlin focused all her energies on the Anunnaki, manifesting a large group of ancient spirits to contain the demons. She had a clay pot at her feet and was close to trapping the first of the two when Josh stepped into her sphere.

'What are you doing?' she hissed through gritted teeth.

'Checking you're okay,' he said flippantly.

'Are you insane? I can't protect both of us!'

'No need,' he said with a wink. 'I'm toxic to them.'

He stepped out of her shield and walked towards them.

Out of the corner of his eye, Josh noticed Bentley and his team setting up their equipment in front of the breach.

He wasn't concentrating on them. His targets were floating three metres off the floor looking at the strange human walking towards them.

'Hello boys,' he said through a smile. 'Want to play?'

92

BREACHED

Caitlin watched as Josh strode towards the Djinn. She held them in the Anunnaki bindings for as long as she could, but time was running out, and she could feel them beginning to regain control.

'Josh!' she shouted, but he wasn't listening.

As she tried to hold on to the connection something distracted her. The Dreadnought team working on the breach were frantically attacking something, men and equipment flying in all directions as they tried to fight off some new threat.

Her concentration lapsed and the Anunnaki spirits faded.

Josh was standing with his arms extended out to the demons, who seemed to be frozen to the spot, each one with a blackened tentacle wrapped around him. Their surfaces had darkened, their internal fires extinguished.

Caitlin looked back to the breach, where a dark figure was carving its way through the Dreadnoughts as if they were toys, and it was making its way towards Josh.

Josh was still locked onto the Djinn, and whatever he

was doing to them was draining them of all their energy. Their bodies were turning to obsidian.

The creature from the breach was through the defences and closing in on Josh. Caitlin tried to move, but time seemed to be slowing, and she called out, but her voice was too weak from the summoning.

As she collapsed to the floor, she saw the entity reach Josh and screamed.

It was Dalton — a hideously distorted version of Dalton.

93

TIME FALLS

There are too many breaches, Sim thought, looking at the map on the table.

It had been a long night, and the timeline was covered in hastily scribbled notes and broken models.

The Dreadnoughts had suffered terribly in the last eighteen hours; half of them were reported missing, and the rest were in Bedlam getting treated for third-degree burns. The Great Fire had taken every able-bodied Draconian to contain the attack.

The rest of Sim's team were asleep under their desks or upstairs in the bar getting drunk. No one wanted to talk about what was going to happen next, not even Derado, but Sim knew they would have to, because as far as he could work out, this was only the beginning.

The latter part of the cascade was imminent. He was in no doubt of that. The previous temporal anomalies were minor infractions compared to the all-out assault of the night before. The continuum had started to collapse, and the Djinn had broken through in vast numbers and multiple locations. They'd used the fire to cover their arrival; it was a type nine cataclysm and was so powerful there was no way to detect it before the event.

And something had taken Josh.

Caitlin had returned to the Draconian HQ with her godfather. She was in a bad way. Her parents had gone with Alixia to the infirmary a few hours ago, and there'd been no news since.

Sim had heard that the founder was also critical, and it felt like the entire Order was holding its breath waiting for the inevitable news.

Astor woke up and raised his head from the desk with a note still stuck to one cheek.

'What time is it?'

'Five,' Sim said quietly.

Astor stretched his arms and yawned. 'Is it over?'

'No, I think it's just starting.'

94

CONFINED SPACES

J osh was in some kind of cylinder. He put out his hands and felt the glass curved around him. There were no lights and nothing to use as a point of reference.

The air inside the pod smelled faintly of ozone, like the air-con in a Land Rover Discovery he'd stolen once. It had been one of the hottest days of the year, and the leather seats were baking when he jumped in. The steering wheel seared his hands when he'd gripped it, leaving welts on his young fingers for days. His mum told him off for playing with matches, which was of course what any normal twelve-year-old should have been doing.

Josh didn't mind confined spaces, but there were a few times when the lift in their block had broken down with him in it. The smell of urine in that small metal box was enough to put off anyone going into it, let alone being trapped in there for three hours while maintenance struggled to wind the thing down to the next floor — it still gave him nightmares.

This felt the same. His fingers swept the inside of the

pod looking for something with a timeline, but there was nothing — there was no kind of chronology in here at all.

He was in the maelstrom.

He concentrated on his breathing, slowing it down the way he used to practice with his mum when she was in pain; counting between breaths to focus his mind on something other than the inside of the tube. As his mind calmed, Josh tried to remember what had happened after he collapsed the timelines of the two fire Djinn, but the last thing he could remember was seeing Dalton.

Josh couldn't quite recall how, but there was no mistaking the arrogant twat's face as it leered down at him just before the world went dark.

At least Caitlin was safe. He was sure of that.

95

FOUNDER WAKES UP

[Citadel, Maelstrom.]

Lord Dee was pale and drawn, his eyes constantly flickering under the paper-thin lids, and every so often he would moan softly. Rufius sat beside him, who wasn't a patient man, and remaining quiet and still was his least favourite activity.

'Will he survive?' he asked Alixia.

She grimaced. 'I don't know.'

'We should convene the emergency council,' Rufius muttered to himself.

'Grandmaster Derado has already initiated it.'

Rufius nodded. 'Always had a lot of time for Derado. He was a good man in my time.'

'As he is here. It's strange to think you have known the founder longer than all of us. I still have trouble coming to terms with the fact you were part our lives in another time.'

Rufius tapped his temple. 'It feels more like three life-times in here.'

'Will you take command? In his absence?' she asked, nodding towards the founder.

He shook his head. 'No, I'm not a leader. Spent too long in the wild. You, on the other hand, would make a fine candidate.'

She smiled graciously. 'I have to admit. It's crossed my mind.'

'The Copernicans may be a little hard to convince.'

'As will the Scriptorians,' she added with a knowing look.

'Yes, they're truly trapped in the past. I don't think they've ever raised a woman above the rank of a senior librarian.'

'Well, if nothing else, this situation shows us we need to change — there are many things we can learn from the twenty-first century.'

'Indeed. Powered flight being one of them.'

'Pardon?'

He waved a hand. 'Never mind. How is Caitlin?'

'Recovering. Lyra has helped her overcome the initial trauma, and the burns are healing rapidly, but I fear the loss of Joshua will take longer to repair.'

'They're saying it was Dalton Eckhart.'

'Or some version of him. Derado believes he was working with the Djinn, controlling them somehow. The breach was sealed immediately after he took Joshua back into it.'

'Which crisis does this come under? Six?'

'Tenth I believe,' Alixia said, looking thoughtfully at the founder. 'But not as predicted.'

Rufius stroked his beard. 'Something I've grown used to over the years. We set too much store in the work of the Copernicans. If there is one thing I have come to rely on it is the ability for the universe to change the rules. That is the nature of chaos after all.'

The founder groaned once more.

Alixia frowned and put her hand tenderly against the founder's cheek. 'If there is one thing I have come to rely on, it's the unshakeable courage and optimism of this man.'

'There isn't another like him,' Rufius said with a sigh.

'What if there was?' the founder whispered in a dry, rasping voice.

'Lord?' Alixia said, gripping his hand.

The founder opened his eyes and smiled. 'My dear Alixia. You worry too much.' He tried to sit up and failed. Alixia poured him a glass of water while Rufius rearranged the pillows and helped him to prop himself up.

'I take it we managed to contain them?' he asked weakly.

Alixia nodded. 'At a terrible cost.'

'And the Paradox — what happened to Joshua?'

Rufius put his hand on the founder's shoulder. 'Gone — taken by Dalton, or whatever he has become.'

'But the others? They are safe?'

'The Dreadnoughts took heavy casualties, but most of the Londoners were safely evacuated. The bridge held until the Duke of York arrived.'

'Good,' the founder said, with a weak smile.

'But Joshua is lost,' Rufius said morosely.

'No. The Paradox is exactly where he's supposed to be.'

Alixia looked surprised. 'You knew this was going to happen?'

The founder took another sip of water and coughed, a rattling hollow cough that wracked his body until it passed. Alixia and Rufius exchanged a look of concern.

'Shall I call Doctor Crooke?'

'No,' the founder said, holding up a hand. 'It will pass. I inhaled too much smoke.'

They waited while his breathing returned to normal.

'I need you to do something for me,' he said, turning to Rufius.

'Anything.'

'Take me to the Djinn.'

'And how exactly are we going to do that?'

96

PLAN

They were all gathered on the bridge of the *Nautilus*.

Alixia, Methuselah, Lyra, Caitlin and her parents were all sat on the various old sofas as Rufius helped the founder to his feet. Da Recco had taken over the controls from Juliana, who had been teaching him how to pilot it over the last few weeks.

The old man stood in front of the viewing port as the fleeting moments of time sped past them. They'd left the continuum a few hours ago, and everyone was wondering what the hell they were going to do in the maelstrom — except Lyra, who was fascinated by the view and really couldn't care less about where they went next.

'My friends,' the founder began, 'there are some things that have always bothered me about the Eschaton Cascade. For years I have puzzled over whether the crises were inevitable or something that could in some way be avoided — I have been working on a number of strategies and all of them appeared to have failed.'

They all looked stunned; this was the first time they'd ever heard the founder confess to defeat.

'Which leaves us with the Nemesis.'

The founder took out a book from inside his long robes.

'I believe Joshua's timeline is an anathema to the Djinn. Its paradoxical nature causes them to experience accelerated time dilation, ageing them — in a similar way to Chief MacKenzie when he held the Infinity Engine.' The founder paused for a moment, the grief weighing heavily on him. 'But even this may not be enough to defeat the Nihil. This is the almanac of Dalton Eckhart, or rather its sympathetic twin. Rufius informs me that we can use it to locate him within the maelstrom — using his observatory.'

Rufius nodded.

'There's a high probability that he will be surrounded by the Djinn horde, so we should be prepared for battle.'

'Glad we had those cannons fitted,' said Caitlin's father, turning to Methuselah. 'It'll give us a chance to test them out.'

'This is going to be a stealth mission rather than a frontal assault,' interrupted the founder. 'Once we have a trace on Dalton it should lead us directly to their base. Assuming that we can reach him without too much resistance, we should be able to reach master Jones.'

'And how strong do you estimate the resistance to be?' asked Caitlin's mother.

'I really have no clue.'

97

DARK WATER

A faint light appeared from somewhere far off in the distance, and like the dawn breaking over the ocean, the rays glistened over a dark rippling surface.

Josh blinked, letting his eyes adjust to the brightness and realising he was surrounded by sea.

The surface of the dark waters was calm, like the pond in Caitlin's moon garden, and he wondered what lay beneath.

Then something nudged the shell of his pod, rocking it slightly back and forth like a boat.

He turned his head, trying to see what it was, but the limited view through the glass door only showed him a sliver of the sea.

A few metres out he saw the surface distort slightly. In the dim twilight, he couldn't be sure if it was a wave or the back of some sea creature diving below the water line.

Josh's breathing quickened as he counted the seconds before it happened again. This time he was sure he heard the grating of claws or teeth along the outer shell. Then the pod began to sink into the luminous green depths.

In the murky waters, Josh could see the hulking forms of giant squid-like creatures as they turned sinuously beneath his feet. Massive monsters rose up from the depths, their tentacles reaching out towards him but failing to connect. It was as if he was protected by some kind of force field, as nothing attempted to take him.

Slowly the pod descended into the deep, the light dimming as it moved further from the surface. The creatures kept their distance but seemed to gain their own internal illumination as he sank.

Internal lights flickered into life inside the pod, and silent fans began to blow cool air over his face. Josh realised he was being pulled down towards the ocean floor.

It was growing colder, and the pressure in his ears was increasing, and still, the pod sank further into the abyss.

98

OBSERVATORY

Caitlin thought Rufius seemed a little distracted when they entered the observatory. He wandered around the large circular wall, studying the notes that had been pinned there as if they were made by someone else — as if he were reading them for the first time.

From what Josh had told her, the old man had been stuck here in a time loop that reset every twenty hours, wiping everything he learned during that time. The notes were the only way for him to keep track of what he'd discovered and by the look of the thousands of pages, there had apparently been many, many loops.

The others were busy marvelling at his research, all except Da Recco and her mother who'd stayed on the ship to make some 'adjustments,' while her father had abandoned them the moment he saw the giant brass telescope.

Methuselah and Lyra were like wide-eyed tourists wandering around with their mouths agape, staring at the sketches of the Djinn and debating whether one was more hideous than the last.

Alixia was helping the founder into the worn armchair

that sat beneath the eyepiece of the telescope. He seemed so frail now, which wasn't surprising considering what he had been through. When Caitlin was younger, she'd always thought that he was the nearest thing to an immortal, and everyone spoke about him as if he would live forever. The idea that he too would die seemed unthinkable, but then her parents disappeared, and everything changed.

Rufius took a monocle out of his jacket, cleaning it before handing it to the founder, who placed it in one eye.

Alixia handed Dalton's almanac to Rufius who opened a door in the side of the giant barrel of the telescope and carefully placed it inside. He pulled a lever and motioned to Alixia to step back. There were a series of winding sounds, as gears and flywheels began to engage beneath the platform they were standing on. The domed metal roof slid away above their heads to expose the swirling chaos outside. The founder put his eye to the lens and was gently spun around on the platform as the tracking mechanisms kicked in.

'We tried to use this to find you,' Rufius said to Caitlin as she came to join them. 'When you were lost.'

Caitlin shuddered at the memory of the Djinn in the ziggurat, the terrible despair she'd felt when they touched her, and tried not to think about what Josh might be going through right now.

'We will find him,' Rufius assured her. 'My Huygens can find a needle in a thousand haystacks.'

Multiply that by a million, thought Caitlin, *and you might be closer to the truth.*

[ERD Basecamp, Maelstrom]

Da Recco stood watch at one end of what was left of Dalton's camp while Alixia, Caitlin and Rufius searched the bodies. The *Nautilus* was hovering ten metres above them, its cannons poised to fire at the first signs of trouble.

Their base camp had been laid out in an unusual way; they observed when they came into land. Someone had created a stable perimeter that should have protected them from most storm-kin but had apparently failed.

Dalton's team were scattered across the ground like discarded dolls, their bodies broken and their unused weapons tossed aside as if they were toys. Da Recco had never seen mutilation like this, even when his men had been attacked by sharks.

Lyra had refused to come off the ship, locking herself in her cabin and complaining about how there were too many ghosts through the door. Methuselah had stayed behind to calm her down.

It was Da Recco's first real experience of the maelstrom, and he was having trouble dealing with the spectacle that was playing out beyond the *Nautilus'* stabilisation field. The landscape reformed continuously as temporal fragments collided, like a tsunami, events and moments crashing into each other, creating a tapestry of random scenes. World war battlefields merged into ancient Babylonian cities leaving soldiers scaling ziggurats and cutting down spear-wielding warriors with machine guns.

'Well he was definitely here,' said Caitlin, picking up Dalton's sword and his almanac.

'I'm afraid that means we've reached a dead end,' said Rufius gravely.

The founder was examining something in the sand. 'Not

necessarily.' He took out a glass vial and dipped it into a dark stain in the sand.

'What is it?' Caitlin asked.

'Aetherium,' he said, holding it up to show her. 'The lifeblood of the Nihil.'

99

___

FATHER

Josh was half-submerged in water when he awoke. He was lying on his side on the floor, his face only just above the surface. There was a searing pain behind his eyes that was far worse than any hangover he could ever remember, but at least he was alive.

'Joshua Jones,' said a voice that sounded strangely familiar. 'Did you enjoy my pets?'

Josh lifted his head from the pool and looked up.

It was Dalton.

Or something that had once been him.

His body was massive and heavily armoured, the skin now plated, like the shell of a beetle, a gleaming black carapace. His face still wore the usual arrogant expression that Josh always wanted to punch.

But there was something different about his eyes; they were dark blue, like the professor's, and Josh realised this wasn't Dalton — he was possessed.

Dalton-jinn lifted Josh from the floor with one hand, holding him like a rag doll up to his face. The talon-like fingers of his hand were rough against Josh's neck, and he struggled to breathe as the grip tightened.

'Do you like my new body,' he rasped into Josh's face. 'I think it once belonged to a god.'

'What are you?' Josh gasped.

'Nihil,' replied Dalton-jinn, speaking the word in a hundred different voices at once.

Josh could feel the power running through Dalton's veins, the familiar patterns of Djinn timelines flowing below the fingers that gripped him, and he let his mind explore them.

But they were different from the others, and Josh couldn't affect them in the way that he could the Djinn; something was protecting his chronology — the talisman he still wore on his finger.

'Nice try, Nemesis,' hissed Dalton, his tongue flickering between sharpened teeth. 'Your powers have no effect on me,' he added, throwing him across the chamber.

Josh hit the wet floor and skidded across it until he connected with a wall.

Dalton rolled his head on his enormous shoulders, like a pro-wrestler getting ready for the final blow. *He's enormous*, thought Josh, pumped up like one of those guys who used too many steroids.

He pulled himself upright, his ribs aching from where he'd collided with the wall, and his throat was swollen. Ignoring the pain, he looked around for some kind of weapon.

They were in a building under the sea. The walls were transparent, and he could see the illuminated bodies of the Djinn swimming blindly around outside. It was a grand hall in an underwater castle, one that stretched out across the seabed. As Dalton walked away, a staircase rose out of the

ANDREW HASTIE

dark water in front of him, and he climbed towards an
ornate obsidian throne that formed at the top.

'You're in my domain now. The infinite worlds of chaos
are mine to command!'

He waved an arm, and two fierce-looking Djinn began to
form out of a pool in front of Josh.

Shit, thought Josh, getting to his feet and trying to
remember the fighting stance Vedris had taught him.

'To think all those years I wasted waiting for you,
wondering how the Nemesis would deliver us, and here you
are, a weak, pathetic human with nothing more than a
single lifetime and no idea of the scale, the majesty, of eternity. I have seen it all — I have seen your beginning and
your end.'

Josh needed to buy some time; he had to keep Dalton
talking. The creatures were shaping up to be some of the
meanest looking demons he'd ever seen, and he knew that
he wouldn't be able to handle both of them at once.

'You've seen my beginning?'

'The whole of your measly life,' Dalton-jinn sneered, his
mouth stretching wider than should've been possible.

'So you know who my father is?'

There was a moment of silence between them, and Josh
wondered if the question had thrown Dalton off his guard.
Caitlin said that Dalton had issues with his own father and
wondered if there was still some part of him that resented
the man.

'I know who your father was,' he whispered, his voice
changing to the deeper, more resinous tone of the Nihil.
'This ridiculous attempt he made to defeat us — The Nihil
have spent an eternity hunting him down, and he sends you
to defeat us!'

Dalton saw the look of confusion on Josh's face and

laughed. 'You have no idea what you are meant to be, do you?'

The first of the two creatures was nearly complete, and Josh couldn't take his eyes off the long spikes that were growing out of its skull.

'I've had no idea my whole life,' he said with a shrug. 'Hasn't seemed to have stopped me so far.'

Josh dropped low as the first creature swung his scythe-like arm at him. The blade passed a few millimetres above his head and unbalanced the beast. Josh took advantage, driving his foot into its side and onto the body of the second beast, impaling itself on an impressive set of chest spikes.

Dalton-jinn laughed as the second creature seemed to walk through the first as though it were still made of water. The beast spread its arms wide to reveal that the chest spikes were a group of secondary limbs all holding dark blades.

'I had toyed with the idea of killing you myself, but this is so much more fun.'

Josh stepped back too slowly as the sharpened arms of the second Djinn swept across his chest. One caught him across the abdomen, and he felt the searing pain as it cut into his skin.

'A strike!' said Dalton like a fencing tutor.

Josh spun around and struck the second Djinn's spindly legs, which were by far its weakest point. He felt something snap as he connected. The creature was too top heavy to support its own weight on one leg and folded.

'Bad design,' noted Dalton from his throne. 'The next will be better.'

As he spoke, Dalton snapped his fingers, and six more creatures began to mould themselves out of the dark liquid.

Josh's belly was on fire, and he looked down to see blood spreading out across his tunic. He was still wearing the underclothes of the fire armour, where a large red stain was blossoming across the lower half.

'Wouldn't you like to know?' Dalton sneered. 'Before you die, wouldn't you like to know about your father?'

Josh felt light-headed, the pain and the loss of blood making it difficult to stay focused. He needed to find a way out of this, but he seemed to be running out of options — other than talking.

'Who was he?'

'You still haven't guessed? Who would be so obsessed with maintaining the continuum that he would sacrifice his own son to protect it.'

Then Josh realised the only man it could be.

It was a strange feeling, not a surprise, but more as if he'd been dreaming and someone had woken him up unexpectedly.

'The Founder.'

Josh thought of the time he'd shown him how to heal the colonel's timeline, the connection they'd shared with the Infinity Engine. They were compatible, like one being working together, harnessing the power of the device.

'Thank you,' said Josh, feeling his strength returning. The memory of that shared moment was like a key, and he let his mind reconnect with the engine and felt the lines of power flood into him.

100

AETHERIUM

The Djinn home-world looked like a planet, a giant black sphere that hung in the void, its outline only defined by the iridescent halo of spectral gas that surrounded it.

'What's it made of?' asked Caitlin, watching their approach from the viewport.

'Aetherium,' muttered the founder. 'Dark energy.'

'They're using dark energy?'

'They're made of it.'

'Do you think Josh is still alive in there?'

The founder nodded. 'I think the Nihil are fascinated by him. He's in a state of quantum superposition, he should not exist, but he does. They won't have met anything like him before.'

'And he can't kill them?'

'Dalton, or whatever he has become, has a talisman. He may be using it to protect himself from the temporal effects. Come, sit by me. I think it's time I told you about the Nihil.'

. . .

The founder drew a deep, solemn breath and closed his eyes.

'When I was much younger, I was an ambitious and impetuous fool, filled with visions of my own achievements and unwilling to listen to those who knew better about the dangers of quantum forces.'

Caitlin looked confused. 'When was this?'

He smiled. 'This was no history that you would recognise, but to tell you more would burden you with a secret I'm not sure you're ready to hear.'

'That there's more than one continuum?'

The founder looked genuinely surprised. 'You never cease to impress me. How may I ask, did you discover this?'

She shrugged. 'When you've been in the maelstrom you realise that there's way more to the universe than our tiny, insignificant lives. It changes your perspective.'

The founder looked out through the glass. 'I have always imagined that the maelstrom was full of wonders: lost times, disconnected pasts.'

'And paths into alternate timelines.'

He nodded. 'Have you ever wondered where the Djinn come from?'

'I've seen ghosts in here, spectres of other lives. I guessed they were remnants of older timelines.'

'Or dead ones.'

She looked puzzled. 'Can a timeline truly die?'

He sighed. 'I am the living proof that it can. My own continuum was destroyed; it was only my research that saved me — although you could say that it ultimately caused the catastrophe in the first place.'

'How?'

'The Nihil is a non-linear species that is drawn to dark energy. Our scientists detected their presence during the early tests of the Infinity Engine. At first, they registered as nothing more than anomalies in their data, unexplained spikes in the monitoring. So we ignored them, as we were too focused on the limitless source of power I had discovered.'

'Infinite power?'

'Yes. Like every other civilisation, we needed energy; ours was running out — my world had consumed every natural resource, and our population growth was out of control. There were few options left, and tension between nations was beginning to escalate. Something had to be done to avoid all-out war. My work with dark energy had been an obscure branch of astrophysics until I discovered a way to harness the energy. It was hailed as the single most important discovery in our history.'

'And the Nihil?'

His eyes were glistening, and she could see tears were gathering in the corners.

'The Nihil feed on dark energy. When my generators tapped into the maelstrom, they became aware of our existence, like a beacon. I painted a target on our timeline, and they swept through it like an invading army. They took everything, a billion souls — including my wife and family.'

'Yet you managed to survive.'

'I did. I used the only escape route — I walked into the breach they created and found my way to your world.'

Caitlin went to the window. 'And the Nihil are down there?'

The founder came to join her. 'I have spent so long trying to hide your timeline from them — it was why I created the Order, to ensure that this reality never made the same mistakes that took my own, but it seems that is unavoidable now. We can do nothing but face our demons and hope that the Paradox can save us.'

Caitlin took his hand. 'I'm not sure Josh is ready for this.'

'He has to be. He's our last hope.'

She turned towards him. 'You knew he was coming?'

He took out the small box that contained the Infinity Engine from his robes and placed it on the low table. 'I realise now that I am the reason he exists.'

101

HOME-WORLD

The surface of the Djinn home-world appeared to be a featureless dark sea as they approached it. Once it filled the viewport it was like looking into night, nothing but the reflection of their ship to show there was anything there at all.

The crew of the Nautilus gathered at the window, each one of them holding their breath.

Strange structures rose as they neared the surface, formed entirely from the dark sea they manifested themselves like the ghosts of ancient castles, their walls covered in carvings of terrifying monsters.

'Is it water?' Thomas wondered aloud.

'No,' the founder answered, 'dark energy, in a concentrated, liquid state. The Djinn dwell beneath in their native forms.'

'And where is Dalton?'

'Somewhere below.'

'Do we have a bearing?' asked Caitlin's mother, staring at the founder.

'Where is he, Lyra?' Caitlin whispered to her sister, who

was sitting holding the vial of aetherium while in a trance. Her eyes were glazed over, and her lips moved silently, but she made no sign that she'd heard her.

Suddenly the Infinity Engine began to glow.

'There he is!' said the founder, jumping up out of his seat.

He opened the box and held it up for them all to see.

'He's initiated a remote connection.'

'Prepare to jump,' commanded Juliana. 'We need to get below this.'

102

BATTLE

Josh took out the six Djinn before they'd fully formed, reducing them to dust with a touch.

He could feel the proximity of the Infinity Engine — it was nearby and so were his friends — and with that the hope he might actually survive.

Dalton-jinn screamed when Josh destroyed his latest creations. Like a battle cry, the sound echoed down the hall, shattering every window and letting in the ocean.

As the water flooded through the tall arches, it transformed. Thousands of Djinn were bursting out of the torrents, and like newly born calves they scattered across the floor, their skin hardening into armour as they climbed to their feet.

The Nihil cursed him in a hundred different tongues as they fell at Josh's feet, none of them able to reach him.

Soon there was nothing left of the building, and the sea was released from whatever gravity Dalton had imposed on it. Their world came apart and reformed.

Josh was surrounded by a sphere of malevolence, circling him like the eye of a hurricane of monsters, biding their time — trying to find a way to hurt him. But he didn't care. He felt like a god — like superman.

Suddenly, there was a massive burst of energy that blasted a hole through a hundred Djinn, and the *Nautilus* swept through it, cannons blazing.

Josh saw the familiar faces of his friends in the viewport. The colonel, Caitlin and her family — all staring out in wonder at him, like children at a toy shop window.

He could feel the Infinity Engine within the ship and summoned it. In an instant, the glowing orb was in his hands, a beacon of light in the dark storm. The Nihil's shrill cries at the sight of it stirred the Djinn into a frenzy.

Josh ignored them, focusing on the multiple timelines that were weaving out from this moment; he could see so many ways this could end, but none of them were good. There were too many of them, and even with the *Nautilus*, it was unlikely they could take out more than ten percent before they would be overwhelmed. He needed to protect them, and as he thought about how, the fields around the orb expanded to encompass the ship.

The Djinn couldn't resist the pull of the Infinity Engine's energy, and like moths to a flame, they threw themselves against its shielding, burning up as they collided with it.

With the barrier holding, Josh turned to see that some of his friends had left the safety of the ship and were coming to join him.

The colonel took his place beside Josh, the book of deadly names in his hands. Caitlin and Lyra both had talismans, while the others manned the cannons on the ship. They looked hopelessly outnumbered compared to the Nihil's horde, but Josh was really glad to see them.

'You should leave,' he told the colonel.

'And miss the big finish? I don't think so,' the old man

said with a grin. 'Anyway, I know how to take out at least seventy of them,' he added, opening the book.

'Hey,' said Caitlin. 'Why am I always the one getting you out of the shit?'

'Guess it's just your destiny,' he said and shrugged.

'Don't use that word!' she said, vaporising a Pentachion with a spectral burst from her talisman.

The Nihil regained control of their forces, pulling them away from the shield. Josh couldn't make out how they communicated, but like a million swarming bees they clustered around their commanders. He could see Dalton-jinn amongst the horde, reshaping his creatures, breaking them down and creating terrible new beasts from their parts. They merged and grew into grotesque giants, like monstrous siege weapons, and he fashioned a new army and sent them against the wall.

The remade were stronger, smarter than the foot soldiers, and tested the shield, finding how to weaken it, coordinating their attacks. Everyone turned their weapons on the new threat, and for a few minutes they kept them at bay, but it was a never-ending onslaught. Dalton had an endless supply of new and more effective weapons, and Josh knew they were trapped here.

The Nihil could sense it too, and broke away, taking half of the swarm with them and heading towards the bright timeline of the continuum.

'They're going for the timeline,' he shouted to his friends. 'You have to go and warn the Order!'

'Not a chance,' said the colonel as he summoned a ballistic missile and sent it into the belly of a tentacle-headed leviathan.

'We can't just leave you,' said Caitlin, her talisman's spectral guardians floating around her.

'You have to. I can hold them, but you have to warn Derado that the Nihil are coming.'

She took out a tachyon and snapped it onto his wrist. 'Don't do anything stupid — I'm not going to be here to save your arse — no matter how cute it is.'

He smiled and kissed her. 'You know me — I'm a born survivor.'

'Just try not to die,' she said, kissing him back.

Caitlin reluctantly let go and headed towards the *Nautilus*, signalling the others to join her as she went.

'Sure you can handle this?' said the colonel.

'It's what I was born to do. It's my dest—'

'Don't say it!' interrupted the old man with a wry smile. 'I taught you better than that!'

The founder appeared beside Josh. 'I'll stay with him.'

The colonel saluted the two of them and followed Caitlin.

Josh turned to the founder. 'I can do this, but I can't be sure it won't destroy you.'

The founder smiled, taking out his Anunnaki. 'I think I've lived long enough.'

103

LEADERSHIP

G randmaster Derado leaned heavily on a stick as he stood in the centre of the Star Chamber, surrounded by the entire membership. He'd refused to let them dress the burns on his face; instead, he bore them as a reminder to all those that questioned his abilities, and it was working. Ten thousand men and women from every guild sat in silence waiting for him to speak, humbled by the bravery of his men during the fire.

Rufius and Alixia stood beside him, their news not unexpected, but still it weighed heavy on him. He was a practical man; if they were going to survive this, every one of them would need to understand the danger and be prepared for what came next.

He cleared his throat and tapped the cane on the floor. 'Our Order was founded for one purpose, to protect the future. We have dedicated our lives to maintaining the continuum, guiding it in the best possible direction for the survival of humanity — and we have failed.'

Derado stumbled, and Rufius caught him before he fell.

A murmur swept around the audience, and Alixia stepped forward, raising her hand to silence them.

'We have failed because we became too closed in our ways. We've become blinded by our own beliefs and traditions. The future is not something that can be codified and calculated — though we have tried very hard to control it.' She looked directly at what was left of the Copernicans. 'We still can only make an educated guess at what might happen a minute from now. Despite our best efforts to predict it, we have done nothing to avert the danger that lies beyond our borders.'

She turned and pointed at Rufius who was helping Derado to a chair. 'We have just returned from the maelstrom where the Djinn are amassing a vast army, and there's no doubt now that the twelfth crisis is upon us; we must prepare for the next assault. If we fail now — there will be no tomorrow!'

The Draconians and the Antiquarians were on their feet, clapping and cheering, but the Copernicans and the Scriptorians were shaking their heads and talking amongst themselves.

Something was wrong. Alixia turned to Rufius, who shrugged. She looked around the auditorium, thinking about the war that was to come.

There were still divisions within the order. If they couldn't heal the rift, there was no chance of surviving this. So many of them were ready to sacrifice their lives defending a world that didn't even know they existed, but without a unified Order, it would be for nothing. They had some terrible choices to make, but all of the founder's plans had failed, and they were all that was left.

104

X9009

[Kverkfjöll volcano, Iceland. Date: 12.418]

They were standing in the middle of Fermi's facility, a hundred different versions of Lenin sealed into grime-stained pods on every wall.

'How?' asked Josh. The last thing he could remember was the Infinity Engine shield failing and a swarm of a thousand Djinn pouring in.

'I designed the engine to help me escape,' the founder said, holding up the weakly glowing sphere. 'All I needed was your timeline to get me here.' He sat down slowly, holding his side.

'You're hurt?'

The founder nodded, opening his robe to show a deep wound from a Djinn strike. 'Aetherium.'

'I can fix that,' Josh said, reaching for the orb.

The founder shook his head. 'We're close to the source of the twelfth crisis. This is the beginning of the Eschaton Cascade. You and Caitlin will arrive here soon, and I've one last mission that must be completed.'

He pointed to a recessed unit in the wall. 'I believe that will do.'

It was some kind of upright med-bay, the recess was moulded into the shape of a body and the words 'TRANSFER STATION 5' stencilled above the console next to it.

Josh helped the founder into the unit and watched as the various probes and needles deployed themselves onto his head.

'Transfer commencing,' intoned a metallic voice from within the booth.

The founder's body stiffened while the readouts changed on the displays. The colour drained from his face, his mouth gaping open as his eyes rolled up into their sockets leaving nothing but the whites — if it wasn't for the heart monitor Josh would have said he just watched him die.

'Complete,' reported the system.

A pod bay opened on the far side of the room and one of the Lenins came to life and extracted itself from the compartment. He was naked except for the number tattooed on his neck.

'X9009'

'I don't have much time to explain,' said the Lenin. 'You will have to trust me.'

He pulled out a knife-like injector and drove it into the founder's chest, an indicator on the side flickering to life as his DNA was harvested.

Josh grabbed his arm. 'Dalton told me it was you.'

'I have to go!' Lenin said, pulling his arm away. 'There will be time for explanations when I return.'

With that the Lenin turned and went into the outer

chamber, Josh following him as Lenin climbed into a time
suit and disappeared through one of the gateways.

105

XII

They had spread sentries over twelve thousand years of history.

Sim and his team had estimated the Nihil would most likely attack the more densely populated part of time, eras with high levels of technology, but Alixia wasn't taking any chances. She posted a member of the Order in every year back to the Ice Age. They would act as sentinels, watching the continuum for signs of an attack.

Derado's remaining troops were garrisoned at strategic points along the continuum, ready to jump at the first sign of trouble.

The Copernicans and the Scriptorians were proposing a truce; they wanted to reach out to Dalton and try and find a peaceful resolution. Derado was said to be fuming, demanding the immediate resignation of all the senior members of those guilds.

Sim had managed to negotiate the use of the Copernican holospheric projection room — so that the entire continuum could be viewed at once. His team sat staring at the fine lines that traced across its domed ceiling, wondering where the next attack would be — Sim could feel the tension growing as the hours passed.

His Eschaton map was laid out on the table, different coloured lines connecting the various crises. He had his own theory, one that he hadn't discussed with anyone else. There wasn't one cascade, but two separate narratives. The first, which he'd marked in blue, was the "Paradox/Nemesis collection", those crises that distinctly involved Josh in some way. This included the first three: Prophecy, Division and Insurgency, and then the fifth, seventh and tenth. The second thread was something Sim referred to as "Anachronisms", which incorporated the others, and all involved the intervention of an external agent.

From what he could see now, the Anachronist was the key to it all; whoever was interfering in the past was responsible for the actual cascade and allowing the Djinn to break through the fabric of time.

Astor walked in with a tray of cups, a teapot and a huge biscuit tin. Sim had come to rely on his unending supply of optimism, especially when some others were having trouble hiding their anxiety. 'Anything yet?'

Sim shook his head.

'Maybe they won't break through,' he said, putting the tray down.

'It won't matter if the timeline collapses,' said another.

'Fiver says they're going to come in from the deep past,' wagered Norman.

'No,' said Sim. 'I think they'll stay just ahead of the cascade, use it to cross the frontier.'

'You're seriously suggesting they're going to surf in on a time wave?'

'Time quake more like,' said Norman, taking a biscuit and shoving the whole thing into his mouth.

'A Time-nami,' said Astor, suppressing a chuckle.

Then they were all laughing, relieving the stress, and helping themselves to tea and grabbing handfuls of biscuits.

'Hey! They have to last all night!' said Astor, grabbing the tin back.

The others shrugged and went back to their stations. It was going to be a long night, and they would need all the caffeine and sugar they could get.

106

LENIN

All that was left of the founder was the physical shell.
Josh was aching to get back to the war, but there
was no way he could leave him unprotected.

He studied the face of his father, noting the line of his
jaw and the shape of his nose — it was strange to finally
look at the person who had made him — quite literally.
He'd no idea how the DNA device worked, nor did he really
care. Just to know that it was this man was enough. Finally,
that question had been answered, and he realised how
much it had mattered after all.

Although right now he wasn't pulling the best of faces.
His freakish white eyes were beginning to disturb Josh, and
turning away he noticed a flickering strip of light from a
door to his right. He went over to it and looked through the
grimy porthole.

Inside the body of Lenin was floating in a large glass
tank. Like some kind of science experiment, he was a
wizened, desiccated version of the man that Josh had once
known.

The signage on the door read 'EXSPEC X0001', and Josh realised that it must be the original Lenin.

Taking one last look at his father, Josh opened the door and went in.

The chamber smelled awful, a pungent mixture of chemical preservatives and shit — somehow they were keeping him alive.

He walked around the glass until he could see Lenin's face. He was sleeping like a baby, his arms and legs folded into a foetal position with tubes and wires plumbed into hundreds of different points on his body.

As he stared at the grey-haired old specimen, Lenin's eyes snapped open, and Josh jumped back.

There passed a few seconds when neither knew what to do next. It took Lenin a moment to recognise Josh and when he did the despair in his expression made Josh look away.

Lenin was too weak to communicate with anything more than his eyes, but that was all Josh needed; he knew what he was asking for — to end it. He looked around the room for anything that could smash the glass or a way to shut off the power, but everything was broken, rusted shut or dead.

Lenin blinked, and his pupils flicked to the clones that were sealed into the pods outside.

'You want to get out of here?' Josh asked, realising what Lenin was saying.

Lenin blinked once.

Josh looked at the controls; they were frozen, the blank display having lost whatever power it used to have. The whole thing was a lump of dead glass and plastic, the systems that were keeping Lenin alive were obviously running on automatic.

Josh remembered the way they'd moved back three hundred years before, how new and shiny everything had been then. He took one more look through the porthole at the catatonic founder and knew what he had to do.

Bookmarking the temporal location on his tachyon, he opened the timeline of the control desk. Weaving through the timeline, he saw how Lenin had been left to rot in this tank — nothing more than a lab rat for over four hundred years.

Josh went back three hundred, just like before, and the room around him was bright and shiny once more — Lenin looked a little less decrepit, but not much.

The control panel lit up with symbols beneath his fingers, but he had no idea what they all meant. It took several attempts before he managed to find the transfer program.

'You sure you want to do this?' he asked, his finger hovering above the button marked 'initiate'.

Lenin looked up, his eyes pleading for Josh to do it, and then, as if the stress was too much, his whole body began to shake. Josh knew that if it'd been the other way around Lenin would probably have just shot him. There were so many times when he'd wished Lenin were dead, imagining a life not corrupted by knowing him, wondering what it would have been like if they'd never met. He looked at things differently now. Lenin was the least most important thing in his life now. It was strange how something so huge could become so insignificant — it was like he finally had taken control of his life, or at least part of it, the bit that didn't involve trying to save the universe.

As he watched Lenin's seizure subside, he realised how long it was since they'd last seen each other.

Josh was eighteen now.

'Happy Birthday,' he said, tapping the glowing button.

Lenin flexed his fingers, studying the way they moved as if discovering them for the first time. His new body wasn't much older than when Josh saw him last — the day he'd let Gossy die. That had been the worst choice he'd ever had to make, and yet the alternatives would have been far worse. Josh had seen the consequences of every possible scenario and none of them ended well. No one understood what it was like to witness the many different ways someone might die; it was like being cursed — choosing the "least worst" option didn't feel the same as doing the right thing.

The right thing would have been to let Lenin die, to just switch off the machine and walk away, but there was part of Josh that couldn't do that to him. No matter how badly Lenin had treated him, he wouldn't let it end like that.

Lenin stepped out of the pod, his naked body rippling with muscle.

Josh smiled. This was a major upgrade for Lenin, who'd never looked as fit in his life — it was a vision of what could have been if he'd stayed off the drugs.

Lenin didn't speak, but just nodded his thanks and walked out the door. Josh knew he had a score to settle with Fermi, and perhaps that was justified — then he remembered the number on the neck of the Lenin that had saved him from the operation.

As Josh opened the tachyon to jump back to the founder, he realised that, by releasing Lenin, he might have just saved himself.

107

THE WAVE

[Cobham, Surrey. Date: 12.018]

M ichael Bates sat in the supermarket car park trying not to think about how he was going to tell his wife he'd lost his job.

This was his third in two years, and there was little chance he was going to get another one any time soon — there were only so many ways you could take 'you're not suitable', or 'we think you're overqualified'. Redundancy was a horrible word, and no amount of sugar-coating was going to pay the rent.

He pulled out his mobile phone and tapped in her number.

She had cried when they had to sell the house, and the kids changed schools after they couldn't pay the fees. Everyone blamed him for ruining their lives.

And now he was going to do it again.

The call failed.

He looked down at the screen; he'd run out of credit — it was the story of his life.

Outside people were getting out of their cars and staring up into the sky. Michael looked through the windscreen and forgot all about the phone and the job.

High above the supermarket signage, an army of hideous looking demons was riding giant flying serpents while behind them a tidal wave of futuristic cities was falling out of the sky.

108

FATHER

The founder's breathing was weak and shallow when his consciousness returned to his body. The Lenin he used was still in the timesuit, standing motionless in the centre of the chamber, his expressionless face bruised and battered from the fight in Josh's mother's bedroom.

'You nearly ruined my plan,' said the founder with a weak smile.

'Why?' was all Josh could manage, staring at the trickle of blood that seeped from the side of the old man's mouth.

'Because,' he began in a hoarse whisper, 'you're the only way to defeat the Nihil.'

Josh frowned. 'Except I don't know how!'

The founder coughed violently, and Josh could hear the blood bubbling in his lungs.

'You live between two worlds: the past and the future — you're a duality — the only one who can survive and live to tell the tale.'

'And you created me with that?' asked Josh, pointing at the DNA device in the Lenin's hand.

'It will be the only way to defeat them.'

'How? I don't know what to do.'

'My son,' he said tenderly, 'I have so much to tell you, but little time to do it.'

Josh reached up and put his hand against his father's face. 'Show me.'

The founder's timeline opened to him, and Josh found himself in a vast network of intersecting timelines, like being inside the Infinity Engine once more, a four-dimensional map of all his chronologies.

WHO ARE YOU?

He could feel the weak presence of the old man's consciousness guiding him towards a cluster of time. It was thousands of years ago, and not within their continuum, but a strange and alien one with structures that looped and branched in ways Josh had never seen.

THIS IS MY ORIGIN intuited the founder. MY WORLD

Suddenly Josh was surrounded by a crowd of robed academics. Each one taking turns to shake him by the hand. He realised he was experiencing one of Dee's milestones. They were all congratulating him on something, speaking a language he couldn't understand at first, but as the engrams embedded their words began to make sense.

'Phenomenal work!' said one.

'Outstanding!' said another, clapping him on the shoulder.

Josh turned to see a blackboard filled with formulae, reminding him of Heisenberg's work in Germany.

TIME TRAVEL?

Josh asked.

QUANTUM DISTORTION.

The founder replied.

YOU CREATED A TIME MACHINE?
AND BROUGHT THE NIHIL.

Time accelerated as the founder's mind took him forward fifty years.

They were in some kind of council meeting; everyone was shouting at each other, pointing fingers at Josh and calling him names. The long table was covered in reports and papers he knew instinctively said the same thing: that their world was coming to an end. It was their own version of an Eschaton.

HOW DID YOU SURVIVE?
Josh asked.

The events shifted again, and suddenly he was standing in a laboratory, the equipment nothing like anything he'd ever seen. It looked more organic like it was alive, but somehow he knew what it was capable of. The connection between him and the founder was filling in the gaps, passing him the missing information. They were quantum state machines, each one 'grown' from designs of their own making.

He felt the information flow between them increase, the founder moving hundreds of memories into his mind, downloading everything he could into Josh, without explanation or understanding. He tried to keep up with the fire-hose of information, but it made his head ache. Whatever he was gifting him would have to come out in its own sweet time.

109

OGLETHORPE

'They've broken through in 12.018,' Astor said, marking the spot on the projector with a chinagraph pencil.

'Deploy the twelfth,' Sim instructed the two scribes, who hastily copied down the temporal coordinates into their almanacs, knowing that somewhere deep within the Draconian Headquarters a squadron of the Dreadnought elite would be scrambled.

Sim read the report as it came in from the field agent. It was a watchman by the name of Oglethorpe. He'd never met him, but Sim could tell from the shaky handwriting that he was scared. The details of the events were sketchy, but he mentioned there was a wave of debris flowing back through time with the Djinn as if objects were being dragged back from the future.

'Second attack vector coming in. This time it's from 7.800,' reported Astor.

They're coming at us from both ends, thought Sim, a *classic pincer movement*.

'Doctor Shika is reporting increased activity in her specimens. She's asking for assistance.'

'Tell her to evacuate the Xeno department and join the Augurs. Send a note to Grandmaster Derado that we're seeing signs of temporal backflow.'

110

NEVER ENOUGH

J osh felt the darkness approaching, a creeping void at the edges of his consciousness, and he quickly disconnected from his father's timeline.

There were tears in the old man's blue eyes.

'You can't go,' Josh whispered. 'I need more time.'

The founder took Josh's hand. 'You're ready. I've given you everything I know. The knowledge will present itself when you need it.'

'But I've spent so long wondering who you were.'

The old man smiled. 'You have so much of your life ahead of you, so don't waste it worrying about things that might have been. I have often wondered what it would've been like to have a child, to watch them grow. I would've been proud to call you my son.'

Josh thought about all those nights he'd spent in police custody and smiled at the idea of Lord Dee coming to bail him out. It would have been interesting to see how he would have dealt with the social workers.

The founder closed his eyes. 'Be true to yourself,

Joshua,' he whispered, and his breathing slowed until it stopped altogether.

Josh stood staring into the old man's face, still holding his hand. There were a thousand things he still wanted to say, a million questions unanswered, but there was no point now — he was gone.

'You would've been a great dad,' he said, tears welling in his eyes.

The Infinity Engine sat in its case on the floor. The moment Josh's hands came into contact with the case, a whole new set of memories opened in his mind. Instantly he knew all about the device, all of its functions, even how to make another one. The knowledge was there as his father had said, just waiting for him to unlock it.

He took the box and tried to lift the limp body of the founder out of the med-bay, but he couldn't hold both at the same time — and he couldn't leave either of them behind.

Lenin X9009 stood staring blankly out from his timesuit, and Josh realised he could use the powered system to carry the body.

He pulled the mindless clone out of the suit and climbed inside; it felt remarkably light to wear, nothing like the clunky suit of armour it appeared to be.

There were a series of sharp pin-pricks in the back of his neck and then the system came to life. Commands and data flooded his vision, and a calm female voice began to relate the pre-flight instructions — which Josh ignored entirely.

He scooped up his father's body with one hand and the Infinity Engine case with the other. There was no way to weave from inside the suit, so he used his eyes to select the appropriate icon on the head-up display.

'Temporal coordinates?' asked the system.

Josh had no idea where he was going.

He walked out onto the main deck and chose the first tunnel he came to. Whichever point in history it was wired into had to be better than staying here.

The portal powered up as he approached and Josh could feel the energy pulsing through the suit's shielding. It was nothing like the way the Order moved through time; he could feel the raw energy tearing a rift in the timestream, drawing power directly from the maelstrom.

Fermi had brought the Nihil to their timeline, just as the founder had done.

He watched the graphic displays on his visor as the fields stabilised; most of them meant nothing to him — except one.

In the right-hand corner a small icon was blinking — a pause symbol beneath a musical note.

'Play.'

A question mark appeared.

'The way you make me feel. Michael Jackson.'

The beat kicked in as he carried his father into the glowing disc of light.

111

UNABRIDGED

[London. Date: Present day]

There'd been no word from Josh in over twenty-four hours. Caitlin messaged Sim, and his curt reply just confirmed that there were multiple breaches being reported and no sign of a let-up — which meant he'd failed.

Her parents had taken the Nautilus and a crew of Dreadnoughts to help rescue a unit trapped in 7.700.

Caitlin had chosen to stay near the frontier. She'd spent the last seven years close to the present and went to the Chapter House with Alixia — it was the nearest thing to a home.

Alixia had intended to send her children with the others being evacuated to the Citadel, but they all refused. There was a glimmer of pride in her eyes when she reluctantly accepted their decision.

The house was unusually quiet when they entered through the back door. Lyra walked out of the study in her pyjamas, her hair a tangled mess, as if she'd just woken up.

'Hey. Where have you been?' she asked through a yawn.

Alixia hugged her tightly. 'Have you seen your father?'

'He's with Rufius, fiddling with the Parabolic Chamber. They're trying to reach the founder.'

Alixia combed her fingers through her daughter's hair and kissed her on the cheek. 'Put the kettle on dear, make Caitlin some tea.'

'Okay,' Lyra said, pulling a face at Caitlin as her mother rushed off. 'What's up with her?'

'Er. The world's going to end.'

Lyra tutted. 'You have to have a little more faith.'

Caitlin had insisted they go via the library so that she could have one last chance to say goodbye and pick up a book.

It was the original copy of the Eschaton Cascade, the one her uncle had presented at the Royal Society all those years ago. Not the abridged version that had been circulated by the Copernicans, but the handwritten journal that Marcus had left on the lectern when he had been laughed out of the auditorium.

It looked like the work of a madman; his notes were written at different times and out of sequence, the diagrams and temporal formulae scribbled in corners of dog-eared pages.

As she flicked through his work, it became clear there were more than twelve crises originally, that Marcus had considered hundreds of different events, visited thousands of different points in time, trying to rationalise the visions he had seen from the talisman.

And what she saw, even though he wasn't named, was Josh's journey — a random sequence of events that only made sense in retrospect.

She opened the last page, simply entitled 'The Eschaton', and began to read.

112

SOLOMON'S TOMB

[Jerusalem. Date: 9.070]

Josh laid the body of the founder inside the sarcophagi. It seemed a fitting place to leave him. As Dalton had once pointed out, the Egyptians really did know how to plan a funeral. The chamber was nearly complete now; every wall and column was covered in gold leaf and surrounded by the treasures of the Pharaohs — thousands of years of history stored in one room.

His father looked peaceful lying inside the silver sarcophagi, like an old wizard in his long robes. He was nothing like the dad Josh had imagined for himself.

He thought back to all those times he'd laid awake at night trying to conjure up an image of his father. Sometimes he used to borrow other people's, but most of the time it was an actor from the movies. Liam Neeson was a favourite for a few years, as he'd wanted a cool dad, one that would come and get him out of trouble.

Except he didn't, and Josh got into a hell of a lot of trouble.

'Josh?' said a ghostly voice that made him jump.

'What the hell!' he said, turning to see the colonel's ghostly image wavering at the bottom of the steps to the throne.

'Where are you?' the colonel continued. 'Where is the founder?'

'He died,' Josh explained, his voice tightening as he choked back the tears.

The colonel nodded. 'Joshua, we need you to come back. The Djinn have overrun the frontier, and the cascade is in full effect.'

113

WAR

S im sat at the head of the table, the remaining
commanders taking their seats around him. Alixia
couldn't help the pride she felt in the way they deferred to
her son. Some of the hardiest Draconian commanders
waited on his orders.

'Ladies and gentlemen,' Sim began, his voice business-
like and unwavering, 'the collapse of the timeline is imminent, our forces are diminished, and the Djinn have closed
off any chance of retreat.'

They all nodded gravely. They knew there was no way
back into the deep past and the cascade had collapsed
everything down to the seventeenth century.

'And the founder is dead.'

There was a collective sigh. They'd all heard the news
when Joshua had returned. Many of the council had openly
wept when he'd told them, and those who had petitioned
for a peaceful resolution were now openly criticising the
leadership. Copernican and Scriptorian emissaries were
already preparing to make a diplomatic mission to the Nihil
blockade in the seventh. There was talk of surrender, of

concessions and parlay, and nothing Alixia could say would change their minds.

Sim continued. 'I have been studying their strategies, comparing it with the Eschaton Cascade, and trying to understand where their weaknesses are, looking for a potential resolution to our situation.'

He stood up and walked around the table, on which was spread his entire Eschaton map.

'There aren't twelve crises, as we've been led to believe, but two separate timelines of at least six, and neither show any direct indication that the Djinn are responsible for the collapse. They are merely capitalising on it.'

He picked up a chess piece that stood on the twelfth symbol and held it up. 'The only certainty we have is the Nemesis, or Paradox, as the Augurs call him. The founder trusted him with the future of our Order, and we've reached the point where all we have left is faith. There is no way to know what the next few hours will bring, and for the first time in our history we are at the mercy of fate.'

The men and women around the table began to talk amongst themselves, and Sim let them. He walked over to his mother and put his hand on her shoulder, and whispered, 'Mother, would you mind if I told them now?'

She nodded. His sense of timing was perfect.

'So,' Sim continued, raising his voice, 'we have only one course of action, a King's Gambit. We must offer up our most valuable piece.' He held up the King. 'And put our trust in him.'

114

THE WITNESS

The knowledge the founder had passed onto him was vast; it was like having a thousand libraries crammed into his skull, and just as when they'd cured the colonel, the relevant information seemed to surface only when he needed it.

All the books the old man had ever read, all the strategies and theories to combat the Djinn, it was all there waiting for him.

'The Djinn have taken the first seven millennia. A combined legion of Dreadnoughts and Augurs are holding them in the edge of the eighth,' explained Sim, waving his hand in the air at the domed ceiling. The projection of the continuum was covered in marks where he and his team had been keeping track of the battles.

'As for the frontier, everything down to the sixteenth century has gone now. The cascade is collapsing the timeline, and Dalton and the Nihil are sweeping up behind it.'

Josh stood and listened to the reports as they came in from the various divisions: one defeat after another, and nothing seemed able to stop them. Every one of their defensive strategies was failing. Josh could remember all of the founder's plans, recall the conversations with Grandmaster Derado and Nostradamus, and amongst them all, was one that he'd discussed with the Grand Seer.

Sim looked frustrated. 'Is any of this triggering anything?'

Josh wasn't listening.

Lord Dee was sitting in his study with Edward Kelly years before, and they were talking about the presentation Marcus had given — the first time he'd proposed the Eschaton Cascade.

'Do you believe it possible?' asked the founder, taking a long taper from the fire and puffing away on a pipe as he lit it.

'Like night turning into day,' replied Kelly with a casual wave of his hand.

'The collapse of the continuum initiated by a future event. The odds of that are astronomically small.'

'Infinitesimal,' agreed the seer.

'How would we stop it?'

Kelly thought for a few moments, staring into the fire. 'You would need to rewrite the future. Call back yesterday. Turn time on its head.'

'Reset the timeline?'

Kelly nodded. 'Indeed.'

'We would have to start all over again, but what's to say that the Nihil won't find us in the next iteration?'

'Something must survive to mark the restoration. A witness.'

'And how do you suggest one might survive a temporal event of that magnitude?'

'There is only one way. To create a Paradox.'

'The first crisis of the Eschaton Cascade?'

'And the last.' Kelly held up a finger and drew an "O" in the air. 'They must complete the circle.'

'Let's hope it never comes to that. I wouldn't even know where to begin.'

'Hope for the best, prepare for the worst.'

Josh looked at the Ouroboros on his arm, the dot standing out like an island in the middle of the ring of the snake.

'I'm going to need the Infinity Engine,' he told Sim.

115

PREPARATIONS

'Are you seriously going to face them alone?' Caitlin exclaimed.

'Not completely,' Josh said with a shrug. 'I have a head full of other people's plans. It feels as if there are at least half the high council in there.'

They were in the engineering bay of the Citadel; the *Nautilus* was in for repairs, its hull scarred and battered and one of the cannons was being replaced.

The timesuit Josh had brought back from the future was standing on a platform surrounded by excited techies trying to work out how to open it. They watched the Augurs of the eleventh fighting over it with the Draconian artificers as both were keen to examine its workings.

'So the founder was your father?'

'Yeah. From a genetic point of view anyway.'

'Did he tell you why?'

Josh shook his head. 'Not really. He dumped his entire knowledge base into my head, but didn't really have time to give me any instructions on how to use it.'

'So, basically, stuff just surfaces when you need it?'

'Basically.'

'And now you're going to take on the Nihil single-handed.'

'The colonel's going to be there.' He nodded to the old man who was busy helping with the installation of the new cannon and annoying Caitlin's mother at the same time.

'Why do you call him that?'

'He used to wear this ridiculous old army coat,' Josh said and smiled at the memory. 'Even in the middle of summer.' Josh realised then that the colonel had been there throughout most of his childhood, watching over him.

'All the kids used to take the piss out of him, but he never seemed to care.'

Caitlin took his hand.

'I've been reading Marcus' original manuscript. It's your story, all of the experiences you've told me; everything revolves around you.'

'No pressure then.'

'I'm not blaming you. I'm just worried how it's going to end.'

'And I'm guessing the book doesn't say.'

'Well, it's obvious that Fermi's experiment went wrong somehow.'

Josh thought it wise not to mention how he'd released Lenin and left him to take his revenge.

Caitlin hugged him. 'I've got a really bad feeling about this.'

Josh wrapped his arms around her. 'Sim has a good plan, and I've got the founder squatting in my head. What could possibly go wrong?'

116

KING'S GAMBIT

Dalton-jinn strode into the Star Chamber as if he owned the place.

Josh stood in the centre of the empty space, the walls of the auditorium shaking with the battle that raged outside. He held the Infinity Engine out before him, the shimmering orb floating in his open hand.

Behind Dalton came the other Nihil, each one hosted in the body of a senior member of the council; the ones that had tried to surrender and found that this version of Dalton had even less mercy than the old one.

'Nemesis, ' Dalton said and sneered, stopping a few metres away from Josh.

'Nihil,' Josh said and nodded.

'Do you still believe you can save them?'

Josh shrugged. 'Can't blame me for trying.'

The other Nihil were spreading out around him, forming a circle. Josh counted twelve, each one of them moving as if they were finding it difficult to contain themselves within their host body.

Just a few seconds longer, he thought to himself.

Dalton-jinn held out his hand. 'Why bother? You have nothing left. Your timeline is collapsing around you and all those that you care so much for have deserted you.'

'I still have this,' Josh said, holding up the Infinity Engine.

'It has brought you nothing but oblivion.'

Josh looked around the room, the Nihil now evenly spaced out around him.

He nodded to the colonel, who'd been standing behind the door. The old man slammed it and bolted it shut.

'There were many reasons why we chose this place as our last line of defence,' began the old man, walking into the centre. 'It is, of course, a splendid debating chamber and capable of holding the entire membership in one sitting. But,' — he paused, holding up one finger — 'many are not aware of its rather interesting architectural properties.'

The Nihil screamed as a circle of energy burned around the outer edge of the floor.

'I see a Dilatino field is not something that you were expecting,' said Josh with a smile.

They writhed inside the field, their host bodies unable to contain the forces that were struggling to break free.

Josh stepped forward, the sphere of the Infinity Engine expanding as he focused his mind on channelling its power. He opened every one of their chronologies and unravelled them, breaking them apart like twigs. Just as the colonel's had been corrupted, their timelines lost cohesion, everything they had ever been, ever experienced disrupted and decoupled. The creatures fell to their knees and howled as their lives were ripped apart.

All except Dalton; the ring was still protecting him. The

Nihil leapt forward in an effort to take the Infinity Engine, but Josh was ready for him. As he reached for the device, Josh grabbed his ring hand and opened up its timeline.

117

DEFEATED

[Date: -654,000,000]

Dalton-jinn towered over Josh, his body twisting and distorting as the aetherium pushed its host to the physical limit. Black filaments threaded through his face, turning it to ebony, and his eyes glowed blue.

Josh was kneeling in the snow before him, the cold burning his face. They were surrounded by a gleaming white tundra, a snow-scape carved by freezing winds.

'There is nowhere to go now, Nemesis. It's just you and me,' the Nihil taunted.

Josh could hardly feel his face and his teeth were chattering so hard that speaking was near impossible.

Cradled against his chest he could feel the heat of the Infinity Engine, and somewhere from the back of his mind he recalled what Kelly had said to the founder: 'They must complete the circle.'

There was nothing to do now but restart the timeline — everything would begin again, and he alone would remember everything — he would have to become the new founder.

'Give me the engine!' demanded Dalton-jinn, leaning down and putting out a large, taloned hand, the ring glowing brightly on one finger.

And watch you destroy everything? Thought Josh, trying to stand.

Dalton laughed maniacally as Josh struggled to his feet.

'Such a weak and feeble species! This world was never meant for pathetic apes; you're nothing more than children playing with matches.'

He grasped Josh by the neck and lifted him out of the snow.

'Just like your belligerent founder, you all seem to cling on to this hope of a better future,' he leered. 'But, there's nothing but death and oblivion. When are you fools going to realise that chaos will always triumph? It's the natural state of the universe.'

Dalton's grip tightened, and Josh struggled to breathe as the pressure increased.

'Your body is failing you, Nemesis. I can feel your tiny heart beating, such a delicate fluttering, like a moth. Wouldn't you like me to end it now?'

'No,' croaked Josh.

He was close to Dalton's face. His skull had elongated giving him a long, demonic jaw, and there were bony, horn-like growths developing across his forehead. His canines had pushed out through his lips. It was as if Josh was seeing the real Dalton for the first time, the monster that had been trapped inside him for so long.

There was a sound from somewhere below them.

Josh looked down to see a figure in a timesuit holding a Japanese sword, and knew instantly it was Caitlin.

She sliced into one of Dalton's tree-trunk legs, and Josh felt his grip weaken.

'Put him down!' she barked, the suit's intercom boosting her voice ten-fold.

'Gladly,' replied Dalton-jinn, throwing Josh at her.

She stepped aside gracefully, and Josh landed in a nearby snowdrift.

Caitlin crouched into a fighting stance and raised the sword above her head. Josh was half-blinded by the snow but could make out her tiny figure as she parried a mighty blow from one of Dalton's hands.

She blinked in and out of existence, using vorpal combat to avoid his attacks. Striking from unexpected directions, Caitlin made him look slow and stupid. Each hit she made seem to stun the massive creature for a few seconds, while he swatted at her as if she were an annoying bee.

Josh pulled himself out of the snow, his chest aching where the impact had cracked his ribs.

He took the Infinity Engine out of his jacket and held it up towards Dalton-jinn.

'Take it!' he screamed at the monster.

'Josh. No!' Caitlin said as she brought her sword down and sliced off Dalton-jinn's ring hand.

Dalton looked at the stump and laughed. They watched as another grew back in its place, but this time instead of a hand his arm ended in a scythe-like blade. His body shimmered as his ebony shell of armour grew spikes.

On Caitlin's next attack the sword simply glanced off the surface, causing her to lose her grip as the weapon span off into the snow.

Dalton swept her aside with one blow of his sword arm. Her limp body went flying into the white and out of sight.

'You see?' he said, moving towards Josh. 'The power of the maelstrom knows no bounds. You cannot defeat me!'

Josh held the sphere out towards him.

'But you aren't in the maelstrom now.'

As Dalton-jinn reached for it, Josh opened his mind and connected with the Infinity Engine.

Time slowed.

He watched the individual flakes of snow, glinting in mid-air until they hung motionless between them. The Nihil's breath billowed in a cloud of vapour around them, his black armour turning slowly white as the ice clung to it.

Josh let the power of the continuum draw him in, feeling the aeons of time at his fingertips, millions of years stretching back into eternity. There was so much still to understand about the device, what it was capable of and the other timelines it could take him to. It held the secrets of the universe, the very beginnings of everything.

But he could only think of one thing — how Dalton would use it. Josh knew he was supposed to reset the timeline, but first, he wanted to send a message to the Nihil — one that they would never forget.

Josh looked into Dalton's dark eyes. 'You wanted infinite power. Be careful what you wish for!'

He grabbed Dalton's left hand and opened his timeline. Now it was no longer protected by the talisman. He could see how the history of the Nihil had woven itself around Dalton's lifeline like ivy entwining a tree. It was a parasite, burrowing into every part of his life.

Josh followed the path back into its past, into the many other lives it had ruined, the thousands of worlds it had destroyed. The entity would have been millions of years old if it had lived in the linear, but it was born outside of time, and Josh could taste the hunger it had for aetherium — it needed dark energy the way Lenin needed smack.

And that was when he realised how to destroy it.

Using the Infinity Engine, Josh went into the dark void at the end of his own timeline, felt the primal dark energies that lingered there, and let them flow through him and into the demon. Dalton's eyes glowed as it tasted the power.

While the Nihil was catatonic, Josh used the engine to accelerate time, watching the frozen world around them change: the snows receded, as grass then flowers and bushes flourished around them. Thousands of years passed in the blink of an eye as Josh dragged the creature through linear time.

The founder's training protected Josh, but it was not the same for the Nihil. The first signs of ageing began to show, its long mane of dark hair starting to grey, cracks opening in its carapace armour. Dalton-jinn's eyes returned to normal, a look of astonishment replacing the ecstatic grin, followed by terror.

'Stop!' it bellowed, but Josh ignored him. He pushed on: herds of animals lived and died around them in a heartbeat, nomadic tribes flowed over the countryside replaced by farms and villages that turned into towns. Dalton-jinn tried to wrestle his arm free, but it was withered and old now, the being that was trapped inside Dalton's linear body subject to the same laws of time. His knees weakened, and he fell to the ground, shrunken to a withered old man. It looked up towards Josh. 'What have you done?'

Josh knew that the creature had never experienced the flow of time. Not from within the continuum, the maelstrom had no concept of ageing, and it was a terrible, unforgiving weapon — as the founder's memories had told him, it was the curse of mortality.

Josh slowed the flow of time and the world around them followed suit.

'You've just lived ten thousand lifetimes — getting old is a bitch, and I guess even Djinn have to die sometime,' Josh said and smiled.

'But not you?' Dalton-jinn croaked.

'No. Just a little secret my father showed me,' Josh said, tapping his head.

Dalton stared down at his hand, the fingers crumbling as he tried to flex them. 'The Djinn are eternal.'

'Only if they stay in the maelstrom,' explained Josh, letting go of his withered hand.

Josh looked down at the Infinity Engine, which was nothing more than a small clockwork sphere now — its energy spent. He raised his hand to strike Dalton, but there was no need. The wind rose, and the desiccated body turned to ash and disappeared in a cloud of dust.

He was standing alone in the lush green valley, one that reminded Josh of Boju where Caitlin had disappeared. Remembering he'd left her back in the Pliocene — Josh located her timeline in the continuum and jumped back.

118

DECISIONS

Josh followed his timeline back to the spot where he'd left her. He no longer needed a vestige or the engine. It was as though he'd absorbed every part of the continuum, carrying the entire map of time inside his head.

Caitlin was lying awkwardly on her side. The timesuit ripped open where Dalton-jinn had struck her with his blade. Blood was seeping out through layers of metal.

'Cat?' Josh whispered, lifting her helmet off.

He pulled her out of the snow. Her lips were blue, and her skin was deathly pale.

'Can you hear me?' he asked, tenderly kissing her cheeks and brushing the hair from her face.

Her eyelids fluttered open, and she looked into his eyes.

'Josh?' she said weakly. 'Is it over?'

Josh smiled. 'Yeah, we did it.'

Caitlin tried to sit up, but the pain was too great, and tears began to run down her cheeks.

She shivered, her breath freezing as it left her lips. 'So, that was your plan? Bring him back here and freeze him to death?'

Josh laughed. 'Where did you get the sword?'

Caitlin sucked in a breath through clenched teeth. 'Dalton's, he left it behind. Don't suppose you have any power left in the engine?'

Josh shook his head. 'All gone. We're on our own now.'

She winced. 'Shame could really use a repair right now.'

Her breathing was shallow, and Josh could see the blood spreading across the white snow.

'Hey. It's okay,' he tried to reassure her. 'I've got a plan.'

She smiled. 'I know that look. You've always got a —' She coughed, and a trickle of blood ran out of her mouth. 'I'm getting cold.'

He looked at the suit. The power indicators were all dead, and he had no idea how to get her out of it.

Josh looked into her eyes as she closed them sleepily.

'Don't go to sleep Cat, stay with me. You need to stay awake.'

He held her close. Her body was limp, like a broken doll.

'It's okay,' she said dreamily. 'I know you'll find a way to fix it.'

He didn't know what to do. She was dying in his arms, and he knew that she wouldn't survive the long jump back to civilisation — they were too far back in the past, and there was nothing he could bring back here to fix her.

The arctic winds were picking up, and he could feel the cold leaching the heat out of her body.

Josh opened up the continuum in his mind. There were so many pathways and too many choices; if he chose the wrong one, it would undo everything they'd done to destroy the Nihil. He knew that somewhere in the future the Eschaton was devouring the timeline. His only option was to start again, but he couldn't bear the thought of having to go through all the agony of Caitlin not recognising him, of his mother's illness, the death of Gossy — they were all memories too painful to repeat.

But he could feel her slipping away.

'It's okay Cat, I'll find a way,' he said, rocking her gently as he heard her breathing weaken.

It was a terrible choice he had to make.

'Cat!' He buried his face in her hair.

119

BEGINNINGS

[London, UK. Date: 12.016]

J osh sat on the grass in Churchill Park with his eyes closed, letting the morning sun warm his face. He could hear the laughter of the kids playing on the swings, an innocent, natural sound he'd never realised could be so beautiful.

It was a moment of peace, one that would be broken shortly by the arrival of the community service team and Mr Bell.

'Are you seriously going to go through with this?' asked Caitlin, coming back with two ice creams and sitting beside him.

He took one and smiled at her. She was so beautiful, even when she was looking at him like he was a crazy person.

'I already have,' he replied, taking a bite of the flake. 'This is my fifteenth reboot.'

'I thought you were supposed to know the future?'

'Yeah, not sure who came up with that one. Do you

know how many variables you have to take into account? It took six attempts just to get back to a reality I even recognise.'

She laughed. 'You're beginning to sound like Sim!'

'Maybe I should bring him along next time.'

She punched him on the arm. 'Anyway, what happens to us every time? Do I remember who you are?'

'No,' he grinned, 'but I've got very good at convincing you.'

She put her arm around him and kissed his neck.

'Sounds like Groundhog Day.'

He nodded. 'All I need to do now is get mum the right treatment early enough.'

'How is she?'

'Better, but there's one more thing I want to try.'

They watched as a white, beaten-up Bedford van pulled into the street — Mr Bell was at the wheel. The council spared no expense when it came to transportation.

'You're going to stop yourself going in there?' she asked, looking over at the colonel's house.

Josh shook his head. 'No. That would be too weird — you are,' he said, standing up. 'I've got an appointment with a neurologist back in 12.010.'

'But, if I do, won't that stop you from discovering the Order?'

He smiled. 'I think you'll find that's why I'm called the Paradox.'

THE
INFINITY
ENGINES

AEONS
ANDREW HASTIE

1

THE KILLING

The silver blades of the weapon were buried deep into his back, a crimson stain spreading across Josh's white shirt like a red flower.

Caitlin sat huddled in the corner of the room, her eyes wild and filled with tears, screaming. 'It's not him. It's not him.'

Armed men came out of the walls; out of the bookshelves, out of mirrors, emerging from every vestige in the room. They wore the uniform of his Praetorian Guard, each one sworn to protect him, none of them believing that she could take his life.

He was their messiah, their founder, an immortal and yet there he lay, pallid and lifeless on the floor of the royal bedchamber, his existence extinguished with a many-bladed knife, ended by the woman who loved him the most.

'It's not him,' Caitlin screamed manically as they fought to restrain her. 'They've taken him.'

Swords were drawn in anger, every fibre of the guards' being was aching to exact revenge for their failure. Only their years of training prevented them from killing her where she stood.

Dragging her away, she pleaded with them. 'He's not in there. They've taken him.'

Lyra woke from the nightmare, her bedsheets soaked with sweat.

She shivered, not from the cold night air that moved the curtains of her open window, but at the memory of her dream.

2

CAITLIN

[The Great Library]

C aitlin was sitting in her office, hidden behind a fortress of books piled high on her desk. She should have been enjoying the latent energies of the dusty tomes, excited by the opportunity to explore the centuries of uncharted timelines contained within them, but she couldn't concentrate. Something else was bothering her.

There was nothing specific that she could put her finger on, but the irritability had grown over the last few days now, like a scratch she couldn't itch.

And it was getting worse.

Caitlin had been feeling out of sorts all that morning and when Penwynn, her new assistant, burst in with the news of a new discovery in Knossos, she had bitten the woman's head off for entering without knocking. The look of shock on her happy little face was still painful to recall. Caitlin apologised later, but it was inexcusable and totally out of character.

She found stupid little things really annoying: the order

of the books stacked on her shelves, the way the morning sun made patterns on her desk, the overpowering smell of Penwynn's perfume from the outer office.

So she decided it was time to reorganise.

It was usual practice for the newly-appointed Head of the Library to insist on changes. Every curator began their term of office by imposing their personality on the collection, some with radical and wide-ranging consequences. Caitlin hadn't gone so far as to initiate a dreaded re-indexing of the stacks, but that wasn't off the table, once she had got her own space in good order.

Taking one book from the top of the pile, she read the title.

'La Chanson de Saisnes by Jean Bodel.'

She closed her eyes, feeling the worn leather of the twelfth-century binding, letting its chronology slip through her fingers. The centuries rolled back as she wove into its timeline. The epic poems of Charlemagne, written at the time of the First Crusades, unwound temptingly, reminding her how much she loved medieval France and how she and Josh could really do with a holiday.

It would be their four-year anniversary next month and she wanted to do something special. Something that would distract Josh from his relentless search for a way to cure his mother.

'Hey,' Sim's voice broke Caitlin's reverie. 'You off somewhere?'

Her eyes snapped open. 'No,' she replied, putting down the book. 'Well, yes, maybe. I was thinking about taking Josh away somewhere, just for the weekend.'

Her stepbrother smiled, sliding a stack of books aside so he could sit on the desk.

'Ah, yes. Four years of marital bliss.'

She scowled at him. 'Don't start that again.'

'Well, it's about time he made an honest woman of you!'

'What does that even mean?'

Sim shrugged. 'No idea. I'm guessing it's something to do with the Victorians.'

'I don't need a ring on my finger. What I do need is someone to sort all of this out!' She waved at the piles of books scattered around the room. 'Master Dorrowkind's cataloguing of the indices was eccentric to put it mildly.'

'Pressures of the new job getting to you already?'

She laughed, pointing to the enormous diary open on the desk. 'Do you know how many meetings I've had in the last week? There are at least four department heads trying to resign over my appointment; a whole sub-guild of classicists threatening to go on strike and that's before we get to the fact that every librarian and his grandmother seem to think they have a better idea of how to re-index the collection than I do.'

As she spoke, a list of new messages appeared across the pages. Inscribing themselves across the smooth vellum in fluid copperplate, as if being written by an invisible hand.

Sim watched the notes move down the page.

'I heard there was a minor altercation last week.'

'Minor altercation! Master Ellerton tried to set fire to the lost scrolls of Herculaneum. Honestly it's like managing a bunch of school children, not respectable senior academics.'

He folded his arms. 'Well, if anyone can get them under control it's you. Your grandfather would be very proud of you. Youngest librarian to ever wear the chains,' he said, nodding to the heavy necklace of thin safety chains hanging on the back of her door.

She rubbed her neck, remembering the weight of them

during the investiture ceremony. 'They're purely ceremonial. No one could ever actually use those on the stacks.'

'Which brings me to the reason for my visit,' he said, his eyes glinting as he took out his almanac. 'My graduation is less than two weeks away and you've been avoiding my messages.'

'I've been a little busy,' she replied.

'Are you and Josh coming?'

Caitlin reached for her diary. 'I'm pretty sure I can,' she said, flicking through the pages. 'Josh might be harder to pin down. You're probably seeing more of him than I do.'

'Not me. He spends all of his time with Eddington. There are rumours he's close to finishing the engine.'

She sighed. 'He's been saying that for nearly a year.'

'Are you two okay?'

Caitlin found it impossible to lie to Sim, he knew her too well. There were no secrets between them and he used to joke that it was probably best she became a librarian because he could read her like a book.

'We would be, if we ever saw each other for more than ten minutes. He comes in to bed in the middle of the night and leaves before breakfast. Sometimes I don't think he even notices that I am there.'

'Well in his defence, the infinity engine is an important project.'

'So are people!' she snapped. 'All he seems to bloody care about is the Napoleon test!' There were tears gathering in the corners of her eyes.

'And the future of humanity,' Sim reminded her.

'I know, sorry. It's just that sometimes the Order seems to take all of him and there's nothing left for me.'

Sim put his almanac away and held out his hand. 'Cat, why don't you come and stay at the house for a couple of days? Lyra would love to see you and Mum has an entire pod of Spinosaurus in the baths. They make the most amazing symphonies at feeding time.'

Caitlin wiped the tears away with her sleeve like a ten-year-old.

'Does your father still cook the boar every Wednesday?'

'And most other nights. Mum and Lyra have persuaded him to go meat-free on Mondays.'

She stood up and closed her diary. 'Fine, let's go. I'm starving.'

～

Get the next book in the series at Amazon

Other books in the Infinity Engines universe.

The Infinity Engines

Infinity Engines Origins

Infinity Engines Missions

You can download 1776 for FREE plus get updates and news by subscribing to my mailing list (simply scan the QR code below).

ACKNOWLEDGEMENTS

Thanks to everyone who continues to support me. You're all amazing, but most of all to Karen and the girls!

This has been an interesting year. Leaving my full-time job and starting my own company feels like the start of a whole new adventure. I'd like to thank everyone that's bought my books (and especially those that have left me a review!), without your support I wouldn't be able to do this...

ABOUT THE AUTHOR

For more information about The Infinity Engines series and other Here Be Dragons books please visit: www. infinityengines.com

Please don't forget to leave a review!
Thank you!
Andy x

Printed in Great Britain
by Amazon

19962951R00257